A Katie Delancey Novel - Volume 2

NO PLACE TO Run

J. A. TAYLOR

NO PLACE TO RUN
Copyright © 2013 by J.A. Taylor

This is a work of fiction. Names, characters, places and incidents either are the product of the author's imagination or are used fictitiously, and any resemblance to actual persons, living or dead, businesses, companies, events, or locales is entirely coincidental.

Unless otherwise indicated, all scriptures taken from the Holy Bible, New International Version®, NIV®. Copyright © 1973, 1978, 1984, 2011 by Biblica, Inc.™ Used by permission of Zondervan. All rights reserved worldwide. Scripture quotations marked KJV taken from the Holy Bible, King James Version, which is in the public domain.

ISBN: 978-1-77069-786-7

Word Alive Press
131 Cordite Road, Winnipeg, MB R3W 1S1
www.wordalivepress.ca

WORD ALIVE PRESS
Just Write!

Library and Archives Canada Cataloguing in Publication
Taylor, J. A. (John Alexander), 1956-
      No place to run / J.A. Taylor.
(A Katie Delancey novel ; 2)
ISBN 978-1-77069-786-7

      I. Title. II. Series: Taylor, J. A. (John Alexander),
1956- . Katie Delancey novel ; 2.
PS8639.A9515N6 2012   C813'.6   C2012-907903-0

POST LOG TO ONE FIRST WAVE

It was twenty feet above the trickling creek, running through the belly of Denman's Gulley, that I did a gut check. The Rebel 250 motorcycle had launched from the sweet spot I had chosen on one side of the small canyon, but now it was bucking me like a bronco determined to unleash its load.

For a few nanoseconds, my feet slid free of the footrests and I was left to wrestle my mount back under control. As I went nearly horizontal above the motorcycle I looked down into the small Red River valley basin below and noticed things I would never have seen if I'd just walked past this Minnesota farm.

Above the roar of the whining engine, hanging on for my life, as the lightning flashed, it was like I was super sensitized to the world around me.

A four inch northern leopard frog was squatting on a rock in the middle of the stream. Its rich green coloring and rows of dark spots may have been good camouflage in the tall grasses on the stream banks, but on this rock it was easily visible to the three foot garter snake slithering up behind it.

While the flickering tongue of the yellow striped green reptile guided it toward its prey, a bull snake twice its size was approaching from the opposite direction. A fox, with neck craned and ears erect, was honing in on the frog's position and a blue heron was striding swiftly along the creek bottom.

As my movement passed above them, the frog gave a screech and began frantically leaping away. One never really knows the dangers we're in and one never really knows how we are protected at crucial moments.

I watched the heron flick her wings as the massive frame of the black Arabian stallion I was racing came lurching down the bank and right into her path. The flaring nostrils and wild eyes of the majestic champion betrayed the determination that drove his heart to race for victory.

But today was my day.

The proud black Arabian stallion belonged to my Uncle Jimmy, my mom's only brother, and this farm was the place I came to time and again to heal and recover from the bangs of life. It all started when I had to leave my birthplace of Kenya unexpectedly and continued as I rebounded from poor life choices and sorted out a new budding romance.

My work as a counsellor in Washington and British Columbia exposed me to the most beautiful of the world around me and to the darkest of the world inside.

For two weeks I anticipated this moment of racing Lancelot. I had suffered some serious injuries failing to clear this part of the ride when I first faced it unexpectedly on a stormy Minnesota summer's day.

That crash had been the start of finding my life again. During my recovery days, I had rediscovered my journals from my last days in Kenya and through that journey had opened myself to a lost past and a future that I would be sharing with my almost fiancé, Bruce.

Bruce saw my intensity and energy building during these past two weeks and continues to tease me about where my love really lies. If only he knew how hard the choice might be if things really did get bad again.

This is my third day on the Minnesota farm and I don't want it to be my last. The first day, I walked out to this field to show Bruce the secret place where I truly come alive. Lancelot watched us as we approached hand in hand. His head began to toss. He pawed the ground and snorted his warning. I gave him time and after fifteen minutes we walked away.

The second day, I came with Bruce on the motorcycle and Lancelot immediately caught the vibes that another race would soon be happening. Both of us had been through a lot since our last fling with wildness. I spent several hours that afternoon getting familiar with the motorbike again as I showed off the countryside.

Around mid-afternoon on the third day, I was ready to race. Yesterday, the sun was intense. Today, the clouds were rolling in as if setting up a replay of my first race with Lancelot and several of our races since. There is nothing like lightning and rain to bring out the wildness inside.

The breached dam inside me was about to release a torrent that surpassed all I've known. Bruce's last words to me were, "stay safe". I tightened my chin strap and told him that was his job.

The racing pulse, the breathless wonder, the spiritual terror is no longer something to be feared. I am at peace with my Maker and the world I live in. The first lightning strike seemed to be a signal to move on out. Bruce watched me anxiously from the road, but there are some things I cannot resist.

As I tore out into the field, Lancelot was already rearing up on his haunches, pawing defiantly at the sky. When I made the turn for our familiar race track, he was moving toward his full gallop.

The black Arabian's mane was flying in the wind. So was my hair. His muscles were aged but the fight was still in his eyes. The thunderclaps began as we passed the lone oak in the field. The pelting rain came soon after. The wind whistled across my black helmet and leather jacket while it streamed over the glistening satin hide of the stallion.

We crossed the ground as if we were one. Closer and closer, he moved as we pressed on. Finally, we were side by side and eye to eye. Our souls connected.

The wildness began to surge through me. Life emerged with a force that almost blinded me to what was ahead. I felt free and invincible. But today, I will not forget about Denman's gulley, the place where I crashed and almost died, during our first race. This time, I will not be taken by surprise. I see my sweet spot. I give the bike full throttle and will it to fly.

And from my vantage point, in this briefest of flights, I see Lancelot stretching himself to charge down and through the dip in his track. I see the heron, the snakes and the frog. I find the footrests just in time as I sail through the tall grass on the lip of the gulley and land the motorcycle like a veteran stunt rider. Without padding, the shock on my back and neck is intense, but the victory is secure.

I wait for the proud stallion a hundred yards on the other side of my landing spot. I shut off the engine and set the motorcycle to rest on its stand. This time, the horse slows to a trot and walks straight toward me. I hold out the sugar cubes and he extends his neck and accepts them without hesitation.

Now, I have one more relationship to settle.

CHAPTER ONE

Today, of all days.

I could visualize the paint peeling off the duty-free shop across the way. The tires, hissing by toward the Huntingdon-Sumas border crossing, sounded like they were sucking tarmac off the roadway with every turn. Every bird had vanished from the skies for the shade of a barn or a tree. This place in Whatcom County, Washington, smelled like the tar sands.

It was Tuesday afternoon, just after five o'clock, weeks before the summer solstice, and I was frying like an egg on a hot griddle. Half my vanilla-almond ice cream bar dropped onto the sidewalk outside. I couldn't get it into my mouth fast enough. By the time I bent down to wipe it up with a Kleenex, only a vanishing smear on the concrete remained. I would head back to Bromiley's to get another from my friend Dora, but I'd probably evaporate along the way.

A quick glance at my reflection in the entrance mirror of Buffalo Bill's revealed my suspicions. Strands of a strawberry blond ponytail were plastered helter-skelter down my neck by sweat. The peachy-pink author interview ensemble, which I'd picked up at a consignment shop just last week, looked like it had been resurrected from an abandoned recycling bin. A streak of melting chocolate highlighted one of the ruffles. I didn't have to see my feet to know that I should have slathered on more sunscreen.

I was hiding my face behind a hamburger in the restaurant, less than three blocks from the border, when I felt the nudge. It was almost physical, like a vibrating cell phone. I actually looked down toward my ribs. I'd been on edge a lot lately. I sensed, rather than saw, the shadow. I snatched up a few fries and moved into the back room before anyone noticed. I had an understanding with the owner.

The reporters seemed to know my schedule; they could spot my car in the neighbourhood without any effort. The knocks on the door and the incessant phone calls had pushed me to hide out until I could sneak in my back door under cover of darkness.

Only a few months had passed since my place was trashed, and I knew those responsible were no longer a threat, but I couldn't help feel that shiver in my spine whenever I turned the key in my lock. The darkness always seemed worse inside, and colder. The walls seemed closer than before, the escapes a little further away.

Bruce, my soon to be fiancé, had crutched his way through my little rented bungalow a dozen times, reassuring me that everything was okay. I still couldn't shake that shiver of fear. A place like Buffalo Bill's was a perfect hideaway. Until now. Not even the smell of grilling steak could bring me comfort.

The pressure against my right temple increased in a slow, circular motion. I could smell the fear in the girl's sweat. She stood close behind me, her breathy gasps floating like lost balloons across my eardrums.

"Ghost towns don't make great neighbourhoods!" the teenager said.

"Or hideaways," I responded. Even with my eyes closed, I could see the young girl's haunted hazel eyes dilating larger and smaller. Even before I had known her, I was mesmerized by her. Her survival story was legendary among the other girls in town. Now she stood behind me, giving me a massage. I perched precariously on the three-legged wooden stool.

I now knew what Thanksgiving turkeys felt like in those first moments of baking. The desperate teen had closed the windows and drawn the gingham drapes in the back room of the restaurant. The fan was turned off so we could hear every sound. A sauna would have been cooler.

"Do you think he'll find you here?" I asked.

"He always does." She applied more pressure to both sides of my head.

It took me a minute to let the massage on my temples take effect. Yessica kept whispering in her gravelly way.

"He hasn't changed. Humiliation. Yelling. Criticizing. Fear. I hate the way he grabs me by the back of the neck. I hate feeling like I'm a bad dog or something."

The tension increased and the massage began to hurt.

"Easy, girl," I said. Her fingers relaxed their pressure. "I know he can make you feel like it's all your fault and you start feeling like you have to walk on eggshells. You start realizing that some topics aren't worth the pain."

"You got it."

The fingers pulled away from my temples, dropped to my shoulders for a moment, then slid away. I sensed her moving around me—a shadow temporarily blocking the light from a shaded window, a soul flirting with life and death, an apparition with the faintest aroma of cheap Chanel.

The drop on my wrist was like the brush of an eyelash, but it was enough to pry my eyes open.

She stared into me without restraint, a raven-haired Barbie doll who had run into a cement truck. Tears streamed from those puffy, blackened orbs that had once drawn men to her. Another dropped onto my arm.

"Am I crazy?" she asked. "Will I ever feel again?"

I looked down at her torn yellow blouse, hanging open, top buttons ripped away, right sleeve clinging by a few threads. Tight jean shorts, made to be noticed. A Firm and Friendly wristband nestled next to a ten-dollar watch.

"Does he still threaten to kill himself if you run? Does he still take all your money as soon as you earn it? Does he still go crazy if he thinks you've looked too long at another guy?"

Yessica slinked into a chair and pulled her knees up to her chin. She rested her head on her right wrist. Her mumbles were clear enough. "He ran over my cell phone. He accused me of stealing an iPod and smashed it against the stairs. He hid the cord on my laptop so I can't Facebook anyone. He's a jerk, but I don't want him to die."

"When you're tired of looking at that face in the mirror, come see me again," I say. "In the meantime, you can decide whether I report this, or you."

When the door closed behind her, I stood up and looked at my own face in the mirror. The eyes were like ice.

CHAPTER TWO

My passport may read Katrina Joy Delancey, but my friends called me Katie.

To those who look for heroes, I was a heroine of 9/11 proportions. To sceptics, I was a somewhat histrionic, delusional, wild woman. To those who flirt with the law, I was about as wanted as a yard full of dandelions. To myself, I was just a truth seeker looking to find a balance of roots and wings.

An empty town like this one didn't make it easy for your dreams to come true—dreams of loving, and being loved, in a way that makes your best friends drool. Dreams of being romanced and rescued by your Prince Charming. Dreams of having all your prayers answered.

I slept in a town with a name that means "place with no trees." In a former trading post like Sumas, there was simply no room to be romanced, nothing to be rescued from, and no prayers that had a chance. Of course, the impossible could still happen. It started happening to me. But I wanted more.

I was the kind of girl who looked for adventure and wildness. I just didn't always want it alone. Yes, I was into beauty; just ask my hairdresser and my mirror. I wanted my blue eyes to be irresistible. I wanted my hair to match my mood, whether it was strawberry blond, chestnut, or just highlighted that way.

Yes, I wanted to have my guy see me as eye candy. Irresistible. Inviting. Alluring. Mysterious. Comforting. Inspiring. But that was only on the good days. And usually not first thing in the morning.

Somewhere at heart, I wanted to do something significant with my life. I wanted to embrace the great causes that could transform my world. I wanted something that would put my restless spirit at peace. I just didn't see it here.

The economic downturn, among other things, crippled my home of six years in Sumas on the Washington-B.C. , border. This former marshland huddled on the prairie and still dreamt of the 1890 gold rush that saw it double in size. The towering trees on the surrounding hills gave it a sense of isolation. Now, the descendants of Dutch dairy farmers manned the farms and milked the cows.

For the past few months, I had been away chasing romance, escaping death, wrestling with doubt and faith, and pursuing my passion for wildness. Now I was back and this place looked like it would never recover. The Canadian traffic surging down State Route 9 seemed to be all that was keeping this place on life-support.

I was amazed how much a place can change when you're gone a short time. I used to hear a lot of laughter on the streets. Now, I rarely saw anyone on foot even looking for a conversation. Even the truckers never seemed to stop and gab anymore.

Everyone was passing through and those who passed through now seemed like they were giving this town the same value as the old crumpled fast food bags that lay discarded along the streets.

A new and improved road, and a strong Canadian dollar, lulled cross-border shoppers to the bargains in Bellingham and Seattle. Apart from a few regulars who grabbed gas, dairy, and maybe a few things at Bromiley's supermarket, no one new was settling here anymore.

Having only a few people living in this border stop didn't mean Sumas was safe for me. After all, I wasn't a ghost. Somehow, my name was connected to every tragedy that had happened here in the past year. Curiosity grew easily when there wasn't a lot of distraction.

Tommy Lee's murder had shaken this little town. Most of the women I know here had owned memberships in his Firm and Friendly Fitness Center, since it was the only show in town. The papers were merciless in pointing out that, although I was currently a professional counsellor, I had once been one of "Tommy's girls." And they weren't talking about his fitness center when they labelled me that way.

The publicity of the upcoming trial wasn't helping. My role in the death of Stephen, known on the streets here as "the Monk," transformed me into a local celebrity with hero status, at least to Dora, at Bromiley's, where I used to shop. She and I intervened so many times with the battered girls who didn't perform well enough for the harsh trafficker that, when he died, she praised my name to every customer who came through her register.

It was clear from my encounters that cleaning up the street would be harder than erasing a few thugs and counseling a few battered women. What I needed was a real, honest to goodness superhero. There was only one problem: honest to goodness superheroes usually didn't materialize in ghost towns like this one.

CHAPTER THREE

Odd things happen in bunches, at least in my life. Take the encounter with Yessica two days earlier, followed by Juanda yesterday and Elli just a few hours ago. Just because a girl dressed to survive the heat, did her guy have to prove how macho he was? The bruises on those bodies were unbelievable.

I quit my after-dinner walks, just to avoid bumping into another desperate journalist, and I felt that old flabbiness start to kick in. Too many hamburgers and ice cream cones. I hated that. At least it would give me an excuse to hit the malls again—taste an Orange Julius, check out the perfume counter, and listen to some up-to-date music. And maybe I'd get to visit my friend Sarah, in Seattle, while I was at it.

Last night, after seeing Juanda, I took a chance and strolled by the empty building where the Firm and Friendly used to be. Tommy Lee had been discovered in one of the closets six months ago with a broken neck. Most of the equipment had been auctioned off while I was away.

A few doors away stood the old dojo. Also vacant and gathering dust. It was right by the doorway where I'd first met Bruce. Who could miss a six-foot-four-inch tower of muscle standing in your way? His Tae Kwon Do outfit did nothing to hide his powerful chest and confident swagger. A black brush cut just looked good on him.

His stint in Afghanistan as part of a Special Forces medical unit had created quite a whirlpool of emotional chaos for us both. I didn't even know his whereabouts when the accident happened.

I could feel the tears streaming down my face as I looked into the window once again. The man preparing to marry me had lost his leg below the knee through an Improvised Explosive Devise as he triaged a fallen soldier. His slow recovery left me lonely, but there was nowhere else to run. Both of us needed healing as he waited for his prosthetic limb on the other side of the country.

Bruce had co-owned the Tai Kwon Do franchise with Stephen ("the Monk") and the police still hadn't untangled the web of intrigue surrounding the partnership. I just didn't know when I'd see him again.

A red Toyota slowed nearby and I ducked around back. Fortunately, no one chased me.

Several of the girls who had been freed from their bondage and battering identified me to reporters as their counsellor and support system, and that led to more calls for interviews. Even though I spent most of my day at my offices in Bellingham, Washington or Langley, British Columbia, the sensationalistic press gave me little room to manoeuvre or disappear. Even the people who knew me here were asking too many questions.

Most of my life was shaped dramatically in Kenya, where I grew up as the daughter of missionaries. That's where my thirst for wildness and adventure was nurtured. Losing my dad and brother in a car accident after we returned to North America put me into a space where I made some significantly bad choices that almost cost me my life, my faith, and my healing. I had to admit that if it hadn't been for a horse and a guy, I might not have made it.

My soul and my feet had been getting that itchy "time to go" feeling. I also had to admit that my expectations for this ghost town had been sliding down to zero.

I was just glad to be sitting here again in Buffalo Bill's, anonymously, with the sweat dripping down my back. I ordered the combo just so I could have an endless supply of Coke—and the ice, which I used strategically to keep cool.

At the very moment I was feeling safe, a woman strolled into the diner with a little girl in tow. The reluctant child must have been about five. There wasn't anything obviously suspicious about this young mom and her little blond angel, but my trust was low. Any time I saw a parent use extra pressure on a child, my counsellor hackles went up. And they were up.

The brunette sported a navy halter top and white capris, something I might have worn on a sizzling day like today if I'd wanted the whole world to notice me. The red slip-ons were out of my league, but to each her own. The gold chain around her neck suspended a locket about the size of a quarter. A second necklace featured an Egyptian cross inset with blue topaz gemstones.

8

I wondered if she'd dyed her hair, since her daughter's mane was pure sunshine. The woman seemed nervous, as her left hand constantly tucked her long hair behind her ear. She fidgeted with the blue topaz earring in her left ear. She definitely had a wedding ring on, but I couldn't see the size of the diamond clearly. Her left hand cradled a cell phone to her ear as she attempted to speak in whispers.

She looked casually around at the dozens of empty tables, but locked her eyes on me a bit too long. With her eyes still focused on me, she reached behind her and grabbed for her little princess. The girl had wandered over to the gumball machine near the washrooms, forcing the mother to twirl and chase after her.

It only took that one look. I dropped my burger on my plate, laid down the twenty-dollar bill I always stashed in the back pocket of my shorts and slid out the back door before the woman could look my way again.

I just knew I had to get away. Panic worked its way into my soul. The air seemed harder to breathe. My legs felt like cement. My brain grew foggy. For a minute, I wondered if my food had been tampered with. I swung around the side of Buffalo Bill's—and that's when I spotted the yellow Porsche.

I scrambled across the parking lot like a gecko dropped on an iron-corrugated roof under the midday equatorial sun.

Within a minute, I was in my Honda Accord, heading for the border. The only yellow Porsche I knew belonged to Tommy Lee.

I was about as calm as a cork in a tsunami by the time I reached the Canadian border. Only two of the eight booths had the green arrows for accepting traffic and I tried hard to see if one of the regulars I knew was on-duty. Newbies who didn't know you could really make it hard while they're trying to prove themselves.

I kept forgetting that my car wasn't an automatic and I didn't handle the shift well at first. My little Honda started doing an imitation of a toad escaping a stampeding herd of buffalo as it sputtered and jumped toward the crossing while I waited for the SUV in front of me to get clearance. The interrogation ahead seemed to take longer than usual.

The border guard was a woman I hadn't seen before. I couldn't see her smiling as she handed back the documents to the driver in front of me. Not a good sign. I hoped she wasn't a university student doing a summer placement. I hoped this wasn't her time of month. I hoped that her boyfriend hadn't betrayed her. I hoped she wasn't that one person determined to find the next terrorist crossing at this border.

I scrounged in my purse and popped a breath mint into my mouth. Finally, it was my turn and I managed to corral my beast into place below the window. The piercing eyes almost made me swallow and choke on my candy.

I wondered if there was something I could do to compliment her. I took off my sunglasses quickly to take away the impression that I had anything to hide. My interrogator had jet-black hair, cropped short, and four gemstones pierced into the top of her left ear. Her name tag said "Feona." I knew if I said anything right now, I'd probably get it wrong.

Usually, I have my Nexus Pass to automatically cross the border, but I'd left it in the trunk because of my hurry. Fortunately, I had my purse with my enhanced driver's license and passport. Feona must have noticed how distraught I was and got suspicious. She snagged my paperwork and began to scan the latest information showing up on her computer screen.

Maybe it was my tendency to snatch looks back toward Buffalo Bill's, where the yellow Porsche and young brunette mother hid just three blocks away. Maybe I just plain looked guilty and on the run. I took quick peeks into my rear-view mirror to see if there was something unexpected in my back seat. She just kept typing and looking and typing and looking.

When Feona asked how long I'd been in the States, I told her I lived in Sumas, but came back and forth to work several times a week. She wanted to know how I had a Canadian passport if I lived in Sumas. I told her that my dad was Canadian but that I was born in Kenya, in Africa, and that my dad and brother had been killed in an accident in the States; my mother was in Minneapolis, dying of cancer, and my sister was getting married and my future fiancé had lost his leg because of a bomb in Afghanistan and he was in the U.S. Special Forces and somehow he'd been caught up with a wanted criminal who had been killed, and now I was waiting for the trial but someone suspicious was following me and I needed to get to my office in Langley quickly.

Of course, I was almost certain she had most of this stuff on the computer screen in front of her and I didn't have all day to fill her in on my life. The whole time I was talking to Feona, I felt like I was having a seizure, since my head was snapping back to look behind me so much.

Her furrowed eyebrows should have stopped my tongue, but at this point it had a life of its own. I had the distinct image of the last time I had plugged in my mixer without first checking to make sure it wasn't on a high-speed setting. That time, the egg and milk and flour had taken a good thirty minutes to clean up. I still found a speck on the light fixture when I cleaned up two weeks later. The chocolate chip cookies for Bruce never did get made. I instinctively knew in my gut that today was going to require a similar clean-up effort.

CHAPTER FOUR

Instead of handing back my passport and telling me to have a good day, the young border guard spoke into her lapel phone and spent a minute dialoguing with someone. Only then did she tell me to please pull over into one of the inspection lanes. I could hardly believe what was happening.

I stuck my head out the window and saw the brunette in the red slip-ons standing out on the street looking away from the border. Her left hand was still trying to tuck that hair behind her ear. Fortunately, she was distracted by a tall African-American man down the block who was getting into a silver-grey Mercedes. The little girl was nowhere in sight.

With all my adrenaline pumping, I accelerated a little too quickly and almost ran down another border services officer who had stepped out in front of my car to wave me into my parking spot. I always seemed to make a mess of things when I got stressed out like this. The grim look on his face, when I finally got my seat belt undone, the engine turned off, and the door opened was not a welcome sight. I looked around him, and at least the brunette was no longer in view.

It took an hour before I was cleared. I even had to hand over phone numbers so my story could be verified. The stern looking Canadian Border Service Agent called my friend Sergeant James of the Bellingham Police, who was in the middle of making an arrest and couldn't talk at the moment. He called Devlyn, my employer in Langley who, as usual, was in an important meeting of some kind. He called my sister Lizzy in Minneapolis, who just happened to be in the shower and was left dripping in her towel when she found out what was happening with me. The border agent also called Bruce, who was debriefing at the Langley Air Force Base in Virginia.

All of which created a frenzy far beyond the need of the moment. The agent didn't seem to be bothered by any of this.

Finally, he called the local Sheriff's Department, and this meant more waiting as my claims were checked out down the street on the American side. It was during this time that I discovered a ketchup stain dead center on my blouse. I just knew the agent had noticed this right away. I couldn't imagine what he thought. When I asked to use the washroom, I had to wait for a female officer to accompany me. She sympathized with my agony as the stain spread while I tried to wipe it off with soap and water. I never did get it completely off.

The interviewing agent listened to the return call from the Sherriff's office some twenty minutes later and stared me down as he nodded intently. Apparently no one at Buffalo Bill's recalled seeing a brunette with a little girl or a yellow Porsche within the past hour.

I tried explaining about the shift change at the restaurant between 5:00 p.m. and 6:00 p.m. each night, but by now it was clear the authorities felt they'd wasted enough time on me. Three of the authorities huddled for about ten minutes before the chief officer gave me the signal to repack my car and go. He was probably reluctant to let another psycho into Canada.

As I pulled away from the border, I noticed a white Subaru fall in behind me from a side street. I deliberately drifted into the right lane to let him pass, but he continued to stay a few hundred yards behind me. When I stopped for a coffee at Tim Horton's, the Subaru went through the drive-thru at Wendy's right next door.

I adjusted my speed several times on Highway 1 but didn't really get a glimpse of him again. A bronze Buick Century followed me for a while, but when I pulled onto the shoulder and glanced over I could see it was just a cautious senior gripping his wheel and letting the car in front lead him on.

The sun was setting on the horizon as I pulled into the office parking lot in Langley. I spent half an hour standing in a coffee shop near Abbotsford, holding my purse in front of me in order to cover up the stain on my blouse. I tried again to rub that ketchup smear out in the washroom and succeeded a little. For all I knew, those passing by assumed I had just loaded up my Starbucks card and was guarding it with my life.

With the surprise visit at Buffalo Bill's, I didn't even get to bring a change of clothing. That meant another shopping trip. Fortunately, I knew the perfect mall close to my Langley office. That took another hour.

As I shopped, I thought through what had just happened at the border. The whole time I couldn't work up the nerve to call Bruce. It should have been automatic. He was my protector. My go-to guy. And still, I didn't want to bother him.

I let myself into the office building where I worked and turned off the alarm with the help of my security card. I scanned the cars passing by, but none of them slowed or seemed to show an interest in what I was doing. It was now past midnight in Virginia, where my future fiancé struggled on without realizing how much I needed him. How ironic. Bruce and I were both in a place called Langley—three time zones apart.

I checked my cell phone. My message box was full. Three from Bruce. Four from Lizzy. One from Sarah.

Sarah had no clue what was happening and just wanted to set up some time to chat in the next week or two. She had been one of my best friends at school in Kenya. I had been at her wedding not too long ago and I hoped she'd soon be at mine. We had a lot to chat about, but not tonight.

Bruce expressed concern about the trouble I was having crossing the border but didn't seem to connect with how serious things were. He let me know that he'd pray for me and call me in the morning.

Lizzy seemed almost frantic, so I naturally called her back. I assured her everything was okay and then we settled into a sisterly chat about our guys.

"Is Bruce a romantic, like Dean?" she asked.

"I suppose," I answered. "He brings me roses and cards. Of course, with everything that's gone on lately, and being a whole continent apart for the past month, neither one of us has had the chance to be romantic."

"How long can they debrief this guy? Are you sure you shouldn't just fly out there and surprise him?"

"I'd love to, but I've got a lot of clients to catch up with now that things are settling down again. And every time I talk with Bruce, he seems preoccupied with some kind of rehab or strategic initiative or whatever these Special Forces guys do together. Right now, he just seems a lot more passionate about planning a mission for the guys than about planning a wedding."

"Give him time, Katie. You know how guys are when they get their heads wrapped around their work. Dean's like that sometimes. Once Bruce sees you face to face, you'll be the only thing he can think about."

"Sure hope you're right, Lizzy. It's taken me a long time to get on this road and I don't want my heart stuck in the potholes the moment I give it a chance."

"Don't worry, girl. I've heard the way you talk about your Prince Charming."

I could almost see my sister in some dramatic pose with her right wrist pressed against her forehead. Watching Lizzy on the phone was like watching a choreographed musical. She was always moving as she spoke. And once she got talking, she could talk on and on.

Sometimes I just needed to be up front with her. "Lizzy, I better call Bruce. He's probably going crazy worrying about why I haven't returned his calls."

As sisters, we knew how to talk straight with each other and not take offence. None was taken and Lizzy signed off. "Say hi from Dean and me. Love you. Call you in the morning when you've got some time."

"I'm in my Langley office with clients all morning. I'll call you at lunch, my time."

"Sounds good. Night, night."

My ten calls to Bruce were disturbing. I was sent straight to his voicemail. I didn't blame the guy for getting his sleep, but I couldn't imagine how you could sleep when someone you cared about had just gone through a life-threatening experience. I sat and played Hearts on the computer until my eyes couldn't stay open anymore.

I set up a couch and blanket from the conference room and settled myself in for the night. Throughout the dark hours, my dreams were disturbed by images of red slip-ons and a yellow Porsche chasing me. Through it all, I was desperately alone. Unprotected. Unguarded. Maybe even unwanted.

Believe it or not, it wasn't until I sat alone in the dark that I finally thought about praying. This trusting God thing was new again for me and it wasn't my first response when things got tough. I had seen a lot of unanswered prayer in my life and it would take time before I sorted it all out again.

CHAPTER FIVE

awn stretched itself out as innocently as a month-old kitten. The tongue of first light licked across the snow-capped mountain peaks and groomed away the final traces of darkness. The purr of life arose in the birdsong, the sway of tree branches in the breeze, and the sounds of joggers calling their greetings. I sat out on the balcony of the office complex, wrapped in a blanket, and took it all in.

It might have been mid-June, but the Pacific Northwest could still be cool early in the morning. I tugged the blanket closer and rose to scan the gardens below. The security lights were blending with the first light of day. I could almost hear the flowers stretching out for their share of rays. I could definitely smell their efforts for attention. I loved the layout.

Bright yellow and white Cala lilies. Variegated maroon viegella. Fragrant lavender. White, mauve, and purple hydrangeas. Butterfly blue scabiosa. Pink bleeding heart ascending from a forest of ostrich fern. Primroses and buttercups. Pansies in their prime. The white flash of a Moscow lilac caught my attention. I hadn't noticed it before. God was at work painting his masterpieces for his own glory and pleasure, whether anyone saw them or not. Someone had at least arranged this garden well.

Traffic noises picked up and I decided it was time to quit staring at the work of other people and start staring at my own. I needed to change, wash up, and try to disguise the traces of a mostly sleepless night. Besides, Bruce should be calling anytime.

I'd heard it said that a man has about six things that he uses to prepare himself in the bathroom each morning. A woman has about 337 things at her disposal. With my minimal handbag accessories on this unexpected trip, I felt a bit limited regarding how much repair I could really do.

My first client was due at 9:30, so when Bruce hadn't called by 8:30 I decided I couldn't wait any longer. I punched in his numbers and he picked up on the fourth ring. His enthusiastic greeting erased half my fears. But then, nothing remains the way it appears to be.

Bruce caught me off-guard. "Katie, wow, ten times last night. What's with all the panic?"

I hated being questioned like this. It made me feel attacked, like I'd committed the unpardonable sin without even knowing what I'd done wrong. It wasn't like I was some histrionic personality. Most days.

I should have learned some peaceful response because of my Tai Kwon Do lessons with Bruce, but this felt too personal. My defences were up.

"What do you mean, panic?" I snapped.

He ignored the strain in my voice and continued to jab. "I mean, you know the time difference. I told you I would call you in the morning."

It really bugged me when guys thought they were the only ones in the world with important things to do. Words were my defence mechanism and the breadth of the English language was soon doing its work for me.

"Bruce, I need to meet with Devlyn in a few minutes to sort out new intakes. I don't need this right now. Why didn't you phone me yet? I was interrogated for an hour at the border last night. Weren't you even worried when that guard called about me? I'm sure I saw the woman Tommy was training to take over his operation. She had his car and she came looking for me. She had on these red slip-ons and I've been dreaming about them all night. I've hardly slept and now I have to focus on helping people who are probably doing better than I am. When can you get here?"

He did the typical guy thing of fixating on one thing I said. "Whoa, girl! You can't be serious. You think someone is after you? Tommy Lee and Stephen are dead. The police are cleaning up the rest of the group. You haven't got anything to worry about."

I tried to engage his protective side a little. "But what about the woman I saw?"

Bruce almost seemed demeaning as he ignored my question. "Listen, Lieutenant Saunders and I have been tasked with formulating a new operation near Kandahar to help set up protected areas for girls wanting education. We're on a tight deadline. I know you have work to do. I'm not sure when I'll be free over the next week, so could you just drop me an email?"

17

"But, Bruce, I need you now!" I said it very clearly.

He continued as if I was an answering machine. "I'll try to call if I can. It's good to hear you. Don't worry about anybody coming after you. It's all under control. I'm really glad everything's fine. You almost had me worried. Don't forget to keep praying. I really need to get back to my briefing. Thanks for calling. Please take care of yourself. And Katie, please try to stay out of trouble."

And just like that, he was gone. I couldn't believe how many times I did this. It was like a weight around the neck of every relationship I ever tried to have. Or maybe I was a ghost—one that scared people off, a ghost whose voice no one heard, a ghost with dark circles under her eyes. I needed to take care of that.

My meeting with Devlyn was quick and easy. She asked about the call from the border and I told her that with all the extra security these days, and the complications around the trial, there was a new guard who was being overly cautious. She asked how things were with Bruce and I told her he was still busy at the base. She asked if there were any engagement or wedding plans yet, and I told her that Bruce and I were still working things out and hoping for some quiet time in the next month or so. She nodded and then dumped two files on the desk in front of me.

"Just two files today. Hanan Faisal. Saudia Arabian woman. Twenty-five. Married off by her father at fifteen. Had a son at sixteen. No choice in either event."

I picked up the file with a passport-sized photo stapled to the corner. I saw the beautiful skin tone of a proud Arabic woman who had been robbed of her spirit. I could see it in her eyes. Haunted. Another ghost.

Devlyn continued her overview. "When her son was born, she was thrown out of the house by her husband. Her father wouldn't take her back. She was left on her own and beaten by the local men. She fled to a village in the country where she taught school to girls. The religious leaders eventually found out about her and gave her a beating. She escaped the country and ended up here as a refugee. Lots of emotional scars and loss. Not sure about funding, but she's worth our time. She'll be in at ten. Just do a standard intake assessment and we'll talk about what we can do later."

My boss then slid the other file in my direction. "This one's a classic. Anthony DeSuza. Jamaican. Thirty-seven."

The face on this file captured me immediately. As black as coal. Teeth like the snow on Mount Kilimanjaro. A smile as big as an ocean. Twinkles in the eyes. No obvious sign of trauma. I looked up inquiringly at Devlyn.

"Victim of Christopher Coke. Some drug lord down in Tivoli Gardens, in Haiti. They used to call his group the shower posse because they'd shower everyone with bullets. Government cracked down on him after pressure from the Americans. Not sure if Anthony was part of the problem or a victim of it. Somehow he escaped that earthquake. He's been hiding in Toronto and Montreal the past several years and just moved into our neighbourhood. Wants help for his trauma. Specifically requested you. Put red flags all over this one. Let me know if we need to shut it down. Start with a standard intake. He's in at eleven. You have your regular groups this afternoon. No cancellations. Any questions?"

I had none for Devlyn. I had a few for Bruce when I talked to him again. Maybe even a few for God when I found the time.

I sent a quick email to Sarah as I waited for my first appointment.

Sarah, talk to me about intimacy sometime. I can't seem to get it down with God or Bruce. I'm not talking physical here. I'm talking about connecting heart to heart. Things are complicated with Bruce being so far away and I feel a little bit alone in trying to deal with the unexpected. I may even be getting paranoid. Not good for a person in my profession. Love, Katie.

CHAPTER SIX

Some days, I felt as stretched as a foot-long worm playing tug-of-war with a robin. It just felt like there was no way to win. And some days I felt like I was sitting in the shadow of one of those victorious individuals who had become champions against all odds.

My session with Hanan was life-changing. Through my time with her, I decided to start a different kind of journal. Up until now, my journals had been records of my experiences helping others see life as I lived it. And, of course, to help me remember life as it really is. I had the impression that my new journals just might help me see life through the eyes of others. From my notes and recordings, I would craft my first entry for Hanan.

Even though I'd made the transition to this country after living a lot of years overseas, I had never had to see life through the eyes of someone who had no one and nothing anymore. No family. No home. No friends. No country. No possessions of significance even, apart from what she carried in one colourful silk headscarf, her only souvenir of a birthplace that no longer wanted her for anything good.

I recorded the session since I knew I'd forget to take good notes. I took just enough to keep me on track. Although I was trained to practice boundaries and healthy distance, Hanan left my heart twisted and wanting to help. The fifty minutes flew by. I arranged to meet her again in a week.

Anthony was another story. Although he probably reached seven feet on his tiptoes, he glided into the room and immediately moved past me to the window and gushed over the view of the mountains and the gardens—and even the freeway. He apologized for his rudeness and began to float around my office commenting on my African artefacts, my batiks, and even my furniture. He was a man used to being in control.

While I stepped over to my desk to pick up his file, he sat in my chair. He bent his right knee and planted his ankle firmly on his left knee. He held it in place by a left hand that had three massive gold rings adorning it.

He worked his right fist, open and shut, like he was about to squeeze the life out of an orange. I'm pretty sure all this was deliberate, but during this first session I played along. As Devlyn said—red flags. Standard assessment.

His voice was the singsong lilt of the Jamaican people. His words were drawn out and deliberate. "So doc–tor." His smile was captivating. His voice was entrancing. His words were deadly. "When the good peoples tell me that you are de fine–est, I did not re–a–lize that they meant de *fine*–est. Sparkling glass a wine like you must be having the whole world a-coming to your door. I am indeed a lucky man to be safe with you. I am safe, right doc–tor?"

Somehow I got through the assessment as he charmed and disarmed me with his verbal dance. I'm not sure if he was deliberately seductive or if it was just the way of his people, his personality, or his defence mechanisms.

Halfway through the assessment, the massive Jamaican planted his big elbows on his knees and leaned forward. "Doc, it pains me to the heart of my soul to have you kill–ing my name like you are. The name sounds like this: Ann–thone–knee. You have to sing it like a love song. It's the name my momma calls me. It's what my gramma calls me. Even my granddaddy calls me Ann–thone–knee. Course, I don't know what my daddy would have called me, but that don't matter 'cause I'm here wid you. Now tell me. How would you want your daddy to say your name?"

Frankly, no one had ever asked me that question and it took me by surprise. I just stared at him. My eyes watered up, but I couldn't explain what was happening. My professionalism was at risk and I fought to regain control. I didn't realize how much switching chairs could change everything.

"Well, Ann–thon–nee." I watched him wince as I slaughtered his beautiful name again. "My family and friends know what to call me, but we're here to talk about you, not about me. Why don't you tell me your story, about why you're here?"

He winked and began a long, complicated tale of getting his oversized frame into a smuggler's ship while the shanty town around him was under a shower of bullets and explosions. He took his full time explaining the two-week trip that left him to swim ashore in American waters. His time was up before his story even got him to Canada, so I only felt it was fair to finish the assessment the following week. He seemed delighted that I wanted to hear more. He invited me for lunch, or a drink, and I reminded him clearly of the professional boundaries we would operate under.

By lunch, having had little sleep and two emotionally challenging lives to deal with, I was ready for a nap. By the time I got my files put away, and my recordings stashed in my purse for transcribing later, my cell rang. It was Lizzy. I wished Bruce would call. I took the call anyway.

"Katie, you better sit down."

I did. My one thought was about Bruce, but Lizzy took me by surprise.

"How would you and Bruce like to come to Kenya with Dean and me?"

"Lizzy, hold on a minute." My head swirled at the possibility, but my heart was already on the way. "What are you talking about? How in the world is that going to happen?"

"I just got a call from Cousin Billy. He says Uncle Jimmy passed away two weeks ago and they've been trying to track us down."

I felt like I'd been blindsided by a semi-trailer. The world was swirling. Uncle Jimmy and Aunt Rose held the key to my safe place on their Minnesota farm.

Even though I cared mostly about one thing, I asked the right question. "What's happening with Aunt Rose?"

"Billy says she had a mild heart attack when she found Uncle Jimmy in the barn. She made it back to the house to call for help, but she's still in hospital."

"What's happening now?"

"I'm not sure. Oh, hold on a minute. I've got Billy calling me. I'll call you back when I know something. Love you. Bye." And then she was gone.

I just had to call Bruce. I speed-dialled and waited for the ring to go through. Bruce had been seconded to the 633rd Medical Support Squadron. In the Navy, he was Commander Southerland. In the Air Force, he had the rank of Colonel.

I call him Commander most of the time, but I can still hear him a few months earlier as he made his transition: *The mission of the U.S. Air Force is to fly, fight, and win… in air, space, and cyberspace.* I knew Bruce would be in his element learning a whole new side of the Armed Forces.

The sergeant who answered put me on hold. In a minute, he came back and told me that Bruce was off the base for a few hours.

I had used this tactic before with unwanted phone calls and I didn't like it. "Would you please have him call Katie Delancey when he returns?"

"I'm sorry, ma'am, but we aren't tasked with that duty at this station."

I remembered that Bruce had been working with Lieutenant Saunders on a secret initiative for Afghanistan, so I tried a different tactic to get my message through. "May I speak with Lieutenant Saunders, please?"

"One minute, ma'am." I wished the young soldier wouldn't be so proper.

It felt like about five minutes, but eventually the phone clicked in and a voice spoke to me. The only problem was that it is a woman's voice. "Air Combat Command. Lieutenant Saunders, speaking."

I was utterly stunned. I was all for women's rights and equal opportunity, but not once had I imagined Bruce working away day after day with a woman. Not once had he even hinted at the possibility. Not once had he explained how this might be perceived under our current circumstances.

I shut the phone down. The inside of me felt like an overinflated balloon that had just been pricked with a pin. Pieces were flying everywhere. I wanted to crawl into a hole and disappear forever. How stupid could I be?

I was still sitting in the same chair when Devlyn opened the door.

"Katie, your group is all here, waiting. I hope you ate your lunch. We don't need anyone else showing your young ladies how not to eat."

I still don't know how I got through the afternoon. Anorexics and rape victims. Somehow both groups happened. The only problem was that my notebook was blank. So was my mind.

I stood at the window watching the diminishing freeway traffic until my office clock chimed seven. A strong surge of clouds blocked out the setting sun. I decided to wait until tomorrow to cross the border. There was a certain man who needed to hear just how I felt at the moment. I didn't think it fair to take it out on a truck driver or a border guard.

I opened my email and found nothing from Bruce, but there was a short reply from Sarah:

Katie: Hey, girlfriend. Sounds like your heart is being stretched to the limits. Take a hug. As far as intimacy with guys, that just takes time together. Keith and I are still trying to work out the kinks. Give yourself a shower of grace. As for God, you know he's looking to love you, not someone you'd like yourself to be. Whether life is crazy or calm, whether you're mellow or mad, whether you're scared or safe, whether you're feeling precious or persnickety, whether you're feeling friendly or friendless, know that you're loved just as you are. Let me know when you're free for coffee and shopping. Love always, Sarah.

CHAPTER SEVEN

Night slithered in like a hunting cobra. The signs were all there. The hiss of tires furrowing through the freshly fallen rains. The stealthy darkness of storm clouds sending out their forked lightning flashes like a serpent's tongue. Flashing out and in. Out and in. While the tingle in my spine and the knot in my gut knew it was coming, I couldn't see it.

Bruce still hadn't called by nine. Neither had he answered my nineteen attempts to call him.

I finally called Lizzy, even though it was late. She was still up. Her assumptions about my call were all wrong.

"Hey, Katie. Dean's just leaving. We've been working out our Kenya plans. Oh, Billy says that Uncle Jimmy's funeral went well and that they missed us. He says someone else was supposed to let us know. He's just settling the estate."

I wasn't sure I heard right, so I parroted back, "The estate?"

"He says that they're going to have to sell the farm to cover everything. Aunt Rose has to go to a nursing home if she survives the hospital. There's no one left who wants the place."

"What about Lancelot?"

"You mean the horse? Billy said something about Uncle Bob sending him to Europe to a stud farm. Billy said the stallion was one wild critter. He might be gone already, for all I know."

"No one told me." I could feel my body shivering and shaking. I pressed the phone harder to my ear. "Do you think I could still get there before everything's gone?"

Lizzy continued as if she was spouting off the six o'clock news. "Sure, but there's probably not a lot of good stuff left. Call Uncle Bob. The good news is,

Uncle Jimmy and Aunt Rose left us both a chunk of change to use for a trip back to Kenya. Dean's psyched to go. I'm going to take him through all my pictures again so he knows what's coming up. Hey, if we both hurry up and get married we could make it a honeymoon trip. I bet Bruce would love to go."

"Lizzy, I'm not sure this wedding is going to happen all that soon, if at all."

I could hear, from the extra-long pause, that Lizzy was honing in on where this conversation was going. "What's the big guy stalling for now?"

I just couldn't tell her about Bruce and another woman. Not yet. I felt stupid enough. "He's got to get his prosthetic leg finished up. He's been contracted to develop some new scheme in Afghanistan. The trial is still upcoming for Charlie and a few others. I've got some new clients."

"Katie, don't give me those excuses. Do me a favour and pray about it. We've got time."

Praying? Was she kidding? Right now I felt betrayed. No matter what I attached my heart to, it was snatched out of my life before I even had time to feel safe and secure. Where was God when you really needed him?

There was only one thing to keep my mind occupied. In the morning, I would book a flight from Seattle to Minneapolis. Devlyn would have to cover for a while. Tonight, I needed to transcribe Hanan's story. It was good fuel for the rage that was roiling underneath. I secured the headset, loosened my fingers, and pushed play. Word by word, I captured her story in print. I deliberately left out my prompts and interjections.

The girl was obviously educated, but something wasn't in sync with the beautiful face I'd seen. Throughout the entire rendition, her voice was straight-jacketed into a monotone. There wasn't a hint of emotion, as if she was a computer droid blurting out someone else's pain.

* * *

My childhood was happy. My father was a well-respected man. He had three wives. There were eleven children, three girls from my mother. The four boys in the house were sent away to school when they were young. I hardly ever saw them as I grew up. My mothers would all wear the Hajib to cover their faces when we went shopping. Some days we would find the most beautiful clothes. I still feel shame some days for not wearing a veil here.

Usually the servants did the shopping for food because we would always have to have one of my uncles to walk with us when we left the house, and they were often too busy. We all said our prayers and were very faithful. We ate well. We talked and laughed a lot when there were no men around. Apart from my mother, none of us spoke much when the men came.

My father had seven daughters to marry, so he was very busy arranging things once we officially became women. One of the older sisters from another of my father's wives was sent out to be married. She brought great shame on her husband for some reason and was sent back to my father. My father called the women and girls out to the family pool one evening. He was fully clothed but stood in waist-deep water as he prayed to the Almighty for mercy. He seemed very sad. He called this daughter of shame to join him in the pool. She seemed uncertain, but since it was her father she removed her sandals and stepped fully clothed into the pool. One step. Two steps. Three steps. All the way, until she stood beside her father with the water lapping at her underarms.

My father looked deep into my eyes as he spoke. He knew that perhaps I had a wild spirit that needed to be taught a lesson. He told us all that in his house there was no room for shame, that daughters must do all they can to be women who bring joy to his heart and honour to the

Almighty. He put his hands on my sister's neck and pushed her under the water. She was kicking and trying to pull herself up by grabbing at his shoulders, but he held her until she stopped moving. When he was done, he left her floating in the pool and walked alone to his room to change. The servants removed her. That night, at dinner, no one said anything about what had happened. There was no service to remember my sister.

The next day, my father came to the door of my room. I had been crying, but I hid my face and dried my tears so he wouldn't see. He took me by the shoulder and led me out of the house into the courtyard. At first, I was terrified, since I thought he would take me to the pool. I looked up to see the oldest daughter of my own mother dressed up beautifully and realized that today she was being married. There would be a big celebration and, of course, my father would not want me to miss it. He led me to the center of the courtyard where my sister was waiting with her groom. He told me to wait and I did. In a few minutes, he returned with an older man. They stood at the entrance pointing in my direction and talking. Finally, they both walked toward me. My father simply said, "Go. He is your husband. Don't bring any shame on my house."

I was so confused, but I could see the pool at the end of the courtyard. I went. When we reached the man's home, he ravaged me without mercy.

I was in so much pain. There were three other older women and they beat me almost every day. I became sick, but the other wives laughed. I finally realized that I would have a baby. When the little boy was born, the wives took him away and the man sent me out onto the streets. Without protection, I was at the mercy of everyone. I had no food. Even the little boys threw stones at me. I ran to the country.

An old woman took me into her home. She was a grandmother and I helped her with her housework. When her granddaughters came for a visit, I would teach them things I had learned from my mother. She had learned things from overhearing my father talk with other men. The grandmother saw that I had a gift to teach and she invited other neighbour girls into the home for the mornings. The little ones had eager minds and bright eyes and they loved to absorb everything I could tell them. I taught them about the numbers and the basics of letters and reading. I told them all the stories I could remember.

One day, two of the girls were missing from our class. A group of angry men came to the door of the grandmother's home and there was a lot of shouting. I used to do shopping for the old woman and the next time I went to the market the men found me and beat me with sticks until I was bleeding and hardly able to make it home. The old woman took care of me, but no more children came to learn from me.

A few days after I was beaten, the men returned. They told the old woman that the religious leaders demanded that I be brought for a trial. They said I was undermining the Koran and teaching things against God. I could see my father's pool in my mind and I was very afraid. The grandmother told them I was too broken from the beatings and that they would have to come back in a few days when I could move.

Later that night, her brother from another village came and took me away. I know she paid him. He put me into an old cart under some blankets. I felt every bump in the road, but I knew I could not scream if I wanted to live. It took three days until the journey was finished. We stopped many times for rest and we talked about whether life could be another way. He told me that I must run to Egypt where women like myself could live without fear. He gave me money and I was put into the back of an old truck that took me to Cairo.

I do not wish to talk about Cairo. The men there were very bad. Most men have been bad. I do not trust men. I had no place to run. I am here now. I have learned not to have babies anymore. I live in the New Hope Women's Home for refugees. I am safe. I miss my son. That is enough.

* * *

Hanan's story sobered me. I knew Andrew Rooney had once said that death is supposed to be a "distant rumour to the young." The reality in our world is that some two and a half million children and youth, between ten and twenty-five years of age, die every year. Car accidents and childbirth seem to be the leading cause of death. But then there are these other untold stories. Premature deaths have left millions from all forms of faith wondering what kind of God exists and what power he really has.

I think for us women the question always arises, is God different than the men we see? Does he notice us? Does he care?

CHAPTER EIGHT

The hyenas of guilt and rage and betrayal attacked my spirit all night long. I felt their nips tearing me apart, leaving me helpless. The wildness that had sustained and focused me in times of overwhelming sorrow and confusion evaporated like clouds under a noonday sun. The only safe place I could imagine was racing side by side against that Arabian stallion in a Minnesota pasture. I determined to start my journey at first light.

I reached the border by five o'clock with the dawn's early light crystal clear. My face looked like I was fresh from a hangover or a long overdue fix, but I was desperate to get to Sea-Tac Airport as soon as humanly possible.

The line-up at the border crossing was short and I used my Nexus Pass without any problem. The gate lifted and I accelerated forward. Fifty feet ahead, a security officer in sunglasses began to wave me over. I slowed down, sure that he was mistaken. Instead, he continued to block my path and wave me over to the farthest inspection lane. Not again. Not now.

I got out and marched toward him before he had time to reach me. "What do you think you're doing? I need to get to the airport as soon as possible." Probably not a good approach for someone in my situation. I tried to stare into his eyes, but his reflective sunglasses only gave me a poor image of a very angry woman.

He was very polite. "Ma'am, your file has been flagged. I'm afraid you'll have to pull over and let me sort out this situation with you."

It seemed strange that he wasn't making me step into the customs office to talk to anyone else, but I'd never had to do this before. He wanted me to let him sit in the passenger's seat while we went over some forms, but I told him we could do this right where we were.

No amount of arguing would convince him, so I obediently pulled my car into the last inspection lane. I felt like a beaten dog, and if this dog got one more beating I wasn't sure she was going to get up again.

"Ma'am, are you Katrina Joy Delancey?" I affirmed that I was. "I regret to inform you that you need to return to Canada. We are not able to process you through here today."

I tried to give him a look to freeze him in place, but the spark was gone. The best I could manage was an exasperated whisper. "What are you talking about?"

"Ms. Delancey, we have concerns that your safety is at risk and your entrance is being denied until pending investigations are complete."

I opened my car door and stepped out to get in his face. I wanted to yell, but I didn't want to draw any more attention to myself so I spoke forcefully and deliberately. "My safety? All I need to do is to get to the airport and I'll be out of here. No one knows I'm here. I'm fine. Please, let me go. I need to go."

"I'm sorry, Ms. Delancey. We cannot let you stay in the United States."

"But I'm an American citizen!"

"Did you use a Canadian passport to cross into Canada?"

"Yes, but I'm a dual citizen. I have a right to be here."

"I'm sorry, ma'am, but you exercised your right as a Canadian and currently you carry the status of a Canadian. We cannot grant you access into the United States until this pending investigation is completed. For your own safety, ma'am, please get into your car and drive back to where you came from. Otherwise, I will have no choice but to escort you out of the country and impound your car until further notice."

I was beyond numb as I sat back in the driver's seat. They should never let a person in my condition sit behind the wheel. I was dead inside. Nothing mattered anymore. Not the law. Not the traffic. Not even my own life. I was too tired to prove anything, though, so I started the car and pulled back into the line-up for Canadian customs. This time I had no problems getting back into Canada. I just didn't care anymore.

Loneliness tracked me like a hungry lioness sensing the nearness of her wounded prey. My breaths came short and raspy. Looking over my shoulder seemed like an act of lunacy, but I couldn't help myself. Escape seemed impossible. Life's complications closed in tighter and tighter. There seemed to be only one way out.

I drove into Vancouver until I got to the city side of the Burrard Street Bridge. I pulled into the first parking spot I could find. I didn't put any money into the meter, because I just didn't care. I stumbled my way back to the pedestrian walkway. My feet weighed so much. My head hurt. There was nothing left.

I reached the highest point of the arch of that bridge and looked out over the inlet and back at the towering buildings of the West End. A dozen freighters rested at anchor. The little people-ferries skittered like water beetles between their stops. Kites flew. Yachts cruised. The dragon boat crews trained. Sailboats of all sizes skimmed across the waves. People basked on the sand and walked their dogs and tossed Frisbees as if there wasn't a care in the world. Stanley Park loomed like a luscious treasure in a bustling metropolis. Above it all were the majestic mountains. I saw it all and just didn't care.

I started to climb the barrier when I heard the voice. A child. A little girl. "Mom, isn't it all beautiful?" And she started to sing. "God is so good. God is so good. God is so good. He's so good to me."

I turned and she was there looking at me with a flower in her hand. "Lady, want a flower? God made it. Just like he made you and me. Right, Mom?"

I stared at this little angel through my tears. I heard the mom calling 911, but I couldn't move. I heard the sirens, but I couldn't move. I knew my body was being grabbed and restrained and moved into an ambulance, but I didn't feel anything.

CHAPTER NINE

Consciousness felt about as welcoming as a great white shark between me and the surface of a deep sea dive. Staying where I was wasn't a good option, but neither was going where I needed to go.

For the next while, I knew life was happening, but the words didn't make sense. The faces didn't mean anything. The numbness just went on and on. I swallowed what I was told to swallow. I sat in chairs where I was told to sit. I gave my blood. I went through tests. I heard the mumbles of others like myself sitting in a circle of nobodies, saying nothing to anyone who cared.

I faced nightmare stretches where images of red slip-ons, yellow Porsches, and glaring brunettes chased me. I felt myself alternating between falling off bridges, being bound, and gagged by the Monk, choking on muddy water and drowning in a ditch far from anyone who could help me.

There were wonderful stretches of deep dark silence where nothing could reach me, but then the images came back. Bruce and Lieutenant Saunders laughing at me as they carried on their affair. Myself, in the place of Hanan, being held under water because of all the shame I'd caused. I never knew who was holding me down, but I just didn't have the strength to hold them off.

There was my beautiful horse, Lancelot, tied and trapped in a barn where no one understood his wild spirit. I could see him so clearly, trying desperately to run, but he couldn't move. And I was still there, in a stall close by. Also tied. Unable to run. Unable to rescue him or me.

Then there were the border agents. And the voices. Both American and Canadian. "You don't belong here, ma'am. You're not wanted, ma'am. Go back to where you belong, ma'am. You don't belong anywhere, ma'am." And always the red slip-ons stepping, stepping, stepping, closer and closer.

But once in a while through the blackness and chaos there was a voice. The voice of an angel singing. "God is so good. God is so good. God is so good. He's so good to me."

And then, one morning, it was all over. I woke up. The sun shone. I threw off my sheets, put on a blue hospital housecoat, stepped carefully toward the window, and looked out on one of the most beautiful cities imaginable. I knew this place well. The Vancouver General Hospital. Psych Ward. I was at peace with this. I was safe and I was sane.

A phantom figure slipped into the room and stood at the foot of my bed. I caught his reflection in the window and turned to see him. His smile looked genuine. "Good to see you up, Ms. Delancey. My name is Tim and I'm your nurse for today. How are you this morning?"

I decided to engage. "Call me Katie. What day is it?"

Tim gently guided me to sit on the bed while he put the blood pressure cuffs on me and went through his routine of taking my temperature. "It's Canada Day. July 1. You've got the perfect room for the fireworks display tonight. I just might have to extend my shift a little to find out how you're really doing."

The thought actually intrigued me. "I wouldn't mind some company. Do you think I'd be able to have some visitors soon?"

Tim flashed a penlight into my eyes and watched my pupils dilate. He took my pulse. His gentle touch actually felt comforting. "Your sister is in town asking to see you. You've created quite a stir these past eleven days. I didn't know you were such a celebrity."

I watched him stow his gear efficiently and professionally. I could tell he wasn't going to stay much longer. "Let's just say, I'm not the kind they're doing fireworks for. I think I'll take a shower, get some breakfast, and read the paper. Maybe this afternoon I can see my sister."

I just finished lunch when Lizzy walked through the door and threw herself around me. Tears streamed down her face. I was glad that I had a private room because she was soon blubbering and convulsing in my arms. It took a while to calm her down.

In the next three hours, she informed me that I'd been all over the American newscasts. The media were speculating that I'd been kidnapped due to my connections with Stephen and Tommy Lee. Bruce had been frantically searching through Washington and Minnesota to see if I was there. I secretly wondered if

Lieutenant Saunders had been helping him with this initiative, but I shook the thought out of my mind.

It had taken a week for the authorities to find out where I was. Everyone who knew me understood that my schedule was supposed to be in Washington the day I disappeared. Lizzy had informed Bruce and others that I had mentioned going to Uncle Jimmy's farm. No one had thought Canada. Devlyn had assured them I had gone to Bellingham. Someone with authority finally checked and saw that I'd actually crossed into the States but returned to Canada on the same day. No one had bothered to consider my recrossing of the border. This seemed strange to me, when I was told, since it was their authorities who sent me back.

Somehow my impounded car led the Vancouver authorities to link me to the unknown jumper on the bridge. The paperwork on the car hadn't been processed for several days after it had been towed, and for some reason the plates hadn't been put into the system. I had no identification on me and had only given my name as "Kat."

Some alert news watcher linked the bigger stories and I was found. Even then it was difficult to locate me, as I'd first been taken to St. Paul's Hospital and then discharged, under confidentiality, to Vancouver General.

The problem for Bruce and me is that they wouldn't let him cross the border to see me. He was a key witness in Charlie's trial. But so was I. With me stuck on the Canadian side and Bruce stuck on the American, I resigned myself that some things just weren't meant to be. Sometimes I hated rules. Obviously, my prayers weren't about to be answered.

The fireworks were gorgeous and I really did have a great view. Lizzy's oohs and aahs made it feel for a few minutes like we were in a luxury hotel celebrating something special. I just didn't feel the same sparkle or zip as my sister. At least the heaviness was dissipating.

When I finally got released into Lizzy's care the next afternoon, she helped get my car out of the impound and then took me shopping. I had lost a bit of weight in the past two weeks and I needed a pick-me-up. Nothing like new clothes for that. I could hardly believe my ID was still safely tucked away in the trunk near the spare tire where I'd hid it. My laptop hadn't been moved. It was no wonder they couldn't find me.

We strolled down Robson Street and hit the fashion stores. Aritzia, Au Coton, BB Blue and Boutique Legerdemain. Lizzy was still thinking of Dean and looked for some of the edgier wear to get me raising my eyebrows. I tried on just one of her selections and had such a strong flashback that I almost crumpled to the floor. I saw the haunted eyes, the alluring cuts that all of Tommy's girls had used to pull a man in. I felt my inner self transforming before the mirror; it took all my energy to rip off the outfit and discard it on the floor.

From that point on, I decided to hold Lizzy's selections while she tried things on and maybe even coach her a bit. Dynamite, Esprit, and Memosa Accessories gave us more options. As one last fling, we hit Dare to Wear on Granville, but even Lizzy found the avant-garde swimwear and lingerie a little too risqué. She was still blushing as we hit the streets again. She had no plans to wear any of it. At least with her older sister present.

CHAPTER TEN

Pink cotton candy clouds padded like tired puppies to their resting place above the mountains. They were exhausted at exuberant forays to sprinkle on picnics and golf games, soccer matches, and weddings alike. Without malice, they charged into the fray of ordinary lives and scrambled to escape when the winds of change blew them off.

I watched the clouds as I sipped chai with my sister on the balcony of a condo in downtown Vancouver. Lizzy had taken a week off and she helped me lease the unit. Of course we had to shop to furnish it, and that took a few days as well.

It took several days to get my wireless internet and phone hooked up. Then a repairman came back to fix my phone line since somehow it hadn't been connected properly. It was great to be connected to the world again.

Lizzy coaxed me into calling my mother since Mom had been in literal pain over my disappearance. Mom had finished up her last round of chemo treatments and was physically fragile. Lizzy was her main support system in Minneapolis, so I knew Mom had sacrificed a lot to let my sister come. I didn't give Mom a lot of details but assured her I was doing better now after some time in the hospital. I thanked her for Lizzy and for her prayers.

And then she said one thing that got my attention.

"I'm glad you're doing better, Katie. Two weeks ago I had this urgency to pray for you. I prayed that God would help you know how good he was to you, and that somehow he would show you his beauty, and how special you are. I even asked him to send you an angel you couldn't miss. It seemed to be so long, so intense. Are you sure you're okay?"

The image of the little girl singing "God is so good," holding a flower and telling me that God had made me special, flooded my mind powerfully. In fact, I had to sit down for the rest of the conversation. For a few minutes, I almost admitted out loud to Mom that perhaps there were no coincidences. That perhaps God had answered her prayers very specifically. That perhaps the only reason I was still alive is because she had obeyed the prompting to pray.

When I got off the phone, Lizzy switched on a good movie and I was able to let the thoughts about Mom's prayer fade away like a commercial. After the movie, life went on.

When I got the nerve to call Devlyn, she politely and gently informed me that she thought it would be good for both myself and my clients if I took a little while to sort things through. Perhaps I should think about doing some volunteer work in the community and do some people-helping that didn't bring on so much stress. I didn't have the energy to argue with her. I just agreed and hung up.

I left two messages for Bruce with my contact information, and to his credit he did email once each day. He might as well have given me a list of bullet points about his schedule.

For example, he wrote these words to his potential fiancée after she'd just been released from the psych ward for almost jumping off a bridge:

Katie: You had me scared. I've been on seven flights in the past week looking for you. I don't understand why you didn't call me. Your sister and mom are worried sick. With our new situation, I'm being transferred temporarily to the Air Force until this project is done. I'll be praying so keep me in touch as you recover. Love, Bruce.

Did men know nothing about wowing a woman? Did he not understand that when I sent him fifteen pages describing the horror my life had become, I was looking for more than just an account of what was happening in his life? Did he not understand how to read between the lines? Or did he only think that because he ran back and forth across the States looking for me that somehow I owed him?

I didn't need his assumptions and excuses. And now I started to wonder how much I needed him.

When Lizzy left on the Quick Shuttle to Sea-Tac Airport, I pulled out my laptop and secured my wireless connection. I opened my recent documents, and that's when I rediscovered Hanan's file. As I read her life story again, I was pulled by a strong desire to help women like her. I felt like I was really hearing her life for the first time. That's when I noticed the last phrases she had spoken in her session with me.

I do not trust men. I had no place to run. I am here now. I have learned not to have babies anymore. I live in the New Hope Women's Home for refugees. I am safe. I miss my son. That is enough.

It didn't take me long to google the New Hope Welcome House for Female Refugees in Vancouver. Although it was out of character for me, I sent an email to the operations manager asking about the possibility of volunteering. She must have been online, because I had my reply before I had time to shut down the laptop: *Call in the morning and we'll set up an interview.*

I had no job, no home, no fiancé, no horse, no company, no friends, nothing that I could really hang onto, but for some reason I felt free. I pulled up a few shows I'd missed and caught up on the crime dramas I was addicted to. I watched the late-night news. I took a long bubble bath surrounded by flickering candles and soothing lavender. Nothing interrupted me. I slept like a baby all night long. Without pills.

Conscious thought emerged like a Monarch from its cocoon. It was slow and somewhat deliberate, escaping bit by bit, opening up little by little. Everything I thought wasn't always gloriously beautiful, but at the end of the process I was ready to spread my wings and fly again. At least, after I finished my shower, toast, and chai.

My cell rang while I tried to select a necklace. I had two to choose from at the moment.

It was Lizzy calling. She was tired, but safe at home. She needed her sleep. She would call again. Thanks for the prayers.

Prayers? I hadn't even thought of praying for her.

At ten o'clock in the morning, I called the New Hope Operations Manager. There was an orientation session and tour of the welcome homes that afternoon at two o'clock—or in a month, if I wasn't available. I told her I'd be there in the afternoon.

I dillydallied at the Bay and a few other outlets. I meandered through the art gallery and grabbed a salad for lunch in a local restaurant. By then, it was time to find my way to the orientation session.

My first mistake was assuming that the gregarious dark-haired gentleman who first welcomed me was part of the New Hope staff. When I walked in through the door of the church where the orientation was being held, he met me with a confident smile, a warm handshake, and even handed me some promotional material. He walked me into the room where about ten others were sitting and even introduced me to Samantha, the operations manager.

When he sat by me, I didn't even think twice about it. Not until formal introductions were happening and individual life stories were being put onto the table did I realize that he was a volunteer just like myself.

When Samantha asked him to introduce himself, he set the template for me. "Name's Damian. I've worked with World Vision and Food for the Hungry for the past ten years, in a lot of countries, and thought I'd like to see what's happening on the ground back in Canada. I believe that God's heart beats passionately for the orphan, the widow, and the refugee. Don't know anyone yet, but I'm looking forward to meeting everyone."

I was so caught up with this compassionate man that I missed the cue for my turn at introductions. Before I realized it, he rescued me.

"Pardon my rudeness for jumping in again. I was supposed to introduce my wonderful friend Kate, and in my excitement at telling you who I was, I missed giving her the honour she deserves. She really does have an incredible passion for refugees and her own story is worthy of your time. Just before she fills us in on the high points of her life, I have a burning question that I just need to know. It comes from my culture shock after being away from this country so long. Why, in this country, is lemon juice made with artificial flavour and dishwashing liquid made with real lemons? Kate, perhaps you can answer that question."

I felt the biggest smile I'd felt for months coming out from deep within my tummy. I was so grateful for his heroic actions that I ignored his misreading of my name and played right along.

"Damian, I'd love to tell you the secret of that, but then I might have to kill you. Friends, the fact is that I grew up in Kenya and never had to sort out that question. I'm a trained counsellor on a bit of a sabbatical from my practice. It was actually one of your New Hope residents who shared her story with me and sparked my interest in how I can help. I love to learn new things. I'm glad to be here."

As the others introduced themselves, I couldn't help glancing sideways at Damian. He had this strange glowing confidence and carefree attitude. Twice he caught me looking at him and the second time he winked. I blushed, determined not to get caught again.

CHAPTER ELEVEN

Some people are as persistent as salmon on their way to spawning grounds. You could put rapids and falls and bears in the way and somehow they'd only see the prize at the end of the stream. Meeting people like that is transformative.

The New Hope orientation was soul-challenging. There were thirty million refugees worldwide, and twenty to thirty thousand asylum seekers coming to Canada each year. Each needed housing and mentoring and caring. The tours of the homes gave us a good introduction to community living, used by New Hope to integrate refugee claimants into their new culture and the relationships they would need to succeed.

We were just leaving the second home when I met Hanan coming into the house. Although I had been hoping to see her, she was genuinely surprised to see me. She began to shake in front of me. I quickly pulled her aside and asked her if she was okay.

"Doctor, you came to see me?"

Her eyes were so filled with hope and expectation that I didn't want to disappoint her. "I came to see what was happening with New Hope because you said they had helped you." I didn't want to make any promises I couldn't keep, and yet I had been hoping to see her.

She clasped my right hand with both her hands. "When I went for my appointment, they said you weren't going to see me again. You are the only one I can tell my story to. I prayed to the Almighty to please give me a chance to talk with you again. You are the answer to my prayers."

I could feel myself already forming boundaries to guard my heart. And yet I couldn't resist her eyes. "I'm not sure about being the answer to anyone's prayers, Hanan, but I would love to see you again and talk with you. I need to stay with this group for today. Perhaps we could meet tomorrow?"

"Yes, I would like that very much." We exchanged phone numbers and I knew that somehow my life was going to change. Again.

After the tour, we sat for an Iranian meal with a wonderful couple who were preparing for their refugee claim hearing. They shared their story with us. After they were done, a petite Bangladeshi woman shared her story followed by an Iranian man who reminded me of a retired lineman for a professional football team. Finally, a Congolese woman shared. Out of habit I recorded each one with the promise of confidentiality.

Damian shadowed me the entire tour and, when it was done, he sidled up to me in the parking lot. "Hope I didn't embarrass you in the orientation?"

"You saved me. I owe you my thanks." I wasn't sure of the appropriate response, so I fished in my purse for my car keys and kept walking toward my car.

It didn't seem to put him off his charm at all. "How thankful are you?"

"What do you mean?" I turned to face him.

"I hate to admit this, but I bought two tickets for the football game next Saturday and I haven't had time to find someone to go with me. It would help me out a lot if you'd be willing to take one of them from me." He even held up the tickets to prove himself.

"I don't really know that much about football. I did grow up in Kenya, you know."

"So I heard. Didn't I also hear that you were willing to learn new things?"

"Yes, I guess I did say something like that." He was a human recording machine. I wasn't sure what my face was showing at the moment, but it did feel good that some man had actually listened to me. Maybe my open mouth gave me away.

"So, it's a date then?"

"Date? No. It's just 'thanks'."

"Great." He seemed genuinely relieved. "As I said in there, I've been away for the past ten years and I'm kind of rusty at this communication and connection thing. If you've got time, before the game, I sure would love to hear what it was like for you growing up in Africa. I found this great little Ethiopian restaurant near the stadium. Hearing your life in Kenya might really get me in touch with others who will be coming here from there."

Damian handed me a crude card with his name and number on it and started walking away.

"In case you change your mind about coming," he called back over his shoulder, "just leave a message on the machine and I'll understand. I'll hang onto the tickets just in case. I really don't want you to feel any pressure on this one. There are no expectations."

He got into his Mustang and pulled away without a backward glance. I wondered if he checked his mirror for one last look.

Damian's manner was like a magnet for my lonely heart and I knew I better email my friend Sarah to stay grounded. Her friendship and input was one of the anchors that kept me going in the storms of the past year. She had been there for me since Kenya and provided the bridge I needed to connect my worlds. I stretched back into my office chair and scanned my message one more time.

Sarah: I met the most incredible refugees today with an organization called New Hope. One of the Saudia Arabian girls in their homes was also a client. I think I've found a niche for my heart to engage in a compassionate way with people who could use a friend. I've been given a few weeks off to sort some things out, so this was a good focus for my energy. For some reason, the U.S. immigration officers won't let me cross the border. Hopefully, I can sort this out quickly so we can get some shopping time in. I met the most incredible guy who is also volunteering. He made me laugh and I haven't done that in ages. He's taking me out for Ethiopian food before we go to a football game. He's also really interested in my life in Kenya. When does that happen around here? Hope you and Keith are enjoying your new place in Seattle. Love, Katie.

For some reason, I felt great as I reviewed my day. But feelings like this didn't tend to last on me. I was like the Teflon girl when it came to positive feelings.

CHAPTER TWELVE

The cockroaches of shame, fear, and anger crawled out that night as I lay alone, unaware. I sensed their approach and used my best counselling tricks to crush them. But, like real cockroaches, they continued to scurry and survive in the dark recesses of my soul. They clustered together and multiplied over and over.

I would behead the pests, but they would live on. I would starve them, and they would continue to survive. I would blast them, and they would keep reproducing and colonizing every niche imaginable. I didn't have a prayer against them.

And that was probably my biggest problem.

The wounds in my spirit, from my time as one of Tommy's girls, hatched a deep shame in my soul that left me feeling like I somehow deserved any mistreatment I got. I didn't deserve to be loved by someone like Bruce. Sometimes I felt like my soul was in a perpetual state of shock. Some days, I hated myself. Still, I had to do life every time the sun came up. I wasn't going back to the hospital.

I tried to call Bruce early to let him know about my new place, about my time with Lizzy, about Hanan, and about my orientation with New Hope. I didn't think telling him about Damian was the best thing, under the circumstances.

Through emails, he was still trying to tell me that Lieutenant Saunders was just someone who had been assigned to work with him, that no woman like her would want a cripple like him. He seemed to be in a real pity party. Or a state of denial. It also didn't create a lot of brownie points for him to indicate that the woman he was with was too good for a cripple, but that somehow I wasn't.

To his credit, Bruce picked up when I called. He acknowledged me and even sounded happy. The military had fitted him with his prosthetic limb and he was being tested to see whether he could build himself up again to his level of former fitness. He wasn't sure if he could remaster Tai Kwon Do, but he was going to give it a try. And then the fatal comment. "Barbara is working with me to adjust some of the other martial arts that might work for me."

"And who's Barbara?" I had to admit that I didn't like surprises. Especially when it came to women in my future husband's life.

I could almost hear him tighten up in frustration. "Katie, don't do this to me. Barbara is Lieutenant Saunders. I've told you, this is strictly professional. She just has a lot of the skills I need right now. You know how I feel about you. That hasn't changed. I just feel kind of frustrated that we can't ever seem to get together."

So Lieutenant Barbara Saunders just happened to have a lot of the skills he needed right now. I'm sure every person in the world with half a brain would know that this wasn't what I needed to hear. If Bruce wanted to make me feel claustrophobic in his verbal straitjacket, he was going about it the right way.

Somehow, I stumbled through the things I wanted to tell him, left him with a civil farewell, and then got ready to meet Hanan.

Maybe if I just tried a little harder, Bruce would like me more. Maybe our family's constant moving had left me unable to properly attach to people. I knew I had problems with eye contact at times, but I really did like people. All my personality tests said so.

To be honest, I had to admit that I felt God was holding out on me. I knew in my head that it wasn't true, but I *felt* like it was true. If God cared for me like his daughter, where was my champion? Where was the man to cherish me and rescue me? Where was the one to call me by name and run to me as if there was no other person on the planet? I just couldn't believe that God would leave me to answer my own prayers by making me find a worthy man on my own.

Doubt was deadly. Right now, it left me wondering if I had anything beautiful left to offer, inside or out. The idea of shopping for more clothes wasn't doing it right now. Redying my hair felt too routine. Trying another exercise or diet program just felt like admitting defeat. I'd been under the illusion that if I could just keep myself busy, somehow I'd matter more.

I was just so tired of it all. The routine. The senseless repetition of doing the same thing day after day. The demands from everyone I knew. I was a cog in a machine that didn't seem to have an off switch. One of dozens of cogs that could easily be replaced by another. Did I really matter anymore?

The cockroaches were subtle and I shook them off with a call to Lizzy, who talked non-stop about the wonderful plans she and Dean were putting together for Kenya. Maybe I'd just go without Bruce.

Hanan was on time for our lunch and it felt wonderful to be able to talk with a woman who understood my soul without realizing it. She had come to me for strength and hope, but I was the one drawing strength and hope from her. She may have been three years younger than me, but she was age-old with experience.

I was in the middle of sipping my Coke when a flash of red caught my attention. A woman in red slip-ons glided quickly into a booth behind me. There was no question that she was a brunette and that she had blue topaz earrings. Hanan continued to talk on, sharing the questions of her soul, but I could barely concentrate any longer. Several times, I saw her questioning my attention through her wrinkled brow and confused eye contact. I tried to make the appropriate comments, but as soon as we were done, I paid the bill and suggested we walk outside.

As we exited onto the street, I grabbed her arm and dragged her behind me. She stared anxiously behind us, wondering what was happening. I glanced back toward the booth where the brunette sat—and that's the exact time I ran into a tower of hard flesh.

I felt powerful hands on my shoulders, but before I could scream I heard melodious laughter booming out all around me. "Da Queen is back. Hallelujah. Da Queen is back."

I looked up and there was Anthony. He flashed those gold rings on his left hand like they were proof of his identity. I was in a whirl inside, but I tried to remember his name properly. "Ann—thown—nee. What are you doing here?"

His singsong chant was less pronounced than I remembered, but it was still there. "Doc—tor, isn't this a beau—ti—ful land? We can see each other any—where. I see that you are with Hanan. She told me you were meeting for lunch today. I felt such a soul connect—ion with you that I had to take the chance to just say hell—o."

For a moment, he had my total attention and I almost forget about the red slip-on stalker lurking in the booth just inside. But not quite. This big mountain of flesh could be a great protection.

"Hanan and I just had lunch and we're going for a walk," I said. "Maybe you'd like to join us for a minute or two." At least until we got out of sight.

"I saw your name card at the counselling center, but they say you are away," Anthony said. "Yet here you are. I like your name. It rolls off my tongue and out my soul. When I think of you, my lips want to say 'Sweet Sugar,' 'Katie Kat,' 'African Queen,' 'Da Girl Widda True Roots.'"

For a moment, I was stunned. Not from the seductive way he whispered his phrases, but with one specific name he used. "Katie Kat" had only been used by one other person in my life. My grandfather. A man whose prayers I could count on to get me through my hardest times.

I stood my ground and stretched my five-foot-seven-inch frame to its full height. Although he was more than a foot taller, he respected my space. He knew he'd got to me.

"Anthony." I didn't even try to get his name right. "You can charm whatever ladies you want, but I'm not on your list. I'm glad you came to see me, but Hanan and I need to finish our discussion. I'm sure the center can keep helping you with whatever you need."

I could see the intrigue in his eyes and the smirk on his face. I could tell that he knew I was putting on a show for Hanan. He might back off for now, but his interest had been piqued. He played the humbled man.

"I just want to tell you the rest of my story." His eyes almost found a way to beg.

"Not today. Make your appointments."

And I walked away. Hanan and I jumped on the Canada Line Skytrain for an hour and then took the Sea Bus ferry to Lonsdale Quay. The Skytrain was a computerized rapid transit line that flashed through the subterranean tunnels of the downtown core and then emerged to soar on its track high above the city and the rivers. Hanan was fascinated by a train that ran without visible human control. She was just as fascinated by the scenery. This time I was able to hear her heart without distraction.

By the time we settled into the lively open markets of the quay, we were more than comfortable with each other as women. I took her to one of my favourite African craft stores and she explained the arts and crafts that she and the other women in Saudi Arabia did behind closed doors. She clearly relished the freedom to shop without a male escort.

Hanan constantly looked in amazement at the expressions on the faces of the women all around us. In our discussion, she repeatedly mentioned how vulnerable she felt without her veil. She wrestled with shame and guilt and fear. And I saw then that it wasn't only me. The cockroaches had found their way into the souls of women in every country of the world.

CHAPTER THIRTEEN

Finding girls these days who had sailed through life without being abused, compromised, or just plain had their hearts torn apart was about as rare as spotting a Rwandan Gorilla without a guide. The worst thing was when all this happened at the hands of family members.

I was one of those few girls who had been cherished by my dad. I'd been his princess. But so was Lizzy. I guess I always felt like I was competing for the attention I craved. And of course, my dad had been busy with other people, just like every dad. Perhaps men just got a lot more strokes from their work and they didn't always see their little ones as work—in the positive sense, that is.

Mom was the greatest role model you could ever hope for. Every kid on the mission compound felt that way. Every other missionary said so. Every person in the community thought so. Sometimes it took a lot to get her attention, but most of the time I couldn't have asked for more. My mother came to my concerts and games and special events. I was loved. And that's why it was so hard to explain why I turned out so insecure.

During the time with Tommy Lee, my soul had developed a giant dark cavity that sucked up attention to my beauty. I craved for men to tell me I had everything they needed. I looked to them to see if they had everything I needed. I never found one of them who did. It just left me with one big ache inside.

Is it always human nature to hide ourselves? I thought. *Is anybody who they seem to be? Are we all so afraid of risking rejection and being abandoned that we can't even try to be real? Why do we always want to be so safe all the time? Maybe we just don't like pain.*

For that reason, I almost picked up the phone a dozen times to cancel the tickets with Damian. When Friday afternoon arrived, I ran my fingers over the numbers on my cell. The one moment when I finally did decide to cancel was while I was out on my power walk and realized that I didn't have his number with me. By the time I got home, I decided to have a shower. Then Lizzy phoned with more of her Kenya plans.

After Lizzy's call, I checked the email and, as usual, was very disappointed in what Bruce conveyed. I just about shut down when I saw the Facebook friend invitation. It was from Damian Harding. I spent ten minutes hovering my mouse over the little box to confirm, my mind racing at what this might mean. The internal arrows of accusation made me feel like I was being invited into an affair and I had to fight off the false guilt. I had been very careful not to lead this man on.

In the end, I decided that if I was volunteering with the guy, if I was going to a football game with him, if I was going to be truly thankful for his rescuing me from looking like a fool, I could at least admit that he was my friend. Besides, he might be able to help give me a guy's perspective on what was going on with Bruce and Anthony.

The questions flowed through my mind. Were Anthony's seductive nuances harmless or something I needed to run from? How could I discern the cultural, personal, and manipulative ways of men? Was Bruce just busy or was something else going on? Should I be worrying about another woman making moves on my guy or did guys even know when they were being wooed? Did I owe this Tai Kwon Do master anything just for saving my life? Did any of my habits from being one of Tommy's girls still come through and give men the wrong impression about who I was and what I wanted? My pulse began to race at the thought of even sharing these questions.

Only ten minutes after I confirmed his friendship, I got a message alert. Damian had sent me a note. I clicked on it: "Dinner at 5 tomorrow. Meet me at the Stadium Skytrain at 4:45."

He didn't even ask for my phone number or address. Sounded like just a friendship to me.

I decided to spend the evening transcribing another one of the refugee stories. This was regarding Khalid and Fatima from Iran.

Khalid: We were young when we got married. Our fathers arranged things for us. I was taken by my father to Fatima's home. We sat in the room with our fathers and they spoke to each other about us.

At the end of one hour, we left the room with our fathers and were asked if we would like to spend time talking with each other. Both of us said yes, so we were given one hour in a room alone together.

Fatima was very shy, but she still let me talk to her without a veil covering her face. We spoke about a lot of things in a short time.

After the hour, we were taken to our homes and we met with both our parents. We both agreed to be married. The next week we were brought together and we were married. Fatima was sixteen. I was twenty-four.

I became a sailor and travelled the world. I was away a lot, so we have only one child. Things were not very good in my country, but I continued with my work until I became a second officer. At that point, I was allowed to bring along my wife and daughter on a trip. We used to go on the large freighters to many different ports.

I was not very spiritual, but Fatima was very faithful. When we came to Vancouver, I felt a strong urging to leave the ship at two o'clock in the morning. I woke my wife and daughter and we left.

Fatima: We came to New Hope and they took care of us. The church was also very good to us. I had many questions. Especially when Christians spoke about Jesus being the Son of God. I began to read the Bible in Farsi and eventually God's Spirit moved my heart to believe. We are only now just beginning our journey and we hope to learn so much more. We are thankful to God that he is answering our prayers.

There it was again. I paused the tape. God was answering their prayers. Why them and not me? I knew the story wasn't much longer, so I pushed play again and finished up.

Khalid: One of the hardest prayers we have had to pray is for forgiveness. Forgiveness with each other and forgiveness for others who have betrayed and wronged us. We have always known God as the Merciful One, but sometimes we did not realize that he would expect us to show the same mercy to others that he is showing to us.

I wondered if this was a hidden message from God to me or if this was just another case of my overactive imagination and more false guilt. Anyway, the cable news came on and I had a football game to get ready for.

As I sat in the bath later, with the candles flickering and the scent of jasmine tickling my nostrils, my mind began to think through the commitment that Khalid and Fatima were making. Everything was good between them and God seemed to be listening, but what about later on?

I'd had days when I'd prayed for simple things. Parking spots, a short line at the border, a phone call from Bruce that meant something, and even a haircut that was everything I'd dreamed of. Some people said God did those sorts of things for them. For me, it was hit and miss. And if it was hit and miss on small prayers, I wasn't sure how effective my trust level was on the big things. After all, whose prayer hadn't been answered when Dad and Robert had been killed in that car accident? I knew they always prayed for safety before they left on a trip. And whose prayer hadn't been answered as Mom lay dying of cancer? And whose prayer wouldn't have been answered if I had actually jumped off that bridge?

I began to think of all the unanswered prayers from clients I dealt with. Empty wombs. Cribs where cries ended prematurely. Little girls and boys who had lost innocence in indescribable ways. Broken covenants that had led to broken hearts. Tombstone markers with final dates that had come far too early. Lost jobs, bank accounts, and health. Faith, hope, and dreams. Nothing left but smoke and tears.

I guess it was then when I had an aha-moment. I realized that my understanding of answered prayer had more to do with who God was, and what he was doing in the world, than who I was and what I wanted to happen in the world.

CHAPTER FOURTEEN

Insecurity is like a warm blanket fresh out of the dryer. It's been twirling around and around inside and then you get to bundle yourself up nice and tight in it. Mine kept me toasty all night long as I faced my last night before having to explain Damian to Bruce. It was a familiar cosiness that I wrapped around my inner self. It soothed me into accepting that self-doubt and feelings of unworthiness were just normal.

Insecurity also reminded me that most women I knew were anxious about relationships. They all had a deep fear of rejection. They all questioned the legitimacy of their feelings and thoughts. And oversensitivity was just part of the package. These things tumbled around and around and around and if you sat and watched enough, it could really be mesmerizing.

Thursday and Friday were novel days. I devoured two romances and dreamed. Apart from two twenty-minute stretches where I slipped on my bikini and laid discreetly sun-tanning on my balcony, I stayed indoors with the fan blowing on my face. Twice I took cold showers to cool down.

I looked down on all the sun worshippers turning crispy on the beach and wished them well. I had no confidence to even mix with the public like that. People lay on towels patterned almost like the cars in the adjacent parking lot, each claiming their little spot and pretending that no one was looking at or noticing them. I hid in my books.

By 7:30 on Saturday morning, I was completely convinced of my inadequacy and inability to build a relationship with Bruce or Damian. I mentally scanned the rolodex of men I might feel comfortable with, and Dean came to mind. A few others I knew from Kenya came to mind, but I had no contact information for them. Before I could paralyze myself with further doubt, I picked up the phone and punched in Dean's number.

Miracle of miracles, he answered. He was honestly surprised to hear from me and asked if I wanted Lizzy. I told him no, I wanted him. After assuring him that I was doing okay, that I thought the trip to Kenya sounded like it could be fun, that Bruce was busy in Virginia at the Langley Air Field Command Center, I told him I just needed him to listen. He said Lizzy would be by in a few minutes, but that he had time. And so I unloaded on him.

"Dean, I don't understand why God doesn't seem to be answering my prayers."

"Are there specific prayers you have in mind?"

"Sometimes. It's just that things have changed in my relationship with God."

"I don't want to use your counsellor's language on you, Katie, but how does that make you feel?"

"Frustrated, maybe. Untrusting—is that a word? I guess, disappointed. Sometimes, angry and afraid."

"That's a lot of feeling for one person. You must really want this relationship badly."

"Dean, you know my story. God was my Abba when I was growing up. I was the good girl who everyone loved and wanted to have as their daughter. I loved God. When we left Kenya, the world got torn apart for me. My life was chaos inside and out. I made tough choices. Especially after Dad and Robert died. It's been a long journey back. I don't want this to go over the cliff."

"So, the main thing you're feeling is disappointment with God as your Abba?"

"Yes. I expect my Abba to protect me. To listen to me. To be there for me. I expect him to show up when I need him. To let me know that he cares what's going on in my life. And sometimes I really need him to fix some things that get broken."

"Like Bruce and Mom?"

"Yes, like Bruce and Mom. If I'm some precious daughter of his, why doesn't he treat me that way? Why doesn't he act in a way that makes it easy for me to trust him?"

"So, what you're essentially asking me is this: How do you know God cares about you? How do you know God is being fair and just? How do you even know God is there? And how do you know if God has really even said anything we can know or trust?"

"Yes, I think you've got it." I could feel my heart asking why all the good guys like Dean were taken already. I could also feel fear whelming up. "But Dean, please don't just tell me that God sent Jesus to die for us and that's all I need to know."

Dean hesitated a few moments. "Katie, what would you accept as proof for each of those questions?"

Now he had me stumped. I'd never thought about that before. Somewhere inside I felt a little defensive and angry that Dean was stalling me. "How am I supposed to know? That's why I'm asking you."

"Let's both give this a couple of days," he responded. "You think of what you'll accept as proof and I'll start looking for a way to try and answer those questions in a way that will mean something to you."

"Thanks for taking me seriously, Dean."

"Just one more thing, Katie. I think it was Oscar Wilde who once said something like this: 'There are two tragic things in life. The first comes when we don't get everything we want. The second comes when we do get everything we want.'"

"Dean, I just need to know what God has for my life now."

As usual, Dean was a patient coach. "Katie, have you ever wondered if God lives by a different clock than you? Or maybe even a different calendar? He doesn't always seem stressed out by passing time like we are."

I wasn't ready to back off yet, so I responded strongly. "Dean, I'm not dealing with issues of time. I'm dealing with issues of my relationships. I just need to know that God is really noticing and paying attention to the details of my life."

"Katie, when I think of others who've felt disappointed with God, I think of Martha and Mary, whose brother Lazarus died. They were among Jesus' best friends. They believed he was God. He was good enough, willing enough, and powerful enough. Yet he didn't meet their expectations. Of course, later he exceeded their expectations, but that didn't help them in the middle of their grief."

"At least they got him back," I said.

"The thing I've discovered, Katie, is that it isn't really about whether God answers my prayers the way I think I want him to. It's about whether I really trust God and have the faith to keep believing no matter what is being faced."

We finished off that conversation, set a time for connecting again, and then I filled him in on my condo and the view, the weather, and life in downtown Vancouver compared to life in a village setting in Kenya. Then I slipped.

"One of the things I couldn't do out in Kenya was go to a professional football game in my backyard."

"Football? I didn't know you liked football." He sounded genuinely surprised and somewhat pleased.

"I actually don't know anything about the game," I said. "I was just asked to go with one of the volunteers who works with a refugee group I spent a few hours at."

"I don't suppose this volunteer is another woman?"

I felt the hook in my gut. "Dean, let's just keep this simple. I'm going with a friend. There's nothing more to it. I just need something to occupy my mind."

He was soft and clear. "Katie, we love you. Just don't make things complicated for yourself. I better go."

And the one man I could count on was gone.

I took the transit line over to the Stadium Sky Train Station and arrived ten minutes early. Damian was already there scanning the crowd. Vancouver was a very multi-cultural city and it struck me at that moment that Damian and I really stood out from the group that was there. His smile and half-jog toward me almost helped kick my insecurity out into the traffic where it could die an unseemly death.

The Ethiopian restaurant was one I hadn't seen before. The Blue Nile. The greyish, sponge-like wat was good and the familiar flavours of that hot North African land flowed over my tongue, down my throat, and into my tummy. I could see Damian wiping his brow frequently and taking advantage of his water. He was making a valiant effort to help me enjoy myself without wimping out.

As he prompted me, I told him the story of my birthplace in Kenya. I told him about my friends Andrea and Sarah. I told him about our tree fort and sleepovers. I told him about my pets and my adventures and my teachers. I talked on and on until I caught him looking at his watch.

"I'm sorry, I didn't mean to bore you." I could feel myself blushing.

"I'm not bored at all," he replied quickly. "It's just that the game started a few minutes ago and I didn't want you to miss the rest of it on your first chance."

Damian paid the waiter quickly, then grabbed my hand and tugged me through the throngs as we raced toward the stadium. I felt pleasure at having a man show me the way. Protect me from the mobs. Make sure I wouldn't get left alone. Even when I didn't need him dragging me, I just kept holding onto his hand all the way to the stadium gate.

A gorgeous night meant the retractable roof was open to the blue sky. The stadium was filled as a party atmosphere reigned down. I honestly couldn't say much about what occurred between all the athletes on the field, but I sure had fun watching Damian screaming and yelling and trying to tell me enough of what was happening to remind me that he hadn't forgotten I was there. Somehow, near the end, the home team did something to win the game and Damian had plenty of energy for a walk afterward.

We grabbed some ice cream and somewhere on that walk by the seawall I began to tell him about the sorrows of leaving my friends, my birthplace, my school, my home. The tears rolled down my face and I didn't even realize he was embracing me until I was already comfortably settled into his arms.

I didn't want to leave this safe place, but Damian made it easier for me. He had been stroking my hair with his fingers and then suddenly he took hold of my shoulders and stood at arm's length. "Have you ever wondered why the sun lightens your hair but darkens your skin?"

The question caught me off-guard, but it changed the mood quickly. I appreciated this man even more for rescuing me one more time. There was no more touching. Just friendship.

When I finally got home after midnight, the light was flashing on my answering machine. Three messages. Two from Bruce, one from Lizzy. All were concerned about where I had been.

I would have to wait until tomorrow. I wasn't going to forget the time difference and have anyone lose sleep over me.

CHAPTER FIFTEEN

I went looking for God today. Kind of like a treasure seeker unrolling an old map. I didn't know how many others actually did this. My clients didn't mention it very often. I started by sitting in a new church. It was a big church, as Canadian standards go. Somewhere, someone handed me a bulletin. I sat in the balcony under the dimmed houselights. The worship team lived up to their reputation for excellence. I could see that the programs for children were excellent. The video promotions for their celebration of World Refugee Day and their Youth Camps were excellent. Even the preaching was excellent. Maybe my spirit wasn't open enough. Maybe my prayers weren't specific enough. At least I was there.

It was when I opened my Bible and just started reading that something changed for me. I was reading in Deuteronomy 30:11–20 and the message was clear. Choose life.

> Now what I am commanding you today is not too difficult for you or beyond
> your reach. It is not up in heaven, so that you have to ask, "Who will ascend
> into heaven to get it and proclaim it to us so we may obey it?" Nor is it
> beyond the sea, so that you have to ask, "Who will cross the sea to get it and
> proclaim it to us so we may obey it?" No, the word is very near you; it is in
> your mouth and in your heart so you may obey it. See, I set before you today
> life and prosperity, death and destruction. For I command you today to love
> the LORD your God, to walk in his ways, and to keep his commands, decrees
> and laws; then you will live and increase, and the LORD your God will
> bless you in the land you are entering to possess. But if your heart turns away
> and you are not obedient, and if you are drawn away to bow down to other

gods and worship them, I declare to you this day that you will certainly be destroyed. You will not live long in the land you are crossing the Jordan to enter and possess. This day I call heaven and earth as witnesses against you that I have set before you life and death, blessings and curses. Now choose life, so that you and your children may live and that you may love the LORD your God, listen to his voice, and hold fast to him. For the LORD is your life, and he will give you many years in the land he swore to give to your fathers, Abraham, Isaac and Jacob.

I almost looked around me because it felt like God was whispering those words to my spirit: "Katie, what you're looking for isn't hard. It isn't out of your reach. It's near you. Inside you even. I'm setting out a clear choice for you today. Follow me and you'll find life. Walk away from me and you'll secure your own destruction. Please choose me. Choose life."

It was kind of strange. Like God was trying to woo me. To prove he was the best lover for me. Like my other options really would sell me short. Ruin me. Did those other choices include Bruce? I could see God wanted me to love him most, but was he open to letting me love anyone else second? That's what I wasn't sure of. This was one thing I probably needed to pray about.

The whole Sunday experience played in my mind during the afternoon when I went for a walk by myself along the seawall in Stanley Park. I picked up a chilidog at a concession stand and realized that I hadn't had one of those in years. The seagulls captured my imagination as they soared on the wind above all the sails bobbing along below them. I completely forgot about returning the calls from last night. Someone's cell phone ringing nearby reminded me.

For some reason, I'd forgotten to set my alarm last night. I knew the church I planned to attend, but when I finally looked at the clock this morning it was late and I raced through my shower and ran out the door without calling anyone. Now, I was out walking and daydreaming and I still hadn't returned any calls. I'm sure Bruce and Lizzy were frantic.

I'd left my cell phone on the bathroom counter so I quickened my pace home. Sure enough, there were eleven messages. I scrolled through the list of missed messages. Two from Bruce, three from Lizzy, three from Damian, and also other calls from Hanan, Anthony, and Samantha.

The fact that Anthony had called just annoyed me. Hanan and Samantha, I could deal with later. I was sure I could deal with Damian quickly, but I knew that duty demanded I call Bruce first.

I didn't even listen to the messages. I just hit the speed dial. Voicemail. I hit speed dial again. Voicemail, again. I just left a short message in case he was trying to call. "It's me. I'm fine. I've been at church and out for a walk. Sorry I missed you. Call when you can." I immediately regretted ending that way. No "I love you," no "I miss you." Just "Call when you can."

I knew I would have to make it up to Bruce when we connected, but decided I'd better get hold of Lizzy before she worried anymore. Her phone also went to voicemail. Was this a conspiracy? Were Bruce and Lizzy talking with each other about me and refusing to pick up just to pay me back? I was getting worked up as my mind conjured all kinds of scenarios.

'Fine, two can play that game.' I punched in the number shown to be Damian's and wondered at the same time how he had gotten my number. He picked it up on the second ring.

"The sun is shining, the sky is blue. This is Damian. How are you?"

I laughed and before I knew it, half an hour had passed discussing everything from the game and the church service to the seagulls over the inlet. A couple of times I heard the interruption for another call coming through, but I didn't want to stop what I was doing.

And then Damian surprised me. "Katie, New Hope has a special community dinner on Saturday night for new volunteers and residents we're being paired with. Maybe Samantha already told you. I know you'll have Hanan. I'm getting Tomas from Cuba. Do you want me to pick you up?"

One message began to pound in my brain: *"Choose me. Choose life."*

The force of the message was so strong that I didn't respond to Damian's question. He finally apologized for being forward and told me he'd just meet me there. He said his goodbyes and hung up. I sat on the couch and stared at the phone.

I jerked and almost dropped the phone when it rang again. It was Bruce's ring tone, so I knew what I was facing. He was such a man. I survived the hour of interrogation, but I wasn't sure how to feel afterward. We ended well, but I wasn't sure whether to be flattered by the jealousy that motivated him to question my time with Damian. I could tell he was trying hard to be as gentle and compassionate as possible, but he was clearly disturbed by my unpredictability and erratic behaviour.

When I was done with Bruce, I just had to work out my thinking with Lizzy. She answered immediately. After we got through all the panic about how I was doing, I started to spew out my anguish on her.

"Lizzy, I just don't get it. Don't men seem to understand how sometimes we just need to know that we're secure in our world? That our relationships are in order? That we're more important than other things or people who compete with us for their time and energy? That we're protected? That when they tell us things, we need to know that they're sincere in what they say? I don't need to be romanced by friends and I don't need interrogations from my future husband."

She gave me all the right feedback, just like a woman should. Finally she said, "Katie, men are complicated. I can't imagine how hard it is for Bruce, or for you, to be separated from each other at the time you need each other the most. And I know that Bruce spending time with that lieutenant, and you spending time with Damian, isn't making this easier."

Lizzy was right, but I wasn't sure how to respond. "So, what can I do? It's not like either of us can change things."

My sister hesitated. "I think you should talk to Dean and get a man's perspective on what might be happening for these guys. He just walked in. Here, I'll let you talk, but first give me a minute to explain to him what's happening."

By the time Dean said hello, I thought maybe the call had been dropped. I'm sure five minutes passed as I waited. Finally, we slogged through the small talk and got to the heart of his wisdom.

"Katie, I know we're still dealing with these other questions of yours, so I don't want things to get too layered between us. I'll just give you a few brief hints on men as I understand us. You're the counsellor, so you probably know this more than I do. Men are looking for women who can help them feel like men. They want a relationship with a woman who will make their life simpler. One who builds up their strengths and doesn't highlight their weaknesses. They want a relationship that isn't going to make things more complicated. A man doesn't want more unrealistic expectations or commitments crowding his mind and spirit. He's looking for appreciation and affirmation. He wants to be relaxed at the end of his day and just feel good about himself. He wants someone to believe in him."

Dean was right. This was Humanity 101. "Dean, I know this stuff. I just need help with Bruce and Damian. I need someone or something in my life I can count on to be there."

Katie," he replied gently. "You know this stuff in your head, but you need to know what this is like in your life. You continue to challenge Bruce with how much you need him and you're calling him to rescue you. Even though you know circumstances don't allow that right now. You're leaving him emasculated.

Helpless. Feeling like a failure. And then, you get upset when he's jealous that you're running to someone else for help and companionship. It's a no-win situation."

Right then, I would rather have stayed with Lizzy's banter, but I had to finish this. "What about Damian?"

Dean was just as straightforward. "Damian's a lonely guy. He told you that. From what I understand, you haven't told him about your relationship with Bruce. Everything he sees says you're interested and available. Blowing him off without telling him the truth is confusing him."

Suddenly I felt claustrophobic in my condo. I needed another walk. "Dean, thanks for the insight. I need to run. Pass my love to Lizzy. I'll get back to you in a couple of days about all my questions. Bye."

And I ran. Literally. I put on my tennis shoes and ran along the waterfront until I couldn't run any further. I just didn't understand how my life could have gotten so complicated.

CHAPTER SIXTEEN

Problems have a nose for me keener than a bloodhound. No matter where I go, they've already figured out where I'll be and there they are waiting and panting for the next round of chaos in my life.

Samantha called me first thing Tuesday morning. "Katie, I have a problem." Of course, I was always intrigued by people's problems. She didn't chit-chat long. "The counsellor who usually joins us on our New Hope retreat is down with the flu. I know you're taking a few days off work and I'm wondering if there's any way we could tap you to help us talk about things like dealing with grief, trauma, new relationships, and things like that."

I was ten chapters into a good novel, so I responded cautiously. "When's the retreat?"

She kept it straight and to the point. "Thursday evening, overnight. Friday, all day. You'll be home by dinner."

I looked at my novel and considered. I had a dentist appointment Wednesday morning to get fitted for a mouth guard because I'd been grinding my teeth lately. I had my annual physical on Thursday morning with all the joys involved in that. It would take a bit of time to prepare my presentations. I tried to give myself a few more seconds to process it. "Where's the retreat?"

Samantha started to express some hope in her voice. "Cultus Lake. It'll take you about an hour to drive or you can come with me. Katie, it's absolutely beautiful. Hanan will be there. We have fifteen of the new refugees signed up so far."

I fanned through the pages of the novel to see how many pages were left. I quickly did the math to see how much reading I had to get through and then agreed. With a few hours less sleep, I could get all this done.

I was tired by the time Thursday afternoon came. And a bit cranky after the physical. I always got so stressed and tense thinking that maybe this time they'd find cancer or something from my past life that had finally shown itself. I'd told Samantha that I'd drive myself and probably be a bit late.

When I arrived at six o'clock, the group was halfway through dinner. Only twelve of the refugees were there. Hanan had saved me a place beside her and I quickly joined in with the conversation.

At seven o'clock, Samantha took us through some ice breakers and explained that a few more of the group would be coming in by eight. That's when I would lead our first session, entitled "Say Goodbye, Say Hello." It was all about grief and transition.

For our last ice breaker, Samantha had me doing a handstand with two of the men holding my feet while the women twirled a hoolahoop around my waist. The contest was to see who could keep the hoop going the longest while the person doing the handstand stayed upright. The blood quickly rushed to my head and I felt faint, but at the moment I looked through Hanan's legs and saw Damian walking through the door with the last three refugees.

For some reason, my arms weakened and the men couldn't hold me up enough to keep us winning. We collapsed in a heap on the floor. Damian was the first one to prop me up and set my back against a wall.

"You look good in red," he said.

Somehow I made it through my session, although I found Damian's smiles of encouragement a little more distracting than helpful. During the chai time at the end of the evening, I asked Damian what he was doing here and he told me that Samantha had asked him to bring the three latecomers, because they didn't have a ride.

I managed to pull myself away from monopolising Damian's time so I could get in some good chat time with Hanan and Fatima and a few others on women's issues. Later, after Samantha closed with games and a final word of instruction for tomorrow morning's session, Damian caught up to me as I walked to my room.

"They've got a Jacuzzi out back. Are you interested?"

I spun on my heel and looked him in the eyes. I knew what to look for. I wasn't sure if I saw exactly what I was looking for. I backed him off. "I didn't bring a good bathing suit for that."

"So, wear a t-shirt overtop." I kept watching his eyes. He kept focusing on mine. He kept up his bargaining. "I just want to talk. Just for a few minutes. Besides, there will probably be others there."

It seemed like a reasonable request, so I finally consented to meet him at the pool. A three-quarter moon glowed in a clear sky. At least we wouldn't be in the dark. When I arrived Damian was already in the Jacuzzi. No one else appeared. I hesitated and looked around.

"Come in, it's beautiful," he said.

I slowly stepped down into the pool and sunk into its warmth. The massage from the jet stream on my back felt wonderful. Damian kept the conversation focused on follow-up questions for my session on grief and transitions and wondered how I was doing with these things in my own life. I tried to keep my emotions out of it as I shared parts of my life story.

After twenty minutes, when no one else had come, I told him I was tired from a long week and needed my sleep. He reminded me that we had some free time in the early afternoon the next day and wanted to know if I could help him take a few of the refugees on a sailing trip. I told him that sounded like fun and then headed off to bed.

The morning session, on cultural values in North America and the keys to building relationships, went well. We spent much of the time role-playing and learning in small groups. I enjoy facilitating things like that. I did catch Damian looking in my direction several times, but I intentionally tried to ignore him.

After a lunch of Iranian wedding rice, lamb kabobs, mixed fried vegetables, and nan, Samantha released us for three hours of free time. As Damian raced out to prepare the boat tied up at the dock, I recruited a few willing sailors and trudged out after him.

Normally, I would probably have worn a swim suit or shorts and a t-shirt for a sail like this, but I wanted to be culturally sensitive to women like Hanan, who were having a hard enough time showing their face, never mind more of their body. I wore a short-sleeved cotton t-shirt and blue capris.

Damian had me unleash the stern and bow docking lines from the cleats. With his command to "cast off," he started up the motor to power us out. We had a good laugh fitting everyone with life jackets and helping them duck under the boom and sails and rigging.

I learned all about "hoisting the main" and "reducing the jib" and "adjusting the foresail." Once, I pulled on the wrong ropes and panicked Damian since he didn't have us pointing into the face of the wind properly. He was yelling something about a halyard not running free as he scrambled to undo whatever damage I'd done. He was obviously very competent.

The winds were strong. After that incident, Damian seemed to go out of his way several times to help me make adjustments to the sail. On one occasion, he stood behind me reaching for the ropes and hesitated a bit longer than necessary. I looked around and saw the questioning look in Hanan's eyes. After that, I tried to watch myself.

We made three short trips with those willing to try and by the third trip I was actually getting the hang of sailing. We were tacking and running and gybing and luffing and a lot of other things that soaked my clothes, tangled my hair, and left my spirit flying.

While the retreat seemed to have been a great success for New Hope and the refugees, I felt it was a key turning point in helping me to recognize that I could still have fun. And Damian left no doubt that perhaps I could have that fun with guys in a healthy way.

Samantha reminded us about the celebration with all our volunteers, staff, and refugee alumnus on Saturday and then released us. I told her I'd have to confirm later. Sure enough, Damian asked a few minutes later if I wanted a ride on Saturday and I let him know that if I was coming I'd get there when I could.

When I got home, it was almost 7:30, so I unpacked and slipped out the door for a quick run to wear off some of that great international cuisine I'd been stuffing into my face.

CHAPTER SEVENTEEN

The sun was setting in a dazzle of oranges, purples, reds, and yellows. I almost sensed God showing off his ability to overwhelm me with his creative beauty and presence. I started gaining a sense of what I needed to say to Bruce and Damian, but for now my mind was at peace.

I took in all I could, then slipped into the washroom of a diner along the way. When I emerged, I looked out to catch the last glimpse of sun. The streetlamps were on. As I reached for the door handle, I looked up and there, standing against the railing under the lamplight, gazing out to sea, was the brunette in the red slip-ons. My first thought was bizarre: *Doesn't she own another pair of shoes?*

I felt trapped, but quickly regained control of my breathing. I headed back to the washroom and looked at my anxious face in the mirror. My mind raced. *Who is this woman? Why am I afraid of her?*

I emerged when there was a knock on the door about ten minutes later and made my apologies to the Filipino mother and daughter who were standing there. I carefully looked out front and the woman was gone. But just then, I heard a singsong voice that actually gave me relief.

"Doc–tor. Is dat you? Doc–tor. Over here."

I didn't even have to look around to know that Anthony had found me again. The coincidences almost made this city seem small. I turned. The big Jamaican was smiling as he rose from the chair he straddled.

He pulled out a chair at his table and waved me over. He removed his reflective sunglasses, increased his smile, flashed his gold rings, and checked to see if I had noticed. Before I sat down, he enveloped me in a massive hug.

"Katie Kat. Da Queen is here. I have double joy now. I am ready to finish my story."

I hadn't eaten yet, but when he ordered fish and chips for both of us I settled in. The aroma and sizzle of grease securing the dough around a piece of fresh halibut was too good to resist. This isn't exactly how I'd planned to spend my evening, but if I listened I wouldn't have to deal with Bruce or Damian. So I listened.

Anthony was a masterful storyteller. One minute, I felt the fear and helplessness of growing up in a Jamaican shantytown without a father. Next, I felt horrified at the string of girls he had been forced to recruit into prostitution for the local drug lord. I didn't question the need for him to escape when the government's troops moved in. I just kept chewing my chips and all these stories of human tragedy.

I marvelled at Anthony's attempt to hide under a tarp on a fishing boat that took him from the Bahamas to a sandbar off the coast of West Palm Beach. I laughed at his animated displays in pantomiming his near-drowning as he swam ashore in the middle of the night. I was astounded at the organized smugglers who drove him through Georgia, Tennessee, Kentucky, West Virginia, Pennsylvania, New York, and then Vermont.

After a hike through the Adirondacks, the big Jamaican was helped across the border. From there he was taken to Toronto where he blended into the multicultural population. In time, he heard about the better weather and living conditions in Vancouver and decided to head west.

I began to wonder about his status as a refugee claimant. Had he had his hearing yet? My mouth asked questions and my smile engaged the storyteller, but my mind was working on the pieces that didn't fit. Perhaps I was just suspicious by nature, but something didn't seem right with this story. It all sounded a bit too easy. But the hour was late. Maybe I was just tired.

Perhaps Anthony caught me drifting on him. He suddenly changed the conversation.

"Doc–tor, it is getting late. I know that you always get plenty of beauty sleep. Let me walk you to your car."

"I don't have a car here, Ann–thown–knee. I walked. I live close."

"Ah, then let me walk you home. I have not been here long, but I hear that even in paradise there are men you cannot trust. Perhaps even tonight there is danger in the streets."

I accepted his offer and he walked me home. Despite his offer, I didn't let him walk me inside past the front door. I accepted his goodnight hug, thanked him for the fish and chips, and bid him farewell. He didn't argue. He just smiled and walked away.

As I slid the digital key into my condo door, I remembered a file I needed from my car. It was my old client file on Charlie, the man who had betrayed Bruce and me to Stephen. I rode the elevator to the underground parking and stepped quickly toward my car. At this time of night, I always felt a little spooked in this place.

I saw the broken window and still didn't register what could be happening. When I activated the remote keyless entry and unlocked the driver's door, I felt my stomach pretzeling. I released the trunk and realized quickly that it was already unlatched. I raised the trunk and looked for my briefcase of client files. There was nothing.

By the time I'd called 911 and gone through the police interview, it was past midnight. There had been just too much excitement for one night. I was sure the appearance of the brunette in red shoes and the disappearance of Charlie's file wasn't a coincidence.

As I sat in the bubble bath later with my candles and my almond aroma therapy, I wondered if God had sent the big Jamaican as my guardian angel. Every time the woman in the red shoes showed up, Anthony didn't seem to be too far away. For a second I wondered if the appearance of the two together might also be more than coincidental.

Questions perked in the back of my mind. Why hadn't Anthony spoken to me about why he had phoned? And why hadn't he told me how he had gotten my phone number?

I climbed out of the tub and dripped across the floor to grab the phone. I just had to know. I found his missed message and clicked on it. He just wanted to let me know that he'd be happy to finish his story with me sometime. He had been glad to see me with Hanan. Not much more. Maybe this evening wasn't so strange after all. Maybe coincidences did happen.

More messages had come in, but it was late and I could deal with them tomorrow. I looked forward to the New Hope celebration with Hanan, but I still wasn't sure how to deal with Damian. How much should I say about Bruce?

CHAPTER EIGHTEEN

The sun was warm and inviting in the morning, so I took my chai out onto my balcony as I made my phone calls. Sitting in my pyjamas, watching the already busy harbour, envying the seagulls, feeling free of any obligations. I just felt good.

Bruce and I kept it civil. He was working, but he took the time to apologize. He'd received the final version of his new leg and everything was working great. He let me know that he was going to head down to Lizzy and Dean's for the weekend. They apparently wanted to talk with him about a few things. He wondered if I knew what was up and I played sly with him and told him he'd have to find out for himself. We flirted a bit and it felt like we'd made some progress. Perhaps I pushed the flirting a little more because I felt guilty about Anthony and about not telling him about the stolen files.

He didn't ask me anything about the guys in my life and I didn't tell him anything. I tried to affirm him for taking time for me and he seemed to warm up to my words. It only lasted forty-five minutes, but the call helped us make up quite a bit of ground. We both expressed our wish that we could spend time together. I apologized for not answering his emails, but assured him I would do that right away. The truth is, I hadn't even checked my emails since Tuesday, but I didn't tell him that either.

I finally called Samantha and confirmed that I'd be there for the celebration. I also confirmed with Hanan and let her know that I was very happy we'd been paired together for the mentorship program. There was no response at Lizzy's, so I left a brief message. She was probably doing her chiropractor work or massage therapy today.

I answered Bruce's emails and he was definitely more romantic on the computer compared to on the phone. Perhaps he was one of those guys who had to be fully present face to face in order for his true feelings to come out.

The appointment to replace the broken car window didn't take long. While I was waiting, I called Devlyn to report the missing files and let her know the police were taking care of everything.

I arrived at the church hall for the celebration and there was a scurry of activity in the kitchen. The place was decorated with flags and international emblems and artefacts. Tables and centerpieces were already in place. I offered to assist in the kitchen, but was assured that everything was ready and I should help myself to the samosas and punch and meet with others as they came.

Damian was the next person through the door. He greeted me awkwardly, then offered his help to the kitchen staff. They parroted back the same words they had given me. We both hovered over the samosas, munching until he graciously broke the silence.

"Katie, I apologize for rushing you, or for taking your friendship for granted. I was just trying to make it easy for you to be here. I'm glad you're here."

I decided to face him honestly. "Damian, I do appreciate your friendship and I don't take it for granted. I just want to make sure we both understand that this is a friendship."

Just then, Hanan came through the doors and embraced me. She appeared to be happy with life as it was, at the moment. Damian's mentoree, Tomas, came in with a loud "Hola" and shook Damian's hand. They wandered off to talk as Hanan and I shared the punch and talked about our favourite foods from her home in Afghanistan and my home in Kenya.

The food was phenomenal. The program was great. There was clearly a sense of family beginning to develop among the participants in the room. A map of the Pacific Northwest was posted and Hanan and I spent time during a break examining it. I tried to explain some of the beautiful places I'd been to, like Victoria and Whistler and Banff. She drank in all my stories like a parched soul.

Just before dessert, we had another break where we could examine about fifty newspaper articles on the history of Vancouver and British Columbia. The first, from the *London Truth* in 1880, essentially said that British Columbia was a waste of space and would never be of benefit to anyone. Hanan and I reminded each other that sometimes things don't end up the way they first seem to be.

Another article featured a journal entry from a Spanish fleet in 1792 which claimed to have taught the native people to sing a song to the tune of "For He's a Jolly Good Fellow."

Hanan and I understood together that this area had always been the desire of peoples from all over the world. And every group that had come left their mark on those who had come before.

A third article spoke of how Gassy Jack (John Deighton) had built the Globe Tavern in twenty-four hours by promising mill workers they could drink as much whisky as they wanted if they'd help him with the job. Hanan and I agreed that men could be motivated to do what they really wanted to do.

We talked about one last *Province* article written on November 6, 1945. Vancouver's city council had officially cancelled an order which had declared that non-white people had segregated swimming times at the pool. The paper declared that the pool was "now open to everyone, all the time, regardless of race, creed, or colour." Hanan and I agreed that every country wrestled with how to make new people feel welcome.

As Damian and Tomas were leaving at the end of the evening, Damian looked at me inquisitively. When I smiled back at him, he seemed satisfied and waved. I could almost see a swagger in his walk. One day soon I was going to have to tell him about Bruce.

I dropped Hanan off at the women's residence and was home by 11:30. As usual, the phone message light was blinking. I took my time fixing my bath and put away a few things, but finally I turned on the answering machine. It was Dean. "Katie, we just got a call from the hospital. Your mom just had a heart attack. Lizzy and I are on the way. Call our cells."

CHAPTER NINETEEN

I called Lizzy five times before I got a response. It was almost 1:00 a.m. by then—3:00, her time.

"Sorry, Katie," she said. "We were just in with Mom and they don't allow cell phones in there."

I could hear the strain in my voice. "I've got to be there, Lizzy."

Lizzy was calm. "Just come, if you can. Mom's not doing well. She survived all the chemo treatments, but maybe after losing Dad and Robert—and now almost losing you—it may have been too much on her. We'll keep in touch, but if you can make it, we'll pick you up. We're at the Methodist hospital. This is one of the best places for both cancer and cardiovascular care. Katie, Mom's in good hands. We're okay. She knows where she's going if anything happens."

I began to pray like I hadn't prayed in years. I had no choice. God was forcing my hand. I had nowhere else to turn. I prayed for Mom and then I prayed that somehow I'd be allowed to fly to see her. I looked online for the next available flight.

WestJet 448 left for Winnipeg at 9:05 a.m. It was two and a half hours long. That was about 1:30 in the afternoon there. I booked it online, printed my eticket, then sped to the Canada departures terminal at the Vancouver airport. I'd grabbed a week's worth of clothes but couldn't be sure if I'd even get on. I printed out my boarding pass at the self-help kiosk and pushed on toward the WestJet gate. No one stopped me, but I was still in Canada, so I guess I wasn't surprised. I alternated between sitting and wandering for five hours while waiting.

In Winnipeg, I retrieved my luggage and booked a vacant seat on a private charter heading down to Minneapolis. I booked it all online, and at the kiosk no one questioned me. I couldn't believe it when we actually took off without incident. The trip took almost six hours and by the time it landed I was a wreck. Not until the plane nosed safely into the St. Paul's Terminal One chute did I start to relax. I wasn't confident that the authorities wouldn't be waiting for me, so I crowded up close to a middle-aged man in an effort to avoid eyes that might be looking for a woman travelling alone. No one stopped me.

I hid in the washroom for half an hour and then realized that I still had to pass through security and customs on my way out. No wonder I'd made it. I felt like I was going to vomit. So close and yet so far. I spent my time trying to think of how to convince the authorities to let me through. I finally just decided to appear confidant, speak the truth, and act as if nothing was wrong.

My bag was one of the last ones on the carrousel and I grabbed it and bunched in at the end of the line going through immigration. I had my U.S. passport and on this day the attendant hardly looked at it twice. Before I knew it, I was in and taking the light rail transit into Minneapolis. I hailed a cab to the Methodist hospital and not once did anyone stop me. In the back of my mind, I began to wonder why.

I reached the hospital at 9:15 in the evening. I hadn't slept for almost thirty-six hours. I dragged my luggage through the entrance door to the information counter, found out where Mom's room was, then headed to the elevator. The tears were flowing down my cheeks before I even got into her room, and I could hardly see as Dean wrapped me up in a hug.

Mom was strongly medicated, but she reached for me. We hugged and cried and whispered all our favourite words to each other. Mom's words were slurred and mumbled, but I know her heart. One word I understood: "Pray."

And so I did. Right in that hospital room, I prayed. I prayed for God's mercy and grace. I prayed for healing and help. I prayed that God would spare my mom from suffering. And as I prayed, I felt her arms around me start to loosen. I held her tighter and prayed harder, and it felt like she just fell asleep in my arms. The alarms began to sound and the medical personnel came running and began to pry me away, but Dean stopped them. They stood and watched as I sobbed and let my mom slip away.

And it was there, in that state, that I met Bruce again. A hand reached out with Kleenex as my eyes and nose ran and the sobs wracked my body. I heard someone slide the room door closed and I felt someone gently rub my back. Lizzy was suddenly beside me crying as well. I turned to hug her and over her shoulder, through the tears, I saw him. Bruce stood, holding out the Kleenex.

I beckoned him, and he and Dean joined Lizzy and I as we grieved in a way that only Delanceys can grieve. Then, after forty hours without sleep, with mascara and mucous and tears running down my face, I was back in the arms of my prince. It felt like my head was full and my heart was empty. It felt like it had been forever. And it felt like I had never been away.

CHAPTER TWENTY

Mom left me to be with Jesus early Wednesday morning. Lizzy gave me her Bible and said Mom had wanted me to have it. I spent Wednesday evening just flipping through it. She used to underline and highlight all her favourite verses and I could see she had a lot of them. Taped inside the front cover were several pages where she'd kept notes from special conferences or messages that had been meaningful to her. I saw one labelled prayer.

Below a blue-ink scribble that read "Evelyn Christenson conference—1977," I read a short list of principles Mom must have gleaned at her event:

Pray for one subject at a time, be short, be simple, be specific, take time to be silent, and let your small group support you in your prayers.

Another section, entitled 1989, was written in black ink:

Use different prayer for different circumstances. Praise and adoration, supplication, intercession, confession, warfare, meditation, and silence.

I wondered which type of prayer was good for losing your Mom to cancer.

Below that, in blue ink again, was written:

Hindrances to prayer: religion without relationship, ignorance, sin, pride, broken relationships, busyness, selfishness, idols.

There was no question I had a few hindrances in my life.

One other verse at the bottom caught my attention:

Call unto me, and I will answer thee, and shew thee great and mighty things, which thou knowest not. (Jeremiah 33:3, KJV)

Right now, I'd settle for anything, even if it wasn't great and mighty.

I should have just enjoyed being with Bruce, but I was finally grieving Robert and Dad and Lancelot and Africa and everything that I'd let slip through my hands over the past dozen years. I had to leave the planning of the funeral service to Lizzy and Dean. I was so tired, I slept almost all of Thursday. Bruce joined the three of us for supper and afterward we finally got to talk. Most of that time I spent talking about how hard things had been.

For two hours, all I did was talk about Lancelot and how I'd never had the chance to say goodbye to the horse I'd loved to race against. For two hours, Bruce sat there and handed me Kleenex while the well deep inside me emptied. For two hours, I acted like my man wasn't even a significant part of my life.

I'm sure a man, with Bruce's training, experience, and self-control wondered what he was dealing with. The girl he planned to marry had almost jumped off a bridge. She'd been in a psych ward. She'd run off with other guys. She was paranoid about people in red slip-ons and yellow Porsches. She was in trouble with the law. And now all she could think about was herself, while her mother's funeral was being planned.

Sometimes the police could be slow, but they weren't asleep. I wondered if God ever used the police to answer prayers. The knock on Lizzy's door came Friday.

I was in the shower when they came. Bruce and I had made plans to meet for a picnic lunch and a trip out to Uncle Jimmy's farm in the Red River Valley where Lancelot and I had raced so many times. Lizzy was on the phone with her pastor trying to make plans for the service. I didn't hear her knocking on the bathroom door the first couple of times. I was humming and thinking of getting together with Bruce.

When I finally did hear her and turned off the shower, my sister told me that I needed to step out of the shower. The police were at the door wanting to see me. I let her know that I still had shampoo in my hair, then stepped back into the shower for the longest rinse I've ever had. No matter how long I stood there, I couldn't think of any way out of this.

I realized that I wasn't going to get my lunch with Bruce and I began to cry. I realized that I was going to miss my own mother's funeral and I cried some more. I realized that I wasn't going to get to say goodbye to the farm where so much of my healing had happened. I realized that no matter how much I prayed right now, there was just no way out of this.

I had just turned off the shower when a stronger knock sounded on the door. A firm voice came soon after. "Ms. Delancey, This is the FBI. We will give you five minutes, but we need you to verbally check in every thirty seconds so we know you're okay. For your own safety, we need to know you are okay."

And so, for the next five minutes, I slowly dressed and brushed my hair, giving my verbal cues that the "loony" had not yet cut her wrists, jumped out of the window, or done anything more insane than she'd already done.

When I emerged, I expected to be handcuffed and thrown to the floor, but the two officers showed me their badges, identified themselves, gave me space, and asked me to sit. Lizzy anxiously watched me and I asked her if she could please give Bruce a call and let him know what was happening. The officers instructed her not to make any calls until they were finished with me.

For one hour, they asked me about my life from the time I'd last left Sumas to the time I arrived in Minneapolis. They questioned me about every person I spent time with. They wanted to know details of facial features. They were very interested in the brunette with the red slip-ons and the yellow Porsche. They actually seemed to believe me that this person could exist.

The FBI officers asked a lot of questions about Anthony, Damian, and Hanan. They also asked me about my relationship with Bruce. At that point, I realized there was something more going on than me illegally crossing the border. I had to find out what it was.

"Gentlemen, I'm not a terrorist. If you need to deport me, I understand. All I'm asking is that you wait until after my mother's funeral is done. You can put me in detention if you need to, but please let me stay so I can say goodbye."

The spokesman for the two officers appeared to shift uncomfortably. His eyebrows raised and he seemed confused by my comments. He cleared his throat, looked at his colleague, and then stared me in the eyes. "Ms. Delancey, we have been sent to protect you, not deport you."

He examined his iPad, then continued. "We have reason to believe you may be in danger. A man named Charlie Collins was found dead in prison two weeks ago. Do you happen to know Mr. Collins?"

So that was who this was about. I answered quickly. "Charlie was one of my patients, but he ended up being recruited by Stephen—the man they called the Monk. He was involved in my abduction, but he helped me in the end. His files were stolen from the trunk of my car last week."

The officer nodded and made a note in his book. "It looked like a suicide until two other witnesses in this case disappeared. We heard there may be a hit out on you. We're in touch with the RCMP and we need to know the best way to keep you safe. Would you prefer to be with us in a safehouse in Seattle or under protective custody in Canada?"

I'm sure my sigh said it all. I rested my head in my hands and braced myself with my knees. "Can't I just say goodbye to my mother?"

"Yes, Ms. Delancey, you can say goodbye, but you'll have to do that privately with your family and you'll have to do that today. We can't risk having you in a public setting. One more thing, Ms. Delancey: I'm afraid we will not be able to allow Colonel Southerland to be with you. We have had to return him to protective custody at Langley for his own security."

My world was shaken, but somehow I packed my things and waited while Lizzy made numerous calls to organize a private viewing and goodbye for the family. Dean dropped in and helped carry my things out to the trunk of the officer's car. Not even the family would know where I was.

The viewing was short. The body didn't look like Mom, but the clothes were familiar. The pastor said some words and prayed. Everyone hugged me. We cried. Dean prayed for me. I'm not sure what prayer was accomplishing these days. I felt all dried out inside.

I was taken to a building where half a dozen officers sat with me in a room and listened to me go over all the same details again. Everything was videotaped. The authorities still had several people in custody for a trial in Seattle and they wanted me close by. The safehouse in Seattle would mean virtual lockdown. If I wanted to stay in my own condo in Vancouver, they would permit that as long as I had two RCMP constables as bodyguards. I obviously chose to stay in Vancouver.

CHAPTER TWENTY-ONE

Flying over the Rocky Mountains of British Columbia was a glorious sight any time of year, but seeing that snow, even in summer, really made those peaks stand out. The renewal of the earth through the seasons was one of those miracles I never stopped thinking about.

With the time change, I still arrived in Vancouver before 11:30 on Saturday morning. I was just glad all this sun and snow didn't depend on my ability to pray.

As glorious as the mountains were, I spent a lot of the flight thinking about the farm and Lancelot and Bruce and Mom. This wasn't the way I had planned to spend my weekend.

I hadn't even picked up my luggage from off the carousel when I noticed two men of significant stature slip in on either side of me. They were dressed in jeans and t-shirts, but all that did was show that they spent a lot of time in the weight room.

One of the men was South Asian and the other was Latin American. For a moment, they merely stood.

When I reached for my bag, the South Asian man spoke up. "Ms. Delancey, I'm Constable Sall from the RCMP. This is Constable Lopez. We'll be on-call for your protection. I believe you are expecting us. Would you accompany us, please?"

Constable Lopez snatched up my bag and I was escorted out of the building without problem. I turned over my keys to a young woman who stood by their car. Constable Sall introduced her as Constable Chan. I let her know where my car was parked in the long-term vehicle parking lot. She left to drive my car home for me. I was chauffeured all the way and dropped off at the door. I put my stuff away and then waited for my faithful Honda to arrive.

When my car pulled up, I showed Constable Chan where to park it. She handed me the keys and then hopped in the cruiser with Constable Lopez. Constable Sall took a seat in the entranceway of the condo unit. As I moved toward the elevator, he called. "One of the three of us will always be here if you need us. The card I gave you has our emergency response numbers. We'll need a list of who's on your safe list so that we don't impede unnecessarily into your private life."

All the way up the elevator to my twenty-first floor condo, I mulled over who should be on my safe list. Probably everybody but "red shoes," and I didn't have a name for her. I could feel myself smiling as I imagined handing Constable Sall a list that said, "Women in red shoes are unsafe." I really didn't want to get caught up in all the paranoia of thinking everyone was out to get me.

Bruce was probably right when he said that everyone who had been after me was either dead or in jail. Now Charlie was gone. I was sure things like that happened in prison with people who didn't know how to protect themselves.

Of course, my voicemail box was full, so I let the answering machine sound out the messages in the order they were taped. One was from Sarah, who was still trying to arrange a time together and teasing me about my wild social life. One was from Bruce, telling me about my mother's heart attack and his prayers for me. There were other messages from Lizzy and Dean with similar "call me" themes.

Damian left a message letting me know about another New Hope event in two weeks—and a football game in one. Sarah called again looking for a connection. Anthony called, thanking me for taking the time to listen to his story. Someone at the church called, thanking me for filling out a visitor's card and wanting to know if I was interested in a visit. A couple of charities collecting donations in the area left their contact information. Bruce called again, letting me know that he was sad to have missed our picnic and trip to the farm. He wanted a call. He also apologized for making light of the danger I might be in. And there was one from Sergeant James from the Bellingham Police. That was all the space available.

I decided to call in reverse order. Sergeant James was sitting in a bagel shop when I called. He told me he was busy on a stakeout, but I could hear people making orders in the background. And I knew that shop.

I decided to be upfront with him. "Sergeant, it's hard for me to ask you for the truth about what's going on when you can't even tell me you're sitting in the

Bagelry on Railroad Ave. I can almost see that bit of cinnamon cream cheese stuck on your moustache. Oh, now you're trying to wipe it off."

He played his role well. "Delancey, if you're here watching me, you're in a lot more trouble than you realize. What took you so long to get back to me?"

I didn't have to tell him about my Mom's funeral, because I was sure he already knew. I just kept up the game. "The RCMP bodyguards up here wouldn't stop for bagels, so I had to settle for steaks. What did you want me for?"

I could hear him chewing in my ear. "You heard about... Charlie... right? I know they told you. It wasn't an accident. Two other witnesses have run off... at least that's what we hope has happened. You know I'd rather have you here in our house, but after last time I know that isn't what you want. Kind of like living in a cage... and at this point I don't even know whether we're going to need you for anyone else. Almost everyone you knew is gone now."

I wanted to encourage this line of thinking. "Seems I'd be extra baggage for your squad and I know you have a lot happening down there. I'm safe here. The only worry I had is when the FBI said there was a hit out on me. Do you think that's still in play?"

He cleared his throat. Was that a stall tactic all men used? "Truth is, Katie, we're hearing some chatter about a reshuffling of the Monk's old group. With both Tommy and the Monk out of the way, there's plenty of market left to work for. We hear there are players moving up, trying to take everything from Vancouver to Seattle. They may not be after you directly, but they may be making sure there's no competition."

When I hung up the phone and went to look out at the harbour, I felt like my wonderful condo had become a gilded prison. The beautiful people who strolled along with their ice cream and hot dogs might have been undercover shadows watching everything I did. The people I cared about could actually be in danger, if any wrong motives were read into what I did or said. I needed a friend I could trust.

My next call was to Sarah. I sold her on a visit to Vancouver without explaining a whole lot. She was more than happy to come since her doctor husband, Keith, was out of town at a medical conference. Maybe one day Sarah's husband and my husband, if it was Bruce, would have to get together and share their love for medicine while we shared our love for shopping.

Damian was a little tougher. How could I explain that I'd just traveled halfway across the country and smuggled myself across the border only to have my mom die in my arms? Then, just when I was about to make up with my future fiancé, I got arrested by the FBI for my own protection, and now I was back in Vancouver, trapped in my own condo and guarded by the RCMP.

Damian picked up on the second ring, like he almost always did. Why couldn't all the men in my life be so reliable? This guy always seemed to be available and more than willing to take time for me. I let him know that there had been a lot going on for me the past couple of days and things had gotten a little out of my control lately.

Then the man with the perfect record in my life chose his moment to blow it.

"Katie, I know you understand the issue of loss of control better than I do. You know whether your control is being determined by what's in you or by what's outside you. Just take a minute. Take three breaths. Realize. Your anxiety comes because you're refusing to make a decision and take responsibility for your life."

When it came down to it, men always proved to be men. They would finally reach the point where they thought they needed to fix something for us women. They would forget to keep the brake on their tongue while talking through our issues, and they would do the talking for us. Maybe that was one of the benefits about prayer. Women could talk out everything with God and after we'd finally emptied ourselves of all our cares and worries we could sit quietly while our Abba let us know how much he loved us.

I refused to even grace Damian with a response and he finally clicked in. "That's not what you need from me, is it?" I gave him a point for that. "I listen better face to face." Some guys never quit. I took away the point. "No pressure. You just sound like you could use a friend." I gave him the point back.

I caved in. "You know the park bench right in front of my place? Meet me there in an hour. I'll have company, but I don't want you asking any questions. Just listen, okay?"

He agreed, so I finished up my other calls as pleasantly as I could and got ready to empty my soul with some guy I hardly knew.

CHAPTER TWENTY-TWO

From time to time, life seems as tasty as a peach and vanilla ice cream cone. The richness oozes down faster than you can lick it up and no flavour in the world tastes better than the one you chose.

Sometimes you think you've found the one person in the world who's perfect for you. But then you meet someone else. And you wonder. Of course, people will tell you to pray and ask God to show you his choice for you. But if he's in control of everything, why would he bring along two perfectly good choices?

Within an hour of being with Damian, my dull and lonely Saturday began to grow into something magical. The man kept his promise. He let me talk about everything without saying a thing. He gave me Kleenex at the right time. I didn't even know other men who carried Kleenex. He prompted me with just the right amount of encouragement. He laughed at my stories and he held my hand just enough when I needed comfort.

He didn't crowd me or take advantage of me. He walked with me. And then he walked some more. When I got lost in my story, he would gently put his hand in the small of my back to guide me around obstacles or people in the way. He was gentle. Gracious. Supportive. Everything I needed.

And Constable Lopez was great. He hung back and didn't get too close. He let me be. I almost forgot he was there until I saw him standing by the doorway of a coffee shop we stopped at. It was probably a good thing he stayed visible once in a while. It kept me from following through on a desire that was growing inside me—to show Damian that he was becoming much more than a friend to me.

Somewhere along the way, I realized that Constable Lopez had disappeared and instead Constable Chan trailed close by. By this time, Damian and I were walking hand in hand and it just seemed like a natural thing for both of us. No one knew me here and no one really cared.

Damian displayed incredible self-control when he dropped me off at my door. Constable Chan remained in the lobby and let us up the elevator alone. After taking my key and opening my door, Damian looked me in the eye, squeezed my hands, and said, "Friends. It's been good. Thanks." And even though I gave him every opportunity to say goodbye in a more intimate way, he resisted and walked away.

I was smitten. And when I walked through my door and saw the picture of Bruce sitting by my telephone, I felt so guilty that I wished I'd never been born. I couldn't go on living this way with one man who I was supposed to marry, completely out of the reach of my heart, and another man who was now reaching into my heart in ways I had never imagined possible.

My bubble bath was longer than ever. I didn't even bother checking my messages. I decided, in the end, that I needed to get to church in the morning.

For now, I just wanted to forget about my life. As I sat in bed, snug in my pyjamas, I decided I needed to focus on someone else's story. I punched in the track of one of the refugee stories I had transcribed several weeks ago.

* * *

Nafrina: I was born in Bangladesh. My father was a very wealthy man. He owned hotels in Dhaka and Chittagong. There are almost six million people in Dhaka and half that many in Chittagong. My mother was sixteen when she was married to my father. She was his second wife. When I was fifteen, I was given to a man to be his fourth wife.

I have always been a good Muslim and I gave him the sons he wanted. I also cooked well. I became his favourite wife and the other women wanted to abuse me, but he made them raise my sons and he put me to work in his hotels. I knew the hotel business from my father and great cooking from my mother and my aunts. I was of great help.

When I was twenty-seven, my husband decided he wanted another, younger wife. He divorced two of his first wives and rarely came to visit me any longer. I became very lonely. I had to work long hours in the hotel.

At the hotel, there was a Hindu manager who did a very fine job. He and I would often work together through the nights when things were quiet. We began to speak about our hopes and dreams. I was surprised that a Hindu had such aspirations.

Two years after I got to know this man, my husband came and told me that he was going to divorce me, but that he wanted me to continue to work in his hotel. I was very angry to be left after all the work I had done for him. This Hindu manager and I began to talk and we decided that we had grown to love each other. We were both free, so we decided to marry on our own.

My ex-husband was a very rich and powerful man and he soon found out about what we were doing. Three days after my marriage to the Hindu, the room we were in was attacked by men in our own families trying to break down the door. They yelled many threats against us. They wanted to do an honour killing to extinguish their shame. We both escaped out a window before anyone could come in. My new husband ran one way and I ran another.

I escaped to Canada to try and open the way to a new life. I had heard from Canadians who came to our hotel that anyone could love anyone in Canada and it was okay. Now, my new husband was in another country and since I am a refugee claimant I have no rights to bring him and no rights to leave to find him. I am alone—apart from God and these good Christian people who have been kind to me. I am willing to do any kind of work. My best work is to be a chef. Now, my only hope is that I can pray and that God can hear me.

* * *

When Nafrina's story stopped, so did my peace of mind. How could God handle all these broken-hearted prayers? How could he let things go on and on and on? I was hoping the pastor had something special in the morning. And I was hoping I could do some thinking about the questions Dean had outlined for me to think about.

I missed my Mom so much.

CHAPTER TWENTY-THREE

The sun didn't play peek-a-boo very well on this summer weekend morning. By 5:30, it was like a little child checking my eyelids to see if I was really sleeping or just pretending. Just because my curtains had been left open, to allow for the cool ocean breezes, the golden orb took that as an invitation to invade my private space. Like a child, it explored the recesses of my face and under its caresses I finally yielded and opened my eyes.

The scientist Isaac Newton once tried to fool the sun. He knew he couldn't look directly into the bright light, so he used a mirror to try and examine it second-hand. The reflected light blinded him for three days and possibly impacted his vision for life. I wasn't sure how all that fits into my thoughts that morning, but that's what I was thinking about.

Maybe I was hoping for just a little light from God today when I got to church.

Before I left for church, I thought I'd better give Bruce an update. I wanted to email so I could say it just right. Sometimes I got tongue-tied on the phone. I'm brief and to the point.

Dear Bruce: You can't imagine how much you've meant to me during this past year. I've felt things with you that I've felt with no one else. We've had such dreams and memories together which no one can take away. I appreciate you so much for being there when Mom passed away. I wish we could have shared our dreams for that picnic and trip to see Lancelot's home. It seems that every time we move forward in our relationship, things get in the way to keep us apart. Perhaps this is just God keeping us from making a big mistake. Maybe I just felt obligated to love you because you saved my life. Things are rather confusing for me at the moment. I'm wondering if we should just give each other the freedom not to have any expectations for a while. I know you're busy with Lieutenant Saunders and I have the work with refugees up here. Maybe when this trial business all blows over we can see if the space has helped us understand how we still feel toward each other. No matter what happens, I want you to know that I'll always be grateful and I'll always be your friend. Katie.

Tears streamed down my face during most of the email and I definitely needed a shower to get myself in shape for the public. For some reason, though, I felt at peace. As Damian had reminded me, I took control and made a decision. Letting go of Bruce seemed like a logical step as I let go of the rest of my life.

Just before going out the door, I opened up an email from Dean. He told me he was still praying and included a quote from C.S. Lewis to someone he knew named Mrs. Jones.

God could, had he pleased, have been incarnate in a man of iron nerves, the stoic sort who lets no sigh escape him. Of his great humility, he chose to be incarnate in a man of delicate sensibilities who wept at the grave of Lazarus and sweated blood at Gethsemane. Otherwise we should have missed the great lesson that it is by his will alone that man is good or bad, and that feelings are not, in themselves, of any importance. We should also have missed the all-important help of knowing that he has faced all that the weakest of us face, has shared not only the strength of our nature, but every weakness of it, except sin. If he had been incarnate in a man of immense courage, that would have been for many of us almost the same as not being incarnate at all.[1]

I read the quote twice to make sure it registered, then headed out the door wondering if Jesus really understood what it was like to be in my shoes. One thing I knew was that Jesus had spent a lot of time praying. Maybe my starting point was to figure out who he was and why he prayed.

Constable Sall had the privilege of trailing me to the church. Although the music was different than it had been two weeks ago, the service was still excellent in a human kind of way. Not perfect, but real and compassionate. I looked forward to the message.

---

1. Lewis, C.S. *A Mind Awake: An Anthology of C.S. Lewis* (San Diego, CA: Harcourt Brace Jovanovich, 1980), p. 93

This week, Pastor Gary was speaking. The passage was from Isaiah 61:1–3.

The Spirit of the Sovereign LORD is on me, because the LORD has anointed me to preach good news to the poor. He has sent me to bind up the brokenhearted, to proclaim freedom for the captives and release from darkness for the prisoners, to proclaim the year of the LORD's favor and the day of vengeance of our God, to comfort all who mourn, and provide for those who grieve in Zion—to bestow on them a crown of beauty instead of ashes, the oil of gladness instead of mourning, and a garment of praise instead of a spirit of despair. They will be called oaks of righteousness, a planting of the LORD for the display of his splendour.

I got two things from the message. Jesus had come to be actively present in the lives of people like me and he had called me to be actively present in the lives of others who faced the same poverty, brokenness, bondage, grief, and despair.

Between Dean's quote and Pastor Gary's message, I felt affirmed in my work with the New Hope refugees. I also felt that somehow Jesus understood the confusion I was living with. I wanted that crown of beauty, that oil of gladness, that garment of praise. I'd had enough of ashes, mourning, and despair.

During the closing songs, an invitation was given for anyone wanting prayer. Dozens of weeping people wandered down the aisle and I found myself leaving my balcony hideaway to get any help I could get.

A young woman wrapped her arms around me and prayed for my healing and hope. I felt the genuineness of her compassion. When the service was done and the benediction given, I sat in the front pew and thought about all that was happening in my life.

Pastor Gary eventually came and sat beside me. Without his prompting, I poured out my confusion about my relationship with God and Bruce.

He spoke to my heart in whispers of grace. "Katie, your heart has been having a hard time in your fight. The enemy really wants to tie you up in knots through his lies. He hates the beauty God has woven into your life. He hates the life God is weaving into your beauty. He will bind you with shame and fear and guilt until you're left seeing only what you can't do and not what God can still do. Your Abba will never abandon you, Katie. Live with truth and truth will help you live. You will never be alone. No matter what Bruce decides."

When I told Pastor Gary about my mother, he called over his wife and another woman. The three of them laid hands on me as they first thanked God for my mother's faith and the hope I have. They then thanked him for the strength, grace, and peace that would continue to hold me in the days ahead. They thanked God for deep tears that spoke of deep love. They thanked him for the gift of eternal life and the reality of heaven where suffering and pain and tears would be no more. They thanked God for the heritage of belief and truth to rest on during our time of separation. They thanked him that he was an Abba who would watch over his daughter and father me until I rejoined my mother in everlasting celebration.

They prayed like God was right next to them. They prayed like he was truly a father they had loved and known all their lives. My tears weren't just because of Bruce and Mom. My tears were because, more than anything, I would love to know God like this. I would love to pray like this.

CHAPTER TWENTY-FOUR

I was invited for lunch by Dorothy Velasquez, the other woman who had been praying for me. I needed time to think, though, so I suggested that next week would be better for me. I wasn't ready to tell any more of my life story to anyone else right now. I just needed to sort things out. The seawall was becoming a familiar place for me.

The skies were overcast as I grabbed my purse and left the condo for my walk. I took the back exit to bypass the art display in the parking lot of the condominium complex. The crowds were a little smaller along the seawall this afternoon. I was glad I'd chosen jeans and a sweatshirt, even though it was supposed to be summer. The Pacific Northwest could be that way. Cool sometimes. It could be that I still had African blood running through my veins.

Near the entrance to the park, I was almost stampeded by a gang of runners doing their duty for charity. As I stood gawking with others, I saw several joggers dressed up in pink costumes to promote their cause for cancer research. When there was a break in the herd, I snaked my way through and passed into the next section of the park where I came across a gaggle of bikers, skateboarders, and rollerbladders doing another charity for the homeless. One thing I loved about this place was that people were very involved in great causes, and they knew how to have fun while supporting others.

The sun shrugged off its mask of clouds and came out to frolic again. I plopped myself down at the base of an old Douglas fir and watched a group of teens playing Ultimate Frisbee.

I saw the shadow before I saw the man, but the size gave him away.

"Do I believe my eyes? Da Queen is here in da park. Katie Kat. I was sure you had gone and left old Ann–thone–nee on his own. I called you, but I guess you know that."

I looked up and shielded my eyes against the bright light coming down over Anthony's shoulders. "Hello, Anthony. I've been busy."

"And I can see you are sure busy at this moment." He dropped his six-foot-seven-inch frame down beside me and nearly crushed my shoulder in the act. "Sorry, sugar. Sometimes old Ann–thone–nee has got to be more delicate with the flowers."

I really didn't want to interact a whole lot, but the big guy was right there. "Anthony, I was at church this morning and the pastor really made me think. I'm a broken girl. I don't treat people right. I know you have your story, but I have a story, too, and it's not pretty."

He turned on the charm. "Now, what kind of trouble might be clogging up your pretty head today? Old Ann–thone–nee has got time for his busy queen."

I told him about my mom dying and about not being able to meet with some of my family and friends because I had to come back to Vancouver. I was about to tell him about my trouble with the police when I realized that none of my three guardian angel constables were in sight. By going out the back door of the condo I had accidentally slipped away unnoticed.

A shiver convulsed up my back, but at the same time a touch of wildness hit me. I was like an eagle rising up on a thermal.

Anthony seemed to notice a change in me. "I see you have something good in your mind."

I looked him in the eyes and saw how his gaze penetrated me. Analyzed me. Sifted me. My heart felt like it froze and a touch of terror gripped me for a fraction of a second. I dismissed it. I was in control. I programmed my mind.

Anthony is the one who saves me, not hurts me.

Whatever expression my eyes ended up giving, I could see that the impact on Anthony was immediate. The tension drained from his eyes and he reclaimed that twinkle of joviality that he worked so hard to portray. Still, his speech was telling. "Perhaps not everything is good. I have seen your look in the eyes of some of the girls in Jamaica, just after they realized the door on their cage was closing and the key was being thrown away. Katie Kat, maybe you have not always been a Queen. At least, not the kind of Queen your pastor would be proud of."

The Jamaican's words disturbed me. From my background, I already naturally put strange men into boxes. I had become a counsellor to gain healing for myself and others who had been through abuse. I'd been through my share of men who wrapped me up in chains through putdowns, name-calling, yelling, screaming, and swearing. The mix of charm and harm was a toxic poison to my spirit.

I tried not to put Anthony in the categories of men I used to know. Men who terrified me into submission with their driving. Men who threw things and tried to possess, isolate, and control me. I'd been slapped, choked, and touched in too many ways to think about. I'd been forced into fraud by signing phoney credit card applications and making false bank deposits and withdrawals. It had taken a long time to clear my name when I found my way out of that lifestyle.

There was no way I wanted anyone to take me back to that level of anxiety, depression, anger, fear, and confusion. I was so stressed physically and emotionally that weeks would go by without me having any conscious memories of what was happening. I needed to stay clearheaded. My pastor may not have been proud of me back then, but I was living in a community of grace now and I didn't want that to change.

Anthony must have taken my silence for something deeper. His next comments exposed his character more than mine. I saw his eyes burrow into me as he spoke. He held up his gold-ringed fingers and let them flash in the sun.

"There is nothing like fresh fish," he said. "I see that you've had the hook in your mouth before. A fish once caught bites carefully ever after."

I leaped to my feet faster than I thought possible. The man who I'd thought was my saviour was exposing a raw nerve and stepping on it. Deliberately. There was an edge in his tone. The singsong rhythm in his voice was almost gone. There was something else about him that set alarm bells ringing.

Anthony unwound himself and used the tree trunk to support himself as he got back on his size-sixteen feet. He towered over me again. And then he transformed himself back into his charming role. "Girl, I am so sor–ry. I only said that I've seen a look like yours before. I wasn't trying to say that you were loose, like those Jamaican girls. I know you don't play with the minds and hearts of men. There ain't no man controlling you for his profit. I just said that I've seen girls with that trapped look before."

Anthony was talking too much and too knowledgeably for me to let this go as a coincidence. I also noticed that he was physically angling me toward the tree. I was back-pedalling slowly to avoid letting him get too close. My brain couldn't calculate what was happening and I felt my knees getting weak under me.

Tripping over a tree root helped fit all the puzzle pieces for me. The blinding pain in my neck and shoulder distracted me from my situation for a moment, and it was because of the fall that I saw the flash of yellow coming into the parking lot. I looked again and couldn't believe it. Tommy Lee's Porsche pulled in right beside a silver-grey Mercedes.

A sudden picture of the brunette standing outside Buffalo Bill's in Sumas and watching an African-American man stepping into a silver-grey Mercedes flashed through my mind. It felt like my heart was seizing up. I wasn't hyperventilating, but my chest was tight and I sure had trouble trying to catch my breath. I had no doubt that the person I'd seen with the brunette was Anthony.

I should have played it calm and tried to downplay everything, but I'm sure my full stare into his eyes, combined with the gasp, gave me away. I saw Anthony look toward the parking lot and then all masks came off. Instead of a disarming grin, I was met with a sneer and a glare. "So, my Queen, I see that we have reached the time for a discussion."

The brute grabbed my arm above the elbow and yanked me to my feet like I was a rag doll. I tried to ditch my purse behind the tree, so someone might alert the police, but Anthony noticed it and picked it up without releasing his grip on me.

He clamped on tight and warned me to keep silent if I valued my boyfriend's life. He then forcibly marched me toward the brunette, who was leaning back against the door of the silver-grey Mercedes. Her left hand pushed her hair behind her ear and twirled those blue topaz earrings. I noticed her cherry red nail polish flashing as if to accentuate her claws. Although her sunglasses were firmly in place, I could tell she was glaring me down.

Anthony kept up his vice grip until I was about ten feet from the brunette. He spoke in an accent that was not even close to Jamaican. More like something out of New Orleans. "Alexis, meet your competition."

I looked around the full parking lot for some help. A few cars looking for spots were driving by on the road about thirty feet away, but no one really looked in our direction. A playground with slides and swings and climbing apparatus was just fifty feet on the far side of the parking lot, but the three or four families there were preoccupied with taking pictures of their children. Meanwhile, I felt like my arm was about to snap.

The brunette, whom Anthony had called Alexis, walked within three feet of me and took off her sunglasses. The stare of her burnt almond eyes was like ice. Her voice was low, harsh, and tinted with an Eastern European accent. It may have been an act, like Anthony's Jamaican accent, but I couldn't be sure.

"So, you're the one running Tommy's network," she said. "You don't look like much."

I didn't have a clue what she was talking about, but I decided I wasn't going to say anything one way or another. I tried to glare back and refused to back down. Her derogatory challenge reached down to the core of my wildness. I could feel Anthony ease up his squeeze on my arm a bit.

She finally backed off and continued. "We want to work out a deal for another shipment."

Alexis turned and walked back toward the Porsche. I noticed that for once she wasn't wearing the red slip-ons.

As she reached for the driver's door, I decided to engage her. "I'm not sure who you think I am. I know one thing: I don't know you. You need to sort out who you're dealing with."

The pain returned to my arm and an irresistible force pressured me toward the rear door of the Mercedes. Just then, a red van pulled into the area and the driver leaned out the window.

"Are you leaving?" the driver asked hopefully.

"Yes," I said loudly enough to shock us all. "My friend is just leaving, but I'm not. Please wait, he'll be gone in just a minute." I pulled away from Anthony as hard as I could and felt my arm slip out of his grip.

The van driver backed up to make room for Anthony and that's when I felt the muzzle in my ribs. It was Alexis. "Make this easy on all of us. Get in my car. There are kids in that van. I don't leave witnesses."

I was more terrified now than I had ever been, even when Stephen had held me at gunpoint. At least then I knew why things were happening. Right now, I didn't understand anything.

CHAPTER TWENTY-FIVE

lexis opened the door for me and watched me settle in. Anthony tossed in my purse and then ensured my safekeeping by pressing up against the door once the brunette had vacated the space. I watched Alexis wave and smile at the van driver as she scooted around the car in a mock act to make it look like she was helping him out. Anthony was climbing into the Mercedes by the time we made it to the exit road.

Before we exited the park, my brunette captor was already taunting me. "What's it feel like to have your old seat back? Tommy Lee always said he had it moulded just for your body." She looked at me with a sneer. "I never did feel comfortable sitting there."

Alexis swung north over the Lion's Gate bridge and as we inched our way across the spans I watched a massive cruise ship sailing underneath. I wondered whether I'd survive a jump off the edge of the bridge onto the top deck of that ship.

I reached for the handle and Alexis shifted the gun so that it poked firmly into my ribs. I went back to clasping my hands. She spoke with steel in her voice and in her hand. "I've heard of your reputation to outwit and outmanoeuvre everyone who takes you on. I know how you're using the police to take down the competition. I've been sent with a message. The free ride is over. You do things our way or you may soon be flying off this bridge."

As we came to the end of the bridge, Alexis snatched my purse from my lap and threw it into the back. She smirked at me.

"The act is over," she said. "Now, it's time to be who you really are."

While we drove up the steep hill into North Vancouver, I attempted to gain myself some space by being truthful. "I don't know who you think I am, but I'm not involved in whatever you think I'm involved in."

She took a quick glance in my direction, but the sunglasses hid her eyes from me. Her voice vomited sarcasm. "I know who you are. Tommy made it clear to every one of us. At first we thought you must have betrayed Tommy to the Monk and gotten him killed. But when we found out you took out the Monk, we knew you were making a move on your own. Giving the password to the police, so they could track us all down, was a smooth way to cover yourself."

I couldn't believe what I heard. It was like some bizarre video of someone else's life. I could see how some of the pieces might look like they fit, but there was no way to make this go away easily.

The shrinking downtown skyscrapers of Vancouver on the other side of the inlet stood out against the afternoon sun. The evergreens continued to flash by. There were plenty of people looking our way, but no one really looking at me. Not too many yellow Porsches around here.

I tried another stab at truth. "Whoever you're hearing this stuff from needs some serious help getting their facts straight."

The sneer on her face was obvious. "You're not the only one with the police in your pocket. Who do you think stopped you at the border and sent you back into our trap here? How do you think we took care of Charlie?"

The picture of the border guard in sunglasses, stopping me fifty feet past the border crossing and turning me back, filled my vision. It all made sense. No wonder I hadn't been stopped by the immigration authorities or the FBI in Minneapolis. My delusions helped spin my own web of terror.

I had almost killed myself falling for their ruse, and now I was angry. There was a serious boil going on in my soul, but I held onto all the self-control Bruce had taught me through Tai Kwon Do and spoke with as much steel as I could. "Do you ever wonder why you and the brute have been allowed to move so freely up here, even after I saw both of you in Sumas?"

I specifically watched her jaw line, and sure enough, it tightened up. I knew she had been wondering. I wasn't the only one whose imagination played with them.

I pushed my case. "Do you ever wonder why I didn't have my bodyguards with me when you found me?" I could see her eyebrows furrow.

Her tone changed ever so slightly. "All we want is to work out another deal. Maybe work out a truce until we can all rebuild. Ivan just wants to set up a meet. He's getting impatient with how long this is taking."

I tried a stall tactic by focusing on our past contact. "When you first saw me, you had a little girl with you. Who was she?"

Alexis actually smiled. "She wasn't mine, if that's what you're asking." Her smile changed to a smirk. "I didn't know you dealt with stock that young."

My anger was still strong enough to fuel the courage I didn't really have. I tried a bluff. "Pull over at the Horseshoe Bay Ferry Terminal up ahead. I need a coffee."

Alexis didn't even argue. She was used to being told what to do. When the exit came, she pulled off, found a parking spot in front of a busy coffee shop, slipped her gun under the seat, and stepped out. Apparently, violence wasn't going to be necessary for our next step.

I wasn't sure what else to do, so I let her order me a chocolate mocha and the two of us, appearing like old friends, sat at a table overlooking the hundreds of boats docked in the marina next to the ferries. As usual, the seagulls had my attention. The Porsche had everyone else's attention. Two punks who had seen us get out of the Porsche tried to impress us and make a play, but Alexis blew them off with a few icy words.

Couples strolled by hand in hand, enamoured by the view. That could have been Bruce and me if all this craziness had never been. I knew Alexis didn't have a gun with her and I told myself a dozen times to run or scream or do anything besides sit sipping my chocolate mocha.

Then I saw Anthony lounging on the bench across the street. Alexis must have seen that I noticed him. "He's quite the charmer. Makes a lousy date in real life, though. How's your boyfriend treating you?"

The quick jerk of my head in her direction must have given her a message she wanted to see. "Just in case you haven't figured it out yet, friends of Anthony's are taking good care of him. He doesn't know it yet, but if today turns out bad for us, it will also turn out bad for him."

I almost lost my self-control at the thought of Bruce being threatened. How would they get to him on the Langley Air Force Base? I wondered if Lieutenant Saunders was their inside person or if the FBI agents were really FBI agents. Or whether Constables Sall, Lopez, and Chan were really RCMP constables.

I was so locked up in my crazy thoughts that I almost missed the next curve Alexis threw at me. "Oh, we watched you at the football game. We watched you on your walk. You're never alone."

The words were in such conflict with the picture I had of Bruce and I that it took a minute or two to figure out that she was labelling Damian as my boyfriend. I wasn't sure whether she was serious or just being derogatory. No matter what was happening, she had my attention. I didn't want Bruce or Damian hurt because of something I had or hadn't done.

I didn't know when I had last felt this vulnerable. Or violated. Or vicious.

I caved. "What do you need from me?"

Alexis looked at me with an expression of surprise. "You're letting a guy like that get to you so easy? With your power, with your looks, you could take any guy you want. What's the hook? Are you playing me, or has the great Kat Woman finally met her match?"

I could see that left hand of hers working her hair and that earring. Something was about to happen.

I had to ask to be sure. I knew from what the police had discovered through Charlie that Tommy had been spreading rumours that I was his heir apparent, that he had been training me in his secret art. I had assumed that the rumour died when he died. Apparently not everyone thought so. I slid my empty coffee mug to the center of the small table.

My thoughts turned back to Bruce and Damian, whoever they thought was my boyfriend. "What do you know about him?"

Alexis' eyebrows raised and her eyes moved up and to the right—a sign she was thinking. She soon became a computer spitting out memorized facts. "Queens, MBA. Harvard, something religious. Two unsuccessful engagements. Never married. Six years with World Vision. Four years with Food for the Hungry. Fluent in four languages. Moved here a year ago. Loves mountain biking. Hang gliding. Football. Trained as a gourmet chef."

I wanted to breathe a sigh of relief. It wasn't Bruce, but it was definitely Damian. I had nothing much to say. "You talked about making a deal for a shipment."

She stared at me and smiled. "I think he put the hook in your heart by showing you the good side. You know as well as I do that every man has another side. This guy is no different. Either you know that side and you're hooking him to work for you or you really don't know the other side and you're losing perspective. Carelessness costs. Ask Tommy and Charlie." She checked her watch. "Either way, if Ivan doesn't get a positive call from me within another twenty minutes, let's just say that it doesn't matter what you think you know about him."

Alexis stood and waved to Anthony. He stretched himself up off the bench and wandered across to the coffee shop where we'd been sitting.

"Stay put," she said and headed for the women's washroom. I avoided looking at Anthony and finally decided that I, too, needed to use the facilities. I met Alexis, washing her hands at the sink. No one else was in the room.

For Damian's sake, I needed to keep this game going. "Okay, what's next?"

"Nothing."

"What do you mean, nothing?"

"Exactly that. We move some more girls into the area. We set up more clubs. You ignore it. You call off your network. If you're called as a witness for anything, you develop amnesia. You don't remember anything Tommy trained you for. You forget everything about the secret of the art."

My heart was racing. This is exactly what Sergeant James had told me was happening. I just needed to be safe. "In exchange?"

"We give you and your boyfriend a free week in Whistler while things are going down. You get an alibi. We get a free pass."

The thought of a week with Damian in Whistler started a wrestling match between my values and my loyalties. *What kind of a girl would I be to cave in and spend time with some guy I hardly know? How would I ever explain this to Bruce? How could I let an innocent guy like Damian die just because I got myself mixed up in something over my head? What kind of hormonal, irrational person gets herself into these messes?*

The thought of spending private time with Damian was a tad intoxicating to my wild side. The thought of no more time with him was just terrifying. I told myself that anything could happen as long as we were both alive. I stepped into a stall while Alexis leaned against the sinks.

Just before I closed the stall door, I let her know my decision. "I need two suites with kitchenettes. All expenses covered. The best I can offer is a one-week head start."

"I'll get you a good hotel room. Make it worth your while," said Alexis with a smirk. "I'll even get you meal vouchers. You'll obviously be too busy to be cooking."

I pushed the door open wide and took an aggressive step toward her. "Two suites with kitchenettes. Final offer. I like making my own meals. And I need my own space."

I knew I was making an impact when she took a backward step away from me.

She picked up her cell and hit speed dial. The conversation was brief from her side. "Yes… yes… asap… one week… yes… Horseshoe Bay… now? Okay."

Alexis closed her cell phone, fully extended her right arm, and stared at her fingers. She examined her cherry red nails and then slowly raised her blue-tinged eyelids.

"Ivan says you need to call Damian now," she said. "You can say anything you want without mentioning our deal. You must convince him to pick you up within an hour and take you to Whistler for a week. If you're unsuccessful, you won't see him again."

I closed the bathroom stall door in her face.

CHAPTER TWENTY-SIX

Eventually Alexis started banging on my door. "We've got fifty-five minutes. If this boyfriend means anything to you, I'd advise you to call now."

I ignored her. I was convinced part of her upward mobility in the group was tied to delivering me in some way. My mind looked for ways to leave breadcrumbs behind. I used my earring to scratch my cell number into the paint on the stall. Who knew what might happen?

While she was banging a second time, someone else walked into the room and I was given a two-minute reprieve while the other stall was being used. By then, at least I knew the next step. I unlocked the stall door and stared at my nemesis.

I reached out my hand and Alexis looked at me strangely.

"I'll need to borrow your cell, Alexis. I left mine at home."

She instinctively looked toward the occupied stall and gave me a threatening glare. She motioned me outside.

I took the time to wash my hands thoroughly, and by then a jovial senior emerged from the stall. She was ready to chat. Another three minutes went by as she told me she was from Portland, Oregon. She loved the ferry ride over to Vancouver Island and had been making this trip every year for thirty years. The prospect didn't look great, but I left more breadcrumbs.

"I've been living in Sumas in Washington, but I'm living in Vancouver now," I said. "My name is Katie Delancey. A good old Irish name you can remember."

She looked at me with wide eyes and then lowered her head and shook it. "Funny thing," she said. "There was someone with a name something like yours who went missing a month or two ago. Can't remember exactly what the story was. Terrible things happening these days. Well, my grandchildren are waiting for their chance on the ferry, so I better run along. Good to meet you. Have a nice day."

I followed her out the door.

Anthony and Alexis angled me off at the exit door.

"You have forty-five minutes and it takes that long to get here," Alexis said. "You're signing a death sentence for Damian. He won't be the last. We know about your family in Minneapolis. This isn't going to end well if you keep this up."

I held out my hand as we stopped beside the Porsche and she slapped her cell phone into my palm. "Remember," she said. "Say nothing about us, or about why you need to be in Whistler. Just get him here. Promise him anything. And I mean anything."

A chill went down my spine. This time it wasn't a game. "I don't have his number with me."

Alexis examined my face and finally accepted that I was playing this straight. She motioned to Anthony, who had resumed his place on the bench across the street.

"Girl, sometimes you make me believe Tommy was lying. The Kat Woman he told us about never forgot anything or anyone who did her wrong. If this guy is your boyfriend, you have to know his number."

I smiled in her face. "Speed dial," is all I said. "Besides, I never need to call him. He calls me."

Her lips curled up in that knowing smile. I could tell she was a woman who knew how to use her looks to keep her men in line. She climbed into the driver's seat. Meanwhile, Anthony reached over and handed me a card with Damian's number on it. These two had prepared for every excuse.

I called Damian, and as always he picked up on the second ring. He seemed happy to have me call. I didn't give him any time for socializing. "Damian, listen to me. Please don't ask any questions and please don't interrupt me. I need your friendship more than ever right now. I'm in Horseshoe Bay at the ferries. I need you to be here in forty-five minutes. I need you to bring a week's worth of clothes and take me to Whistler. It won't cost you a thing. I can't tell you what will happen if you take too long to get here, but I can tell you that you need to get here as fast as you possibly can. I need you to do this for me. I may never be able to explain this to you. This isn't romantic, but I need you and no one else. Whatever it takes. Please be here in forty-five minutes. If you have to phone people to cancel appointments or to change things, please do it while you're driving. Don't waste a second. Look for a yellow Porsche."

And I hung up.

Anthony nodded his approval, removed the cell phone from my hand, and handed it over to Alexis. Just for a second, I'd hoped I might be able to dial 911 for a little assistance. Maybe forcing Damian to speed would get him stopped by the police and everything could still turn out okay.

I knew it was completely unfair to disrupt Damian's life, but I hoped all the fairy tales were right. I had to believe that men loved to play the part of Prince Charming rescuing their princess. Although I knew I wasn't Damian's princess, I wasn't sure he knew that yet. All I could do was wait and hope that this one man was as good as Alexis said he was. I wondered what the other, unknown side of him might be. I hoped the week ahead wouldn't make me find out the hard way.

As Anthony opened the door for me and ensured I was safely buckled in, my mind tried to prepare for the seven days to come. I needed to shop for some clothes. I needed to let Hanan know that I wasn't abandoning her just because of missing the New Hope event. And somehow I had to connect with Bruce.

I should have been thinking about finding ways to connect with the RCMP, but instead I just hoped my bodyguards had noticed I was missing. I tried to engage Alexis by asking her about her change of footwear. She just smirked and let me know that the shoes functioned as a signal for Anthony to make contact with me.

Alexis was clearly displeased that her car was drawing so much attention, but she was helpless to move us out of there. She told me to stay put, then stepped out with Anthony to handle the curious onlookers who had nothing better to do than gawk at a bright yellow Porsche. There was nothing I could do but pray.

Just for insurance, I poked my fingertip against the tip of my earring and smeared the blood on the inside door handle. I also planted the earring under the passenger seat. Hopefully, some forensic team would eventually catch up with this crew and if anything happened to me there would be some evidence linking Alexis and Anthony to my disappearance. Another breadcrumb for someone to follow.

I tried to recall my last conversation with Dean, when he had identified that my main issue was disappointment with God as my Abba. I did expect God to protect me, listen to me, and be there for me. My current situation was clear justification for my doubt. Where was God when I needed him? Where was his protection? Mom was gone and now it looked like I'd be losing Bruce. If he found out I'd spent a week with Damian, there would be no grace sufficient to help me explain myself.

Does God care about me? Is he being fair with me? Is he here for me? Can I trust him?

As I watched the seagulls out the window, images and memories flowed through my mind. Lancelot, that beautiful black Arabian stallion, had stood guard over me until I was found after a motorcycle crash on Uncle Jimmy's farm. Bruce had carried me when I fell asleep after a nightmare memory in his car. Dean had been there in his small Bible study group explaining carefully how God entered our suffering as he moulded us for the better world to come. I could also see Hanan and Khalid and Fatima and Nafrina, and dozens of other refugees, thanking God for answering their prayers while they were in their most desperate situations. And I relived memory after memory of my time in Kenya.

One image seemed especially relevant to my current situation. I closed my eyes and watched the movie play in my mind. Tommy had me wrapped up tight in his grip. I wasn't only taking care of the men he brought my way; I was organizing the connections for the other girls. He had truly been teaching me the art.

In my mind's eye, I stood on a street corner eyeing a particular man when I felt a nudge on my elbow. A young mother and her daughter were there. I was about to express my annoyance when I saw the most compassionate eyes I'd ever seen. The little girl handed me a cup of hot chocolate and smiled.

"You sure are pretty, lady."

I knew I spent a lot of time trying to look pretty and she hadn't been the first to use those words. I looked up at the girl's young mom, barely older than I was at the time. The woman's eyes were closed and she was moving her lips.

"What are you doing?" I asked.

"Praying for your soul," she said. "God loves you. He has his hand on you. He has plans that are so much better for you than this. There is a key for your chains. His name is Jesus. Do you know him?"

I'd grown up in a missionary school with missionaries. Of course I knew him.

I could feel the tears pouring down my cheeks. The little girl took my hand and I just walked like I was in a trance. I walked away from that street corner and went to a room where people prayed for me. It was like scales came off my eyes that day. God was there, in the form of a child with a cup of hot chocolate.

Just like the child with a flower on the bridge.

I never went back to the streets after that night and Tommy never forgave me. Instead I went to university and trained as a counsellor. I ventured onto the streets of Bellingham, Seattle, and Vancouver, helping the girls there just like that mom and little girl had helped me.

I opened my eyes and nothing outside had changed. The seagulls still drifted on the breeze. The couples still strolled. Families still picnicked. Alexis was still talking with Anthony on the sidewalk outside. Nothing had changed outwardly, but something had changed inwardly.

CHAPTER TWENTY-SEVEN

Alexis' cell rang with ten minutes to spare. I saw her stroll away as she talked. Anthony drifted along behind her, leaving no one to watch me. I felt the urge to run.

I tried to open the car door quietly, but as soon as I emerged some guy gave a wolf whistle in my direction and Anthony turned.

"Any time you need company, let me know," called the admirer with a meaningful look. "And bring your car."

Anthony was by my side within a matter of seconds and the man backed off quickly.

"No harm meant," the man said, looking up at the Jamaican giant. He ducked into the coffee shop and only a few people continued to look in our direction.

Alexis came up and motioned us to follow her.

While we were walking, Alexis handed me a personalized credit card prepared in advance. She gave me room confirmation numbers.

In exchange, Anthony gave me my purse and made sure I handed over all my identification—driver's license, medical and insurance documents, passport, Nexus card, credit cards, and even my library card.

"You'll get it back in a week," Anthony said in a distinctive Louisiana accent.

The brunette was a confident and experienced player who knew how to think several moves in advance. I didn't want to think about what might have happened had I refused her offer. I just hoped Damian, Bruce, Lizzy, and Dean would all be safe.

Alexis informed us that Damian was on his way. Their informants had followed him out to Highway 1; he'd probably be a bit late, but he was moving quickly. Sure enough, twenty minutes later Damian arrived and pulled up across the street by Anthony's bench.

We were seated in a coffee shop a block away from the Porsche when Damian arrived.

Alexis gave her instructions. "We won't be going with you. Enjoy your week. Don't be heroic or come back early. Don't lose your heart and get yourself compromised. I'd rather work with you than against you. Remember your family. Now go, before he starts to worry too much."

I walked out of the coffee shop. Before I had gone half a block, Damian was running toward me. He opened his arms and hugged me in a way that would have convinced any observer that we were long lost lovers. I'm sure I was red-faced, but I needed to keep the show moving. I grabbed his hand and tugged him toward his car.

He asked his first question. "Why is it that the time of day with the slowest traffic is called rush hour?"

"Thanks for coming. Keep walking."

As soon as we were in the car, Damian wanted to know what was going on. I told him to just start the car and drive to Whistler without stopping. He could probably tell by the strain in my voice that I had something on my mind besides romance.

As we started moving, Damian asked his next question. "Why do you suppose they call this the ferry *terminal* when you're just starting out on your adventure?"

I wondered if all these questions served a purpose somehow.

Whether I should have or not, when we got far enough away without seeing a yellow Porsche or silver-grey Mercedes, I began to pour out the events of the past few hours. Damian seemed incredulous as he listened. He kept glancing in my direction to confirm that it was me talking. I gave him a tiny sketch of my former life with Tommy Lee and the complications that had arisen since meeting Stephen. I told him the danger he was in and why it had been so important for him to come immediately without question. And I told him about Bruce. At least, enough to let him know that there was someone else in my life. To his credit, he kept driving. And he was silent.

Along the way we paused at a rest stop to use the pit toilets. I used a stone to scratch my name and number into the wall of the bathroom stall. As I came back to the car, Damian was swinging his arms around his head.

He asked another question. "Why didn't Noah swat those two mosquitoes?"

I couldn't help smiling, then giggling. It seemed totally inappropriate for the situation, but I couldn't help imagine Noah scrambling and chasing after these two tiny pests as they escaped up and around the legs and trunks and tails and horns of the rest of the animals on the ark.

Two minutes after we were back on the highway, I noticed in the passenger mirror that a black Durango was rocketing toward us on the inside lane. I tensed like a drum and gasped. Damian must have noticed where my attention was because he said, "That guy's going to kill someone if he keeps that up."

Within a minute, the Durango had charged in behind us. Traffic was light and passing was easy. Damian accelerated to put some space between us, but the other driver didn't give up an inch.

Damian broke the silence. "He's got a 3.6-liter engine. He's just showing off. I'll get out of his way."

Damian signalled and tried to pull off onto the shoulder, but the driver began to nudge us off the road by banging his right front bumper against our back left. I could hear a taillight crunch. Damian tried to accelerate and move back into the lane but the pursuer waited until traffic was clear and moved into the oncoming lane until he was almost parallel with Damian.

I looked at the speedometer and saw that we were already nudging over 160. The larger vehicle began crowding us toward the rock wall along the shoulder of the road. My lungs felt empty and my eyes felt like they would leap from their sockets. I clung desperately to the safety strap and dashboard.

A small access road for service trucks appeared to our right and Damian cranked the wheel hard and swerved into our escape route while the SUV sped on by. I could feel our car almost tip over onto two wheels as we rocketed onto that gravel road and swerved to avoid a porta-potty and a row of orange and white striped traffic barriers.

Damian finally stopped when he was sure we weren't being followed. He looked angry when he turned to me. "Friends of yours?"

My throat was so tight I could hardly speak. "I hope not. Thanks for saving my life."

"Should we go back?" he asked. "Do we call the police?"

"We can't."

He looked grim. "I sure hope the rest of the week isn't as exciting as the first hour."

During the last half hour of our trip, I tried to work out options with Damian. What might it mean for us to call the police? We'd be in protective custody and there was no reason my family couldn't be as well. And what would it mean for other young girls if we didn't call the police?

We both agreed that we just didn't know how real or widespread the threat was. If Ivan, Alexis, or Anthony did have connections within the police department, how could we communicate without endangering anyone? We weren't sure how much was known about our family and friends.

We had no doubt that we'd be watched all week. Since our rooms had been preselected, perhaps even our phones would be tapped. Maybe our rooms were bugged. We agreed that we'd play this out until we figured something out. There was nothing to do but make the best of it. But from the start I made it clear—this was friendship.

As we slowed to a stop at a red light, Damian put his hand on my knee and spoke sincerely. "Maybe we should think about doubling up here. I don't like the idea of you being on your own with these crazy people after you."

I put my hand on his and assured him, "I'll be fine. I'm grateful you came, but there's no way I'm putting either of us in a compromising situation."

We checked into the suites in Whistler Village and nothing seemed suspicious. I needed to go shopping and take advantage of the credit card to renew my wardrobe and stock our kitchenettes for the week, since I hadn't been given a chance to bring anything along. Damian had managed to stuff enough clothing into an overnight case, but he didn't intend to abandon me at such a critical time.

Whistler was a beautiful Alpine ski village made to look like something you'd find in Switzerland. The high-pitched roofs kept the snow from piling up in winter. The cobbled streets, free of traffic, were always filled with people and you can hear twenty or thirty different languages from the young people who were there for adventure—or maybe love. There were a lot of trendy tourist stores, but some practical outlets as well.

I was looking forward to trying new outfits that actually made me feel pretty again. Most of my purchases were decided alone in the dressing room, but I couldn't help stepping out and getting Damian's approval from time to time. I didn't have to try very hard to get that. Perhaps I'd picked up enough for two weeks, but I didn't know what lay ahead.

Shopping for food took almost as long as the clothing stops. Damian was, indeed, a chef and had been putting together menus in his mind as I tried on clothes. He picked up most of his items without too much difficulty, but there were definitely some herbs and spices that he had to keep searching for in various speciality shops. He finally found most of what he wanted.

As we stood in the checkout line-up, Damian asked, "Why do you suppose they sell hotdogs in packages of ten and buns in packages of eight?"

I assured him I didn't know, but it was probably because men were in charge of the operation. He gave my waist a quick squeeze and I jumped. We both end up laughing.

We agreed to meet for a late supper. I headed back to my room for a shower and a change of clothes. If I was going to survive, I could only think about being where I was and being thankful to God that Damian wouldn't be a nightmare to be with.

He knocked on my door as I was putting on my makeup. I let him in and told him to wait while I finished up. He expressed all the appreciation I needed to hear about the pant suit I'd chosen. I walked away feeling warm all over.

I had just finished my lashes when Damian called out another question. "Have you ever wondered why women can't put on mascara with their mouth closed?"

I looked in the mirror and, sure enough, my mouth was open. All I said was, "No comment."

There was a light sprinkle outside and we'd forgotten to buy an umbrella. We stood in the lobby and looked out at the drops making their presence known in the puddles outside.

Damian just had to say something useless. "Katie, you know how wool shrinks? I've been wondering. Why don't sheep shrink when it rains?"

Fortunately, one of the staff noticed our dilemma and retrieved an umbrella from inside the hotel for us. We had a great time at the restaurant and did a great job pretending that both of us really wanted to be there. I was pleasantly surprised to find out that Damian liked prime rib and mushrooms just like I did. He even ordered Ranch dressing for his salad.

I'd never met a man who knew how to dig into my soul so well. He genuinely seemed to care about my Kenyan experiences. He even remarked on how much of a culture shock it must have been coming back to North America after all those years in Africa. Bruce had never once even asked me about my transition experiences and losses.

I told Damian how on my first trip to the supermarket with my mother, my dad and us kids had been given the chance to choose one box of cereal each while Mom did the rest of the shopping. In Kenya, there may have been one or two choices, and since the supermarket was over an hour away from where we lived, Mom usually needed all the space she could get to buy in bulk. We usually didn't shop in the big stores. Here, there was an entire aisle of nothing but cereals. Hundreds of choices. When Mom came to get us after finishing her part, we still hadn't been able to make a choice.

Damian laughed and said that he'd once had a similar experience with dental floss.

Finally, I came to my senses and realized that Damian had another life as well. I wasn't sure what this week was costing him. As I questioned him over the next two hours, I was amazed at the depth of his knowledge and experience around the world.

Currently, he was working as a consultant for several charities. He'd had to cancel several appointments to be with me. He was building a sailboat, a project which he'd put on hold. He still had tickets to the football game we'd planned to go to; missing the game was going to be a disappointment.

When I pressed to see if he had other interests, and to see how well Alexis really knew him, he did admit to enjoying mountain biking. Whistler had great mountain bike trails. He also enjoyed international gourmet cooking and was looking forward to trying out a few dishes on me—if I was willing to teach him some of the Kenyan specialties I knew.

When I questioned him about his education, he humbly admitted that Queens and Harvard had been good places to keep his mind active and broaden his perspective on the world. He had been to more than twenty-five countries and enjoyed travelling. He'd had enough for now, though, and was looking to put down some roots.

We shared our international adventures and laughed a lot. Midnight came and went. At one o'clock in the morning, we were the only ones left and the staff had cleared all the other tables. The bill had been sitting on our table for three hours, so I paid it and we headed back to our rooms.

Damian walked me to my door. We didn't hold hands or anything. He did look questioningly into my eyes, but I looked away and he wished me good night before moving toward his own door next to mine.

"I'll make breakfast if you're interested," he said.

I checked my watch. "I'll be there at 10:30. We can do brunch."

I got through my door and leaned back against it, trying to deal with all the emotion that washed over me.

CHAPTER TWENTY-EIGHT

Monday morning was almost perfect. I was still dozing when a knock sounded on my door. I heard Damian calling, "Breakfast in bed is being served." My heart pounded in my chest. How would I handle this? I'd never had breakfast in bed before.

My quickly-purchased nightie was in no way decent enough for a breakfast in bed, so I told Damian to hang on. I pulled on a sweatshirt, unlocked the door, then raced back to bed. Damian turned the knob, hip-checked the door open, and brought in a tray loaded with waffles, whipped cream, and strawberries. On the sides were bowls of sliced fruits—mangos, bananas, kiwis, oranges, papaya, and pineapple. The man knew how to score brownie points.

He set the tray beside me on the Queen-sized bed and flopped down on the other side as if this was the most normal thing in the world. He was wearing a muscle shirt and shorts. I tried not to overreact.

His first question didn't ease my concerns. "Is that what you slept in? Aren't you a bit warm?"

My answer probably didn't help my cause. "I'm afraid what I wore isn't appropriate for breakfast in bed." I meant that to push him off, but it seemed to spark his interest even more. I attempted to wriggle out of the awkward situation by focusing on his wonderful gift. "Strawberries and whipped cream on waffles. One of my absolute favourites."

"Help yourself."

"Why don't you pray for us?" I said.

"For what?" he asked. "Do you have something in mind that I don't know about?" His suggestive look and raised eyebrows made me nervous. Absolutely no one who could help me knew I was there. But I had nothing to fear. This was only friendship.

I set him straight. "For breakfast. Nothing else. I'll pray." I kept it short, but I wondered if other thoughts were still filling his mind.

During breakfast, Damian pulled out his Whistler information packet and asked me about the different things we could do. We decided on a hike to Lost Lake, the famous gondola ride from Blackcomb to Whistler Mountain, and a late dinner. We had all week and didn't want to do everything at once.

As we talked, I found myself surprised that this hunk hadn't once mentioned the difficult circumstances that had brought us to Whistler. I was grateful that he wasn't using guilt trips to make me feel bad, but it would have been normal to at least question about how we might be able to get out of this mess. He seemed quite content to just be with me.

After breakfast, Damian seemed to stall so I finally threw back the covers, grabbed my shorts, t-shirt, and underclothes and escaped as he cleaned up. I ignored his whistle, gave him a sly grin, and locked myself in the bathroom to change.

It was on the hike around the lake that he finally took my hand. I didn't resist him. All the other couples were holding hands and it did seem strange that we weren't; I didn't want to draw unnecessary attention to us. While we sat on a bench, watching a few young girls feeding the ducks, he planted his right arm loosely around my shoulders. I felt that it was the least I could allow given he had dropped everything on such short notice.

When we were riding the gondola, he slipped his hand behind me and began to give me a backrub. His hands were strong and he knew how to work the body well. Maybe a bit too well. I enjoyed the eleven-minute trip and didn't exactly do my best to resist him later when we sat on a mountaintop bench as he gave me a neck massage. In that warm sunshine, under his touch, I was putty.

Later, back at the hotel, he didn't push himself on me when I put my hand on his chest and pushed him back while closing the door in his face.

"Give me an hour," I told him.

I was still in the shower when he knocked. I ignored him. It didn't hurt to keep men waiting sometimes. Besides, I needed this cold water to get myself under control.

When I stood in front of the mirror checking out my outfits, I realized there were really only two good options for the warm weather. Although I had been looking at what made me look pretty when I bought these, I could now see why a man might think, in the right circumstances, that he had a shot with me. I decided to go with the more conservative choice. Things had been hot enough today.

Damian eventually called and I let him know that I'd be ready in twenty minutes. He suggested that he could come and help me finish up. I told him that I wouldn't want to spoil the surprise. Sometimes my words were like reflex responses from my old life. I knew I needed to work on that.

When the time was right, I opened the door for Damian. I could see from his eyes that he was pretty satisfied. He was dressed in black jeans and a short-sleeved shirt with the buttons undone most of the way. His muscular chest was only slightly hairy. I instinctively reached over and started to do a few of them up. He put his hand over mine.

I looked up into his eyes and saw his desire. I let him kiss me briefly, but pulled away and reminded him that dinner was waiting. I really hoped that I had befriended a man who might be a little different than the others.

During dinner, Damian seemed to take a different tack in our conversation. He asked me about what Tommy had trained me to do. How the operation worked. How the Monk was involved. How I'd managed to knock off the Monk. How the police were involved. I told him consistently that I wasn't prepared to discuss any of this with him; he was a friend and I didn't want to put our friendship at risk. He told me that he was ready to be more than a friend and I could trust him.

The more he pushed me, the more I wanted to back away, but I stayed and kept deflecting his interests. When dinner was done, we walked hand-in-hand under the moonlight. The snow-capped mountains glowed white in the night sky. A few stars were even visible despite the streetlights. Romance seemed to be pouring from every window and stopping point along the way.

When we got to Damian's room, he manoeuvred me to sit on the edge of his bed. I hesitated, but when he walked away I leaned back and propped myself up on my elbows, warily watching his every move. He pulled up a chair, gently placed my feet on his lap, and began to practice his reflexology. He massaged my toes, heels, and the soles of my feet, melting my weariness and wariness away. I soon lay back on the bed and let him care for me.

As he lulled me into oblivion, I could faintly hear his voice telling me how we'd go sailing in a few days. How there was nothing like racing across the water with the wind pushing you faster than you can control. How, when you're in the middle of nowhere but water, you can slip into the water and float and relax and rest and be calm. I could almost feel it.

I forgot to tell Damian about one thing—that my knees were hypersensitive to touch. He massaged my feet and ankles and calves… and that's when my mind woke up, as he approached the no-touch zone of my knees. Out of nowhere, the words of Pastor Gary's sermon sifted like breezes across my spirit: "Beauty, gladness, praise, righteousness. That's what God has planned for you."

I sat up so quickly that I'm sure Damian was surprised.

"I need to go."

That's all I could say. I left the room without my shoes, shut the door behind me, then sat in my own room on the edge of my bed, shaking like a leaf. What was I doing?

I tried to find something to read, but the only book in the room was a Gideon's Bible. I hadn't realized that was still allowed in Canada. I missed my bubble bath, but I still soaked in the tub. The Bible sat on the floor beside me.

I finally felt guilty enough for not doing my share of reading that I grabbed the book and let it open somewhere in the middle. The book of Job. A book about suffering. I'd already had my share and I thought I'd already answered this issue. I had to admit, my suffering didn't seem to have gotten better just because I wasn't so angry about it anymore.

Being a good kid all my life, I knew that the right thing to do was to read, so I did. God and Satan had a bet. God's best man against Satan's worst torments. The outcome was about faith. Where would Job's faith lie at the end of the contest? Of course, Job had no idea about the action behind the scenes.

I stopped to reflect and wondered if there was something similar happening in my life. Was God holding back his hedge of protection because he believed in me? Or rather, because he was counting on me believing in him when this was all over? I wasn't sure that God—or Satan, for that matter—would waste their time on someone like me.

As I read, I saw that God was setting Satan up. He was taking a miraculous form of fragile dust, carved together into his image, and letting that man stand in his place against the greatest enemy the universe would ever know. The only problem was that God wasn't telling the man who he was really fighting against.

I was amazed anew at the dialogue of the suffering hero and realized that the little choices people make on earth actually have huge consequences in the unseen world. The same thing was happening in my life. Maybe my choices impacted the unseen world's invisible struggle.

The water in the tub had cooled, but I wasn't ready to put down the book yet. In some personal way, God was saying that what I believed and thought and felt and chose mattered. The issue I had to wrestle with wasn't "Where is God when things are bad?" but "Where am *I* when things are bad?" Would I choose to love God or would I choose to love myself—or someone or something else?

I saw the truth clearly again. God and life weren't the same thing. The battle wasn't about what was going on around me, but what was going on inside me. Who I was mattered. What I did mattered. I wondered if I'd blown it with God by coming up here with Damian.

An hour later, I couldn't resist the urge to knock on his door and talk just a little bit more.

CHAPTER TWENTY-NINE

I should have had trouble sleeping, but I didn't. I slept right through until nine o'clock in the morning and then went out for a jog. The early birds were already on the mountains, racing down the bike track, and launching themselves off the jumps. The runs were dry today and in perfect condition for daredevils. I could feel my adrenaline surging in anticipation of a future chance to experience that sensation of flight.

By the time I had showered and changed, I knew breakfast would be ready. I knocked on Damian's door and, sure enough, Mr. Reliable had a beautiful fruit plate, brown toast, bacon, tomato wedges, and omelettes already in place.

For just a second, I had a memory flash to the morning Bruce had gone all out to prepare his crepes for me. It was obvious that both Damian and Bruce could hold their own in the kitchen. Of course, one or two special occasions were a little different than a daily routine.

Neither of us mentioned the night before. After a great breakfast, I washed the dishes while Damian dried and put them away. I couldn't help but notice that he spent his fair share of time with the weights. His sleeveless t-shirt and shorts did nothing to hide the fact. He seemed comfortable and relaxed, despite the harrowing experience I had just brought him through.

I was curious about what made him tick, so I asked about his family. His parents had died in a plane crash while they were holidaying in China. He had already been in college, so he kept looking after himself. He had a brother who was physically handicapped and was being looked after by a family friend in Florida. Both his parents had been single children, so there were no cousins. Family events had always been small.

When I asked about former girlfriends, he stopped drying the bowl he was working on and turned to face me. "Katie, I don't mind going down this road, but you made it clear that we are focusing on friendship. I have to tell you that this is a painful road for me. I'd rather we kept things simple and focused on the present."

His vulnerable honesty actually made me feel drawn toward him. Of course I backed off. I already knew from Alexis that he'd had two unsuccessful engagements. Maybe I was just trying to test his integrity. It was just as well, as I didn't want to go down that road either. Not after my apology and reaffirmation of friendship the night before. I just thought it might open the door for me to say something more about Bruce.

After cleanup, I decided that the outdoors was likely safer for the two of us, so we went on a hike. Just after noon, we turned our attention toward the mountain bike rentals. We picked up some good bikes and protective gear, bought our tickets, and took our place in the long lines.

Damian brought his brochures and seemed to love proving how knowledgeable he was by reading what was already in print. There were over a hundred marked runs on each mountain. The longest run was over eleven kilometres. Eight thousand acres were set aside for athletes and Damian was sure that us bikers could take advantage of a lot of the same space.

Both of the mountains were over seven thousand feet high, which seemed small compared to Mount Kenya, all seventeen thousand feet of which I'd climbed to prove I'd reached womanhood. That was one memory I was willing to forget: humiliating myself in front of the first boy I'd fallen in love with. I wasn't going to do anything desperate today. Maybe a little wild, but not desperate.

When our turns came, I let Damian lead the way for a bit while I adjusted to the bike and terrain. I could feel some of my confidence returning, but I could also tell that my body didn't have the same reflexes I'd once been proud of. On the first two runs, I followed Damian's lead when he chose the launching point for the jumps. By the third run, I felt like he was keeping it a bit tame and I wasn't sure whether he was taking it easy on me or he just wasn't into risks as much as he claimed.

I sailed past him on a less-marked path and chose a riskier launch. I felt like I was twenty to thirty feet up and nearly lost everything when I landed. The feeling was so exhilarating that I repeated the challenge on the next jump. This was almost the same adrenaline rush as racing Lancelot or an African leopard on my motorcycle.

I was an eagle catching the thermal. When I landed the jump, I looked back to see where Damian had landed. I was so fascinated by the terrified expression on his face as he launched that I missed the turn in the trail and drove right into the bright orange fencing. I tumbled and twisted into a contorted blob of uncontrolled pain.

By the time anyone reached me, I was hurting so bad I thought I'd fractured every bone in my body. The brilliant sun directly overhead forced me to keep my eyes closed and to experience an unbelievable level of trust in others.

The first panicked voices who called 911 gave way to calm professionals who worked to extricate me from the fencing. I lay helpless, experiencing my rescue as if watching a reality show. I could feel someone gently poking me in specific areas and I knew this was an old-time method still used in Kenya to assess whether limbs were fractured. Someone else draped a blanket around me to help protect me from shock.

I kept listening for Damian, but I couldn't hear him in the multitude of voices all around me. When I sensed that someone had moved to block the sun from my face, I tried to look up and around. The throbbing migraine kept me from trying that too often. I could hear my voice responding tersely when the prodding got too intense, but it still felt like a dream.

A collar was placed around my neck and splints were nudged into place around both my legs. A backboard was gently worked underneath me and I was then immobilized into place with a series of straps and wrappings. It would have been the perfect nightmare for someone with claustrophobia.

Somehow I was airlifted by helicopter and taken to the Whistler Medical Clinic. I was briefly aware of someone flashing a bright light into my eyes. When I woke again, I was in an ambulance heading for Vancouver. Two nurses were crunched up, sitting alongside where I lay.

It took a minute to process what was happening, but then Alexis' warning sounded in my head: *"Don't be heroic or come back early… I'd rather work with you than against you. Remember your family."*

I worked to try removing the oxygen mask so I could tell someone that we couldn't go back, but my arms were strapped down. I continued to struggle and I saw a nurse preparing a needle. In a moment, there was only darkness again.

Waking up off and on wasn't the best experience. It seemed that every time I opened my eyes, there was a new face I didn't recognize. This hospital experience was getting old. As darkness after darkness went by, I was surprised that I never saw Damian

My world had definitely shifted. I did have a live hero who knew how to rescue me. I did have a man who knew how to respect me and treat me as if I really was beautiful. But where was he when I needed him? I found myself dreaming about his caresses and wishing I had taken advantage of his offer of a goodnight kiss. With Damian, I'd found laughter again. I'd explored thoughts and parts of the world I hadn't dreamed of before. He gave wings to my soul and roots for my heart.

Apart from Dean, I wasn't sure I'd met anyone quite like him. It was like someone had figured out who I was and carefully crafted the perfect partner. He was almost too good to be true. Still other questions came to my mind as clarity improved. Maybe I could thank Damian for teaching me to ask questions. These questions seemed unending.

What was trust, really? Was I supposed to put myself on the line, to let go of my control to determine my own life? Was I really just supposed to open up my hands like a beggar and wait for whatever God dropped into them? Was I supposed to do the same thing with this man I hardly knew? Was I that desperate to be loved?

I remembered Damian's words to me that night in Whistler after I told him a little about my potential relationship with Bruce and my struggle with prayer. He'd become very clinical.

"Katie, in my management practice, we had this thing we called Minimax Regret Analysis. We had to think of the worst possible thing that could happen and then we worked hard to minimize it. What's the worst possible thing that can happen if you decide you don't want to pray anymore? What's the worst possible thing that can happen if you choose the wrong guy?"

That night, after I'd read about Job and gone back to his room, as we were sitting by the fire, sipping cappuccinos, and talking about the upcoming week and all we could discover in Whistler, it seemed like wisdom from on high. I wasn't so sure anymore.

At least Damian had the nerve to kick me out before things got cosy. He was waiting for me to make a final choice—and that was making it easier to choose him. I just wish I'd had the rest of the week to test out the relationship a little more.

CHAPTER THIRTY

Somewhere around the third sunset that I remember, without any sign of Damian, my mind clicked onto what must have happened. Alexis had warned me that Ivan wouldn't tolerate me coming back to Vancouver earlier than the end of the week. If I did, Damian or my family would pay the consequences. They must have gotten to him.

I'd had plenty of time to examine my own injuries. Both legs in casts. A wrist that was broken and casted. My head still wrapped up and sometimes painful beyond belief. I knew they had me on morphine or Demerol and things were a little out of focus.

I knew one other thing: Bruce and Lizzy had to be warned. I asked for a laptop to email, but Nurse Alejandra said there wasn't one available on this floor. A girl named Imelda brought me a food tray. She told me it was Sunday, so I knew I'd missed some time along the way. I tried to tell these people that my name was Katrina Delancey and that I lived in Vancouver. The name printed above my bed in black Sharpie said "K. Delaney."

I told doctors and nurses alike that the name was wrong. Some specialist came by to talk to me and tell me that my real name was Kay Delaney and that I lived in Bellingham, Washington. He said that with a head injury like mine, things could be confusing for a while. Apparently, my credit card was clearly labeled and that was the only identification anyone had found. The social workers had tried to find someone who knew me before the hospital shipped me down to Seattle for care.

When I asked about Damian Harding for the fifth time, a social worker said there was no record of anyone by that name in Whistler. When I asked him to check with Devlyn at the counselling office in Langley, he replied that the office had told him Devlyn was in Toronto at a conference. When I told them about my sister in Minneapolis, they said there was nothing they could do since I couldn't remember an address or phone number.

When I told them to call the RCMP about me, I finally got some action. Corporal Sall showed up with someone I didn't know, Sergeant Richardson. Within minutes, I was wheeled down the hall to a private room. The door was shut and two female constables were placed on guard outside. Sergeant Richardson spent the next hour or two grilling me about every minute of every day I could remember from the last time I'd seen Constable Lopez after church a week earlier.

While I didn't tell them about my intimacy with Damian, I did tell them about the encounter with Alexis and Anthony. I told them about my personal identification being taken and my need to cancel all my credit cards. I told them about the warning against Damian and about the bike accident. I couldn't tell them anything else about Damian. Maybe Harding wasn't his last name. Maybe it was Harder. I'd only heard it once or twice. Constable Sall was designated to contact Lizzy and Bruce to bring them up to date.

Constable Chan brought me a laptop on her shift that evening. She admitted to me that Constable Lopez had been put on leave after my disappearance. I seemed to keep making life hard on people. Damian's disappearance was a mystery. How could he have just disappeared? I was afraid for his life.

It was hard to email Bruce while the constable was sitting in a chair at the foot of my bed, but I'd waited long enough. When I opened my email, there were 139 messages. I could see a lot of them were from Bruce and Lizzy. I spent about half an hour skipping in and out of the messages and saw that most of the early ones were personal updates and the later ones were attempts to contact me. In a moment of desperation, I deleted most of them.

I only had my left hand to work with, so my labour of love to Bruce was slow and tedious. I gave him a brief overview of my encounter with Alexis and Anthony—the lady with the red slip-ons and her personal enforcer. I assured Bruce that I would physically heal and that my injuries were an accident resulting from my own stupidity and nothing more. For now, I didn't have the words or stamina to tell him about Damian.

I must have fallen asleep with the laptop still on. When I woke up, the laptop and Constable Chan were gone. A young redhead stood looking out the window. She turned when I made it obvious I was awake and gave me a big-toothed grin. She had the greenest eyes.

"I'm Constable O'Brien," she said. "Call me Connie. We'll be working together for the next little while. Beautiful view from up here. Makes me want to move offices. Now, how are you doing this morning, Ms. Delancey?"

I blinked against the light, but managed to get my tongue in gear. "Call me Katie. I'm fine for a mummy who's ready to say uncle."

Connie broke into a small belly laugh over that one and we spent the morning becoming friends. Breakfast and potty breaks hardly slowed us down. I just needed someone to talk with and she seemed more than willing to handle anything and everything I threw her way.

When Corporal Sall returned in the evening, he brought the laptop and informed me that Lizzy was on her way. She should be with me in the morning. This time, I managed notes to Bruce and Lizzy with my left hand. I also took the time to read all the new emails before falling asleep. I hoped there was nothing special in the eighty or more emails I'd already deleted.

Constable Chan was there when I woke up and she informed me that Sergeant Richardson would be bringing Lizzy by in a few hours. In the meantime, we needed to go over a few more details of what had happened while I was away. I begged off until I had finished my breakfast, potty break, and therapy.

Lizzy still hadn't arrived when all that was done, so I had little choice. I recounted the details regarding everyone involved in as much detail as possible. I had to state who said what to whom and when and where. All this was recorded.

Sergeant Richardson arrived just before noon but closed the door behind him. I asked about Lizzy and he said she was just outside and would be with me as soon as we dealt with a couple more issues. He brought in a sketch artist and I spent an hour giving details until the faces of Damian, Anthony, and Alexis were identifiable.

As soon as he left with the sketches, my lunch tray was brought in. The girl who brought the turkey sandwiches and vegetable soup looked at me briefly and then moved into my bathroom and closed the door. Her behaviour seemed odd.

Constable Chan said she was just going to bring Lizzy up to speed on things before she came in. She then left me alone.

I had just spent an hour with a sketch artist, so paying attention to detail was high on my mind. There was something oddly familiar about the girl who had delivered the lunch, so I tried to focus on the image of her face. Short cropped black hair; it could have been a wig. Almond-shaped hazel eyes. Porcelain skin. Sharp nose.

The black-framed eyeglasses looked like they could have been picked up in a cheap outlet. There was no jewellery on her hands or arms that made her stand out. But there was something about her necklace. A dark blue Egyptian cross—an ankh, just like the one Alexis wore.

As I reached for the call buzzer to alert someone, the girl emerged from my bathroom. This time she wore a nurse's uniform and she was blond and without glasses. She smiled at me and I froze. There was no question as to her identity. I pressed the buzzer as she walked out of the room.

At that moment, Lizzy walked in all excited and threw herself somewhat gently around my neck. I tried to pay her the attention she deserved, but I asked her to get Constable Chan.

Lizzy smiled. "No need. She's gone for lunch. I'm your bodyguard for now."

A nurse from the station stepped into the room in response to my buzzer call and asked if I was okay. I tried to explain about the girl who had just come in with my lunch. Lizzy scurried out to find the constable. No one at the nursing station had noticed anything. They were busy with updating records or attending patients.

Again, I was left alone and suddenly got suspicious about my lunch. I moved the cover over my meal aside and noticed a piece of paper wrapped around my menu order sheet. When I got it open with my left hand, the message made me swallow hard.

Nice work, Kat Woman. One less for us to deal with. You are ruthless. How about a partnership? When you're out. Wear red shoes. We'll find you. The order is in.

I had no clue what this meant, but the shivers coming down my spine said I had vague suspicions. When Lizzy and the constable returned, I passed on the note and tried to describe again the two disguises worn by Alexis. Sergeant Richardson came by and was furious at the two constables outside who couldn't seem to remember many details about the girl who had delivered the lunch or the nurse who came out of the room.

They had been distracted by a large African man who couldn't speak English. None of the nurses knew which unit he was supposed to be on, but eventually a nurse had come to claim him and take him back to where he belonged. And yes, she had been blond.

CHAPTER THIRTY-ONE

A thorough check of the hospital by a large force of Vancouver police officers found no one and revealed nothing. Again, I was interviewed. This time, by the city police detectives. By the time I was done, I felt like I was the criminal. The detective in charge took the note for analysis after questioning me repeatedly about every phrase.

I reminded the detectives about the yellow Porsche and silver-grey Mercedes. An all-points bulletin was sent out for patrols and the borders to keep watch for these cars.

I wondered if this was a setup. Alexis probably knew I'd turn the note in to the police. Being called *Kat Woman* and *ruthless*—and suggesting a partnership, one less to deal with, and my inside knowledge of an order—all pointed to me as the suspicious party. Alexis and her crew were probably monitoring police action to see how much the net had tightened around them.

I had a great visit with Lizzy, although her nonstop chatter left my head spinning. Mom's funeral service had been packed with people from the church and community who loved her.

Everyone missed me and passed on their greetings. Yes, everyone had been panicking when I went missing again, but no one contacted the papers this time.

She told me that she and Dean had scheduled their wedding for October to make sure I'd be available. They'd been talking to Bruce about the Kenya trip and he was game to go. Even Dean's family was game to spend a few weeks doing a safari. Lizzy and Dean would do a special ceremony and reception for our relatives and friends afterward.

And there was more. Lizzy had found the stud farm in Belgium where Lancelot had been shipped. My sister thought we could visit if I wanted on the way back from Kenya.

Sergeant Richardson dropped by again to say the police were moving me out of the hospital to a more secure location. I'd be able to have visitors, but only if they cleared security and had my okay. The secure location just happened to be my own condominium.

"No use wasting any more taxpayer dollars than we need to," he said as he walked away.

Corporal O'Brien delivered me home with Lizzy around lunch time. My wheelchair wasn't power-driven, so I had to be pushed. I didn't like being dependant on others like this.

Two new constables, casually dressed, were seated in the entryway. Another sat on a chair at the end of my hallway. A nurse would drop by three times a day to check up on me for the next week. After that, I'd have to secure a maid service if no one else was going to be available.

Lizzy did the shopping and restocked my fridge and cupboards. She played with my hair and rubbed my back several times a day. She knew what I liked. We played backgammon, Skip-Bo, and Hearts over and over. Twice a day she pushed me around the building and out to the rooftop garden. I think she needed to get out, so she didn't go stir crazy.

She explored my heart like only a sister or best friend can. She was God's healing touch in the flesh. She brought grace, mercy, joy, and safety. She hugged me through my tears. She understood my life and my heart. Most of it, anyway.

Too many times I had been a controlling, demanding, disappointing older sister. I had expected her to come through for me when I wanted her, but I'd often fallen short when she needed me. And here she was. No guilt, no pressure, no expectations. She was teaching me about love again. Slowly, the lies of the enemy and the wounds of my soul were being exposed.

Whenever we weren't talking, I worked on emails and tried to build up my connections again. Pastor Gary briefly let me know that his church would be praying for me. Dozens of my former school friends from Kenya sent me Facebook sympathies. Sometimes I still looked for a letter from my mom even though I knew she was gone.

After a superficial explanation about my situation, Hanan agreed to take the next month of her life and spend her days taking care of me. I was humbled by her generosity and gracious assistance.

Nothing else exceptional happened during the week of Lizzy's stay except that Bruce's daily phone calls revealed a romantic side I'd missed in the past several months. In my dialogue with Samantha, she said that Damian hadn't contacted her and hadn't shown up to any New Hope events. When I inquired at World Vision about a Damian Harding, the receptionist did eventually locate his name in their database as someone who had worked with them for just over five years. He'd been out of their organization the past five years and the last contact they'd had with him was in Florida. I encouraged her to keep her files updated.

The receptionist at Food for the Hungry said she only had the contact information of people who worked locally and that Damian may have worked for them overseas. They were involved in a lot of locations. I suggested they broaden their communication network.

The detectives I talked to admitted there were people at Whistler who remembered someone who looked like Damian, but no one was absolutely sure. The clerk who lent us the umbrella was the most sure of anyone. No one apparently saw Damian the day of the bike accident. He wasn't reported as an injury. I suggested they call a few more hospitals.

My constant thought was that somehow Alexis and Anthony had contacts who'd gotten to him after I went down with my accident. I felt a lot of guilt for letting my arrogant pride cause me to be careless. Damian's life may have been lost because of me. With all these confusing thoughts, I had trouble responding to Bruce's romantic overtures with as much focus and enthusiasm as he might have wanted.

In my own childish way, I began to pray. I prayed that Bruce would understand and forgive. And if not, that he would be able to find a woman worthy of his love. I prayed that Damian be spared and Alexis and Anthony brought to justice. I prayed for my physical, emotional, and spiritual healing, that somehow God would accomplish all he wanted in the middle of this mess.

Several weeks after my accident, I was sitting alone in my condo on a Sunday morning going over the Isaiah 61 passage which Pastor Gary had used to impact my life. I focused on praying that God would develop a crown of beauty, the oil of gladness, the garment of praise, and the deep roots and strength of righteousness in my life.

Just then, my eyes drifted back to the first verse. The words seemed to speak on their own:

Preach good news to the poor... bind up the brokenhearted... proclaim freedom for the captives and release from darkness for the prisoners.

These were things I'd been doing through my counselling practice and with my volunteer work. Perhaps this was meant to be happening within me. The thought brought me peace.

But the next words hit me differently: *"Proclaim the year of the Lord's favor and the day of vengeance of our God"* (Isaiah 61:2). These words sounded like God was going to do something special. Could this have something to do with Bruce or Lancelot or my trip to Kenya? Or could it have something to do with Alexis and Anthony finally being brought to justice? Maybe it had something to do with Damian. I tried to restrain the excitement that arose within me.

CHAPTER THIRTY-TWO

A month after Whistler, September arrived and Damian was nothing more than a memory wrapped in a dream. Unfortunately, some nights those were powerful dreams. Too much fantasy could be dangerous to a girl's mind. In order to combat this, I tried to become more and more vulnerable in my correspondence with Bruce.

One day, I decided to expose who I was as a woman and see how he would react. I read the message and edited it three times before I pressed "send." I scanned it one more time.

> I've counselled hundreds of women over the years. There's one thing I have in common with all of them. I've never reached a certainty that others will always love me for who I am. There seems to be a deep insecurity that wraps itself like thorns around my soul. I feel the piercing pain each time I dare to stretch and expose my God-given beauty. I'm left hesitant and overly sensitive to any word or action that questions who I am as a woman.
>
> Ever since I've been a little girl, I seem to have that unanswered question that I ask of everyone in my world: do you really see me?
>
> That question has a thousand disguises as it floats from my heart. Am I likeable? Am I pretty? Am I really fearfully and wonderfully made? Is time spent with me worthwhile?
>
> I'm surprised sometimes how little it takes to answer my heart. Someone running their fingers through my hair can fill my soul for hours. So can a hairdresser who takes an extra ten minutes to perfect highlights, or to rinse a little more, or to blow-dry and get my style exactly as I want it.

I can be as mellow as a cat, and just as ready to purr, after a good foot massage. A pedicure can get me dancing. A backrub takes me halfway to heaven.

A single red rose with some baby's breath will definitely get my attention. What I love is some original poetry written with only me in mind. A song works, but that doesn't happen too often in my world.

For adventure, I can get into almost anything. Hikes are fun, as long as the scenery and company is good. I tend not to walk alone too much. I love a great horseback ride, an open throttle on a motorcycle, jet skiing, paragliding, mountain biking, and talking over chai until midnight. I love to stand and gaze at beauty. Nature. Art. Clothes. Sometimes people.

I prefer to shop with someone I trust. I like to try on things and watch people's eyes for their reaction. I like to see where their attention is drawn. I don't shop with guys very often. They're too single-minded.

As you know, I grieve deeply. I have so many losses in my life. Kenya. My parents. My brother. My innocence. My friends. Lancelot. My job. My freedom.

Sometimes I dream about the men who have held my heart. More than anything, I want them to be unable to resist that second and third glance. I want to mesmerize and satisfy, but sometimes I'm happy if they just show up and keep their promises. I long to be protected and wanted. I long to make one special man dream. To stimulate him to be more than he could ever be on his own.

I haven't always handled the men in my life well. One day we'll talk more on this. I know you know enough. If you can see past the coal, I really think God is still polishing up a diamond inside. I'm not begging, just letting you know that I'm prepared to talk about anything.

Sometimes I'm afraid to get out of bed in the morning. I know I have to, but I don't always want to face what's ahead of me. Sometimes I want to take on the world and be a warrior princess like Joan of Arc. Sometimes I just want to be alone as I try to fight what's happening inside me.

Most days, if you're in the room, I'll talk out my issues whether you're really listening or not. I don't really want you to fix me or my problem. Except when I ask, and sometimes I'll just expect you to read my mind and know when I mean to ask. I usually figure things out, eventually. Sometimes I'll cry in the process. Just hold me. If I let you.

You know my faith is growing slowly. God sometimes seems so close and other times so far. Sometimes I have questions I have to get answered and sometimes I can live with the uncertainty as long as I know I'm loved. I don't know my Bible well enough to know where all the answers are, but I know God is determined to grow me up and I'm hoping someone steps in when I need them to help me understand what I need to know. Just be patient. And gracious. And forgiving.

If you want me, I need you. Love, Katie.

For a first effort with Bruce, it would have to do. I sent it. I felt pretty smug about my valiant effort to bridge my heart connection with Bruce.

Just then, I heard Hanan open the door and give me her cheery greeting.

"Katie, good afternoon. It's such a beautiful day. I've got a good lunch planned for you. My mother used to make it for me on special holidays."

My beautiful friend dropped the bags of groceries on the kitchen counter and then handed me the mail. I put the usual bills into my "to do" file. I shoved the flyers and newsletters across the table. If I had time, I would read them before throwing them into the recycle.

Two envelopes stuck out. One contained Lizzy and Dean's wedding invitation, with the date now set for October 25 in Kijabe, Kenya. The other letter had no return address. When I opened it, I almost dropped it. Hanan noticed I was shaking like a leaf and asked me what was wrong.

"Go get the police in the hall," is all that I could say.

CHAPTER THIRTY-THREE

S ergeant Richardson responded quickly to the constable's call. He and three colleagues scanned the paper carefully and examined the wording which I had already burned into my memory.

Your shipment is in. While Ivan may be gone, his memory is not. Guard your family.

The quartet held a ten-minute conference on my balcony with the door closed and finally returned, taking their places in a semicircle around me as I sat in my wheelchair. Hanan was asked to wait out in the hall for a few minutes.

Sergeant Richardson spoke first. "Katie, we need to give you a few updates. I'm glad you're seated."

An assistant handed the sergeant a file folder and this folder was opened and laid on the table in front of me. The folder contained the three sketches of Damian, Alexis, and Anthony with a paperclipped photograph of each attached. No surprises.

Sergeant Richardson tapped the one of Anthony. "His real name is Sebastian St. Jean. Louisiana muscle. He was imported to intimidate while the new network gets established." He pointed next to Alexis. "Her name is Natalia Sarakova. Distant contacts with Montreal and New York Russian Mafia. She's starting out her own show here, now that there's a gap. Tommy Lee was trying to get her started." The sergeant planted his index finger firmly on Damian's picture.

"His name is Pavel Ivanovich Putin. His nickname is Ivan the Terrible. The real mastermind. All I can say, Katie, is that if this is who you were really with, you're lucky to still be in control of your life."

I refused to believe that they had Damian's identity right. Maybe they looked alike, but there was no way the man I'd been with could mastermind anything like the drug and prostitution ring set up by Tommy Lee and the Monk.

I defended him the best I could. "But he worked for World Vision and Food for the Hungry. He volunteered with me at New Hope. He respected me. Alexis made me call him. He had to change his schedule. He helped me escape."

One of the other investigators spoke the words I already knew. "It was a setup, Katie. The ones you knew as Anthony and Alexis were herding you into Ivan's arms. There really was a Damian Harding who worked for World Vision. He's now retired in Florida. They took the chance you wouldn't check that part out. Ivan took on his name and reputation and joined New Hope to charm you into a relationship with him. What happened at the ferry terminal was just their way of getting you alone with him so he could pull you into his circle, or finish you off. That's his modus operandi. You were very fortunate to have that accident and escape."

I was too numb to talk. In fact, I shook so bad that the female constable had to hold me so I didn't fall out of the wheelchair. Thoughts of what could have happened hit me like an avalanche of boulders. I was unable to control the emotional reaction that consumed me. I felt myself convulsing in her arms and only faintly heard a voice calling for medical assistance.

I lay on a stretcher somewhere in a waiting area when I heard the words to a song by Simon and Garfunkel. The words of the refrain were familiar. *It's cloud illusions I recall, I really don't know clouds at all.* Reality hit me. Every man I thought I knew was an illusion. I really didn't know men at all. I couldn't believe how stupid I'd been. Again.

Someone once said that all of us grow closer to God through three phases that are repeated over and over again in our lives. First, we face something tragic that shakes us to the core of our being. Next, we face a time of deep silence and questioning as we examine all we know about our faith. Finally, we face a time where faith emerges stronger and better-equipped to handle the unfairness and injustice of life in a world run by the evil one. Slowly, God trains his warriors for the unseen battle that will either transform us or destroy us.

So far it seemed like I was getting stuck in the second stage over and over. Perhaps I was being destroyed by the battle.

A picture came to my mind. I'd spelunked a year ago with Bruce, Dean, and Lizzy. The cave had had a small entrance and dropped dramatically at times deeper into the ground. It was icy cold and slippery from the water that ran down the walls we were descending. In several places we had to use ropes. Half an hour into the adventure, we stopped for a breather.

Dean had us turn off our flashlights. I'd never experienced darkness so thick and cold. I remembered Dean's words clearly: "What do you want more than anything right now?"

"Light!" I answered quickly.

"Imagine we had no lights. What would you want?"

I reached over to grab Bruce's hand. "I'd want someone to take my hand and help me find my way." I squeezed a hand before Dean informed me that it was his hand I'd found. We laughed.

He continued. "What if there was no one to hold your hand?"

I played along as if I was the only pupil in the room. Which was how I felt. "I'd want a voice to talk me out." Maybe I just wanted to let everyone know I was still there.

"What if there was no voice?" Dean persisted.

Lizzy spoke up. "Dean, you're scaring me."

I could hear the scrabble of moving feet and then a sigh. I knew they had found each other. I found Bruce.

"Most of the world lives like this," Dean said. "No light, no hand, no voice."

Bruce spoke up. "But don't we have a light, a hand, and a voice through the Bible, through Jesus and through the Spirit? Don't we show faith by moving toward the light even without always seeing the path in between? Aren't we following the whispers of the Spirit's voice even when they seem like faint echoes penetrating the chambers of our soul? Isn't the Christian journey about trusting that the hand is near even when you don't feel its touch?"

I had been impressed with Bruce's insights and so had Dean. We turned our lights on and started back out.

Maybe Bruce had something to offer in my current darkness. I just didn't want to get caught putting too many expectations or hopes on another man who would just let me down.

For two days, the police had me meet with one of their counsellors at the hospital. From things I'd overheard, they wanted me moved out of there as quickly as possible.

It was interesting being on the client's side of the room without trying to outguess and outmanoeuvre the one probing my mind and emotions.

One of the first exercises I was given involved circling words that might describe emotions I was feeling. The list included words like accepted, angry, anxious, appreciated, and continued in alphabetical order all the way down to uncomfortable, unsure, and worried. I circled angry, anxious, confused, embarrassed, fearful, frightened, frustrated, grieving, humiliated, hurt, lonely, scared, ashamed, uncomfortable, unsure, and worried. It was fairly obvious where this session was going to go. I wonder if all my clients wanted to leave as much as I did at that moment.

CHAPTER THIRTY-FOUR

s a precaution, the Mounties moved me to a safehouse on Bowen Island. Constable Chan, Constable O'Brien, and Hanan came with me. The twenty-minute ferry ride from Horseshoe Bay, just outside Vancouver, left my Afghani friend an emotional basketcase. She sat by me in the top lounge unable to release her grip on my arm and unable to tear her eyes from the beauty all around.

She'd never been on a boat before and was terrified of water. At the same time, she was enraptured by the huge mountains surrounding us, the hundreds of sails carrying people quickly across the bay, and the seagulls floating on the winds.

A biblical verse came to mind and I shared it with her. "Hanan, when I first came to this island, I looked up at those mountains and God reminded me of a verse in the Psalms that has helped me many times. It says, *'I lift up my eyes to the hills—where does my help come from? My help comes from the Lord, the Maker of heaven and earth.'*"

Hanan crouched in front of my wheelchair and stared into my eyes. She spoke softly and reverently. "All my life I have known only a Creator who keeps us obedient through fear. I would like to know this God who helps."

I realized at that moment what a rich heritage I had. A God who loved me. A family who had raised me in an atmosphere of grace and truth. A faith that spoke to me about a Creator who displayed his beauty, a Saviour who lay down his life for me, a God who was present everyday as my counsellor and friend.

I felt ashamed at the fear that had consumed me in front of Hanan. What hope was I really showing her when I lived this way?

I looked her in the eyes and spoke as clearly as I could. "Hanan, when I was young I followed Jesus without any questions or doubts. When hard things happened in my life, I struggled in my heart with questions and doubts. I wanted to run from God. I was even angry at him. I'm just now beginning my journey to believe again that he's the Creator who helps and heals."

Hanan bowed her head. "We will walk this journey together."

Fortunately, the ride was short enough and her terror was eased when we rode the van off onto the island at Snug Cove. I'd spent many hours in this community, at the top of Cates Hill in a retreat center called Rivendell. I'd wrestled with God here and it was ironic that in my time of desperation the authorities had brought me back to this haven.

The safehouse was nestled halfway up Cates Hill, overlooking the cove. It was an ideal place to watch the ferries and cruise ships plowing through the waters as the smaller powerboats and windcraft choreographed their movement around the larger vessels. I could see that the island had been highly developed in the past few years as the wealthy and artistic discovered a perfect hideaway not too far away from the bustle of a busy city.

Although I was trapped in my wheelchair, I loved to have Hanan push me out onto the deck so I could feel the ocean breezes. There was no smell of freedom and peace like the sea.

The air was so clean and fresh as it filtered its way through the groves of alders, spruce, hemlocks, birch, maple, and endless cedar. In the homes scattered around and below, I could make out cherry, oak, dogwood, and hazelnut trees. In the gardens were begonia, honeysuckle, wiegela, ornamental hop, pink and yellow tea roses, fuschias, and large crops of waist-high white daisies.

On our third morning in this oasis, sirens sounded in the cove below us as an emergency vehicle of some kind raced into the community near the lagoon. Constable Chan strode out purposefully and scanned the area below for trouble. A stag and a doe feeding in the garden raised their noble heads in a brief inquiry at the strange noise in their domain. Within a minute, the usual sights and sounds returned.

Constable O'Brien spent some of her free time down in the library researching about the history of Bowen Island. She shared her findings at dinner and I learned some things I hadn't known before.

Bowen Island had been one of the original fishing grounds for the First Nations Squamish people. Later, whalers and fishing boats from Europe made it their haven. The Spanish explorer Don Jose Narvaez had charted the area in 1791 and called this place the Isle de Apodaca. It wasn't until 1861 that this emerald jewel was officially named after British Rear Admiral James Bowen.

The first white settlers came in 1874 and within thirty years the island became the playground of those wanting to escape the busyness of the city. Church and company picnics were common in the safety of the shores and forests of Bowen. Salmon and herring were so abundant that the government had once claimed that the fish could be raked out of the water. Trout were even abundant in the lakes. Deer and grouse were hunted and fruits and vegetables cultivated for the city markets. A dairy, a schoolhouse, a greenhouse, a slaughterhouse, barns, stables, and even a steam-powered merry-go-round became part of the neighbourhood that grew up in the early 1900s.

Captain John Cates and his steamship company made major purchases of land and turned this hidden jewel into the Shangri-La of the West Coast. Logging was successful and even a blasting company took root on the island.

Now, only new mansions were being fashioned into the island's craggy rockface. Everyone had million-dollar views and, within the past few years, were starting to pay the price for it.

It was in this space that I talked things out with God. I also had great chats with Constable O'Brien and Hanan. As we talked, we took in the scenery all around.

A group of sea otters were playing at the entrance to the bay; we watched them through our binoculars. A couple of kayakers moved out to get a closer look. Four fishing boats were passing by using sonar to locate elusive schools of salmon. A small powerboat raced out of the cove, leaving a rooster tail of spray glistening in the sunshine. More flotilla of small sailboats skimmed toward the cove, reminding me of skeeters on a pond.

The ferry made its return mid-afternoon and I could hear the clanging iron as the ramp was lowered. The boarding call sounded, engines revved up, and farewells shouted. Soon cars were chugging and grinding their way up the hill to homes on the rocky heights. Barking dogs began to alert whoever needed to know that they were on the job and new arrivals were in the area.

The bang and clang of doors arose again as families and neighbours connected. Most of the people were completely unaware and unconcerned with who we were and why we were here.

The voices and barking stopped. Only the swish of the sea breezes through flowers, shrubs, and tree branches continued. The three-foot daisies below us carried on their mystical dance, raising their open faces to the life-giving orb above.

I watched Hanan with her eyes closed, feeling, hearing, and experiencing it all. I looked across the inlet and saw the jagged crevasses and majestic peaks of the mainland coastal range. Sea planes droned by under the clear blue canopy as a paraglider drifted on the winds below the watchful eye of eagles.

Hanan's face was filled with awe as she watched the bird drift above us.

I filled her in. "The eagle is a symbol of God watching over us. The First Nations people have great respect for this bird. Once, many years ago when I was young in Kenya and helping a friend who was badly hurt, an eagle hovered over us just like this. It reminded me that God was watching over me."

Hanan looked thoughtfully at the bird. "It is good to have a God who watches over you," she remarked.

A scar just above the water's edge gave evidence of the highway from Vancouver to Whistler. A helicopter whirled by overhead and once again Constable Chan emerged to follow its path over the hills. Bells clanged from the cove below and the harbour whistle sounded again and again. Something was happening and it made my guardians nervous.

More planes began to buzz in the area overhead. Cars and motorcycles whooshed by us on the roads that led up the steep incline. I assumed that the volunteer fire department had been summoned.

Constable Chan's cell phone rang and she immediately vacated the deck. I could see a neighbour jump on his motorcycle and take off down the road to the harbour. Even Hanan knew something wasn't right.

Within five minutes, Constable Chan was back with a nervous smile. "Headquarters. There have been some developments. We'll need to catch the next ferry and keep a low profile at your place."

Just like that, Hanan and Constable O'Brien packed up the house while Constable Chan wheeled me out to the van. We were on the way home. Not once did anyone tell me what was happening.

The ferry ride back didn't seem to be any easier for Hanan, but one thing had changed; once we were half way across, she looked up at the peaks and said, "We will look to the Creator who helps us."

CHAPTER THIRTY-FIVE

I found myself thinking about popcorn kernels. One moment they were minding their own business, nestled in their bag, and the next moment they'd be exposed to so much internal pressure that they literally blew apart. The first two days back in my apartment, I felt like I just might understand those kernels. These were the times I needed my sister.

Lizzy and I talked about her wedding every day. She'd call me on the run to talk about the dresses, the cake, the decoration, the seating, the ceremony, and the music—but most of all she wanted to talk about Dean. The more she talked about Dean, the more I thought about Bruce. And the more I thought about Bruce, the more shame I felt about my moments with Damian. And the more shame I felt, the angrier I got about Bruce working with Lieutenant Barbara Saunders.

I found myself annoyed and irritated about almost everything. I was frustrated with the nursing care, uptight about my rehab progress, and even sarcastic at some of the plots in my favourite television shows. I tried hard not to take out my bitterness on Hanan. Bruce got the brunt of my complaints in my phone calls and emails.

It was less than two months before the wedding and Bruce was talking to me about joining Dean and Lizzy in Kenya for a couple of weeks. I just exploded all over him. My mind had been especially active since I'd gotten out of bed at daybreak and I couldn't shake it.

My wrist was finally free of its cast and my feet were now encased in walking boots. I still used crutches and I didn't want to wait another week. Everything was itchy and irritable and I just had no excuse for what I did to him.

I accused the poor guy of cheating on me and of making excuses for not coming to see me. Nothing he could say was working. Finally, he broke down and told me that Lieutenant Barbara Saunders had once been his foster sister. Talk about being blindsided and feeling stupid all over again.

Bruce finally told me the story after I loudly let him know how I felt about hearing this piece of news. Apparently, Barbara had just been starting school when his adoptive parents had been killed. Bruce and Barbara had lived in the same house for less than a year. Bruce knew his family was working on adopting her, but instead she was taken in by another family and raised half a country apart.

When Bruce discovered through a family friend that Barbara worked at Langley, he had requested a transfer in hopes of getting to know the only sibling he could remember having. In exchange for rehab services, he had agreed to lend his expertise to the project on educational development in Afghanistan.

Of course, I felt like I could stand on my tiptoes and still not touch the bottom of an ant's belly. Yes, I felt small. I couldn't blame everything on the wrong time of month. After my tirade, I figured I'd just about chopped off any chances I had with this guy.

I did apologize and was just about to bid my farewell when he got really tender and said, "I read your heart on that email you sent me."

I had to admit, part of my irritation with Bruce came from having laid out my soul to him and not hearing a word back about it. I did everything I could to keep my teeth clenched and not dig myself into a deeper hole.

He continued. "I've been thinking that you've been spending way too much time in the hospitals up there. I know all your medical is covered and you're just getting your money's worth, but I've been talking to some people here. If you and I made our relationship a little more official, you could move down here and I could take care of you. I do have a little medical experience, you know."

I didn't always believe that what I heard guys say was what they really meant. I always needed to clarify.

"Bruce, tell me straight what you mean by making our relationship a little more official. Do you want to adopt me as your kid sister or something?"

Sometimes I had no mercy.

He was quiet so long I wondered if we'd been cut off. Finally, I heard him let out his breath. "Okay, girl. You never were very subtle. What I'm saying is that if we're going to spend our lives together, I'd like to plan for enough time in the same space so that you know what you're getting into. I think we've both been changing a lot lately and it's not working this far apart."

This time I was the one who was quiet a bit too long. Finally, I could engage again. "Bruce, I'm no mannequin. I've got powerful emotions that are wrapped up in a lot of tough choices I've made over the years. I know we put a lot of our past behind us a couple of times already, but I have to tell you there's more past to deal with."

Bruce cleared his throat. "Katie, I don't want you feeling like you owe me anything. And I don't want to feel like I'm going to be some charity case. Losing my leg has impacted my life and I need to know you can handle it. I want to make sure we're in love with who we really are."

I appreciated his heart. "Bruce, if you can figure out a way to get us together, I can't think of anything I'd rather do than learn to love a man like you."

Once we hung up, I just had to email Sarah. My heart felt like it was being strangled by the thought of what I'd done, and yet it felt strangely liberating. My words were all about the fear.

Sarah: I think I just almost proposed to Bruce. I'm torn in two and feel consumed by fear. But I don't know why. Am I afraid of commitment? Does sharing love just seem like an unreal dream in the world we live in? Maybe fear is part of being a person these days. I turn on the news and feel fear because of a car bomb in Afghanistan or an IED in Iraq. I feel fear when I hear refugees talk about what's really happening behind the scenes in Iran or the Congo or in some of the other countries they come from.

Fear sells. The medical people sell fear with talk of Alzheimer's, breast cancer, skin cancer, heart problems, and dangerous ingredients in food. The government sells fear with talk of terrorists, gangs, murders, kidnappers, rapes, pedophiles, sex slave traffickers, robberies, and identity theft. The environmentalists sell fear through their talk of global warming and climate change. They highlight tsunamis, floods, droughts, melting polar ice caps, hurricanes, and environmental disasters. The conspiracy theorists plant fear by undermining our trust in the government or the oil companies or the Wall Street bankers. They create hidden agendas for our military leaders and business tycoons. They knit together suspicious motives for religious leaders. It's no wonder that one out of every five people in this country is on pills for anxiety of some kind.

Here's another conspiracy. Maybe the drug companies are financing the news media to focus on fear-based news so they can sell more of their product. Or maybe there's really a spiritual mastermind trying to destroy our society and tear it from its foundation of faith.

Maybe we're all being trained not to trust anyone anymore. Maybe I'm just having trouble trusting that Bruce will be all I need him to be. Anyway, thanks for listening. Love, Katie.

CHAPTER THIRTY-SIX

The next few days were relatively quiet. Hanan could only clean and cook so much and we spent some good times sharing stories of our growing up years. I took the time to read some of my journal entries to her and she could hardly believe the adventures I'd had. Mostly, she could hardly believe the freedom I'd had as a girl to learn, play, and just be myself.

When I shared entries that told of loss, I could tell they hit her deeply. She cried as much as I did. She questioned me about my friendships and marvelled that I could survive a motorcycle crash at eighty-fives kilometres an hour. She loved my account of races with Lancelot, which reminded her of the story of a grand Arabian stallion she had once seen in the villages of Afghanistan. It had been ridden by one of the tribal chieftains and became the topic of many legends over the years.

I still wondered how Lancelot was doing in Belgium.

On Sunday afternoon, I saw Hanan sitting on the deck reading my Bible, so I reached for my laptop. There was a brief reply to my email from Sarah.

Katie: You nailed it on our culture. You might even say we're addicted to fear. Our amusement parks create rides that keep us fascinated with fear. How close can we come to feel like we're going to die without actually dying? Our theaters market horror flicks to feed the fear of the young. How graphic can we be in displaying and imitating and worshipping the gruesome carnage of zombies, vampires, werewolves, and the demonic without actually experiencing the reality? Our youth set up parties with drugs and sexual encounters that keep them flirting with fear. Is this Russian roulette where sexually-transmitted diseases or pregnancy could happen with or without

condoms? Even our extreme sports and game shows push the boundaries of
fear. Is there not enough to be afraid of in real life or are we just trying to
inoculate ourselves against the real thing?

Katie, you and I both know Bruce isn't the one to fear. Concentrate on
building trust. God has not given us a spirit of fear, but of love, power, and
a sound mind. That's what Paul tells Timothy, and that's all I can tell you.
John says that perfect love casts out fear. I don't know how it works, but I
think I'd focus on learning to love. Praying. Love, Sarah.

I decided to relax more. As Sarah had implied, God hadn't given me a spirit
of fear to keep me in chains.

It was Monday afternoon and Hanan and I were both restless. I realized that
almost three months had passed since my first encounter with Alexis in Sumas.
Six weeks had passed since my time with Damian in Whistler. Two weeks since
the last coded message. It all seemed like a dream.

Hanan looked longingly out the window at the bay. The sun was shining
perfectly.

I'd been cooped up long enough. I decided to see what could happen. "Do
you think the police would let us go for a walk?"

When she turned to me, I could see the interest in her eyes. I nodded and she
fell in behind to push me out into the hallway.

Constable Sall was on duty. It didn't take long to convince him to get out
and escort me into the sunshine. When we hit the lobby, he even invited one of
the female constables to join us as an extra pair of eyes.

Being outside again was glorious. The sun was intense but soothing. We
fell into a leisurely pace, with Hanan pushing and the two constables chatting
behind us. Skateboarders, rollerbladers, cyclists, strollers, and even an occasional
senior with a walker mixed with the constant flow of humanity streaming along
the walkways.

We stopped for ice cream. I had two scoops. Maple walnut and moose tracks.
The ice cream was soon dripping faster than I could lick it and Hanan alternated
between licking her own and wiping up my messes. We soon ran out of paper
napkins.

A friendly rollerblader noticed our dilemma and brought by a small handful
of napkins taken from a hotdog vendor. I was so busy licking my ice cream and
reaching for napkins that the flash of blue topaz didn't register as significant until
moments later. By the time I looked up, she was out of my sight.

I handed the napkins to Hanan so she could continue her duties. Five minutes later, she stopped and whispered in my ear so the constables couldn't hear. "Katie, there's writing on one of these napkins."

At first I didn't understand. Then she showed me. In clear black ink were the words:

Everything on track. Cars gone. Restructuring done. Ivan planned for sailing disaster. You got him first. Ready when you are. If all is okay, do nothing.

I knew immediately that the daring rollerblader had been Alexis. I alerted Constable Sall, but by then there was no one in view to chase. None of us even remembered much about the rollerblader. I just knew who she was.

Sergeant Richardson spent several hours poring over the notes I'd received from Alexis. He finally sat down with me and a task force of seven others in a meeting room at the condominium. He addressed us all.

"From my reading of the notes, I believe this woman. Alexis—Natalia, whoever she is—honestly thinks you're trying to take over Tommy Lee's organization. She believes that you somehow eliminated the competition and she's reaching out to work with you. She mentioned wearing red shoes if you wanted to make contact. Where would you meet with her?"

I was stunned by where this seemed to be going. "Sergeant, I never try to meet with her. She always finds me."

"So, she has someone watching you all the time. The red shoes are signals that a connection needs to happen. Up until now the connection has happened through Natalia to Sebastian to you." He noticed my confused look and amended himself. "Sorry, through Alexis to Anthony to you."

I reached for my crutches and hobbled over to the window. "So what do you need me to do?"

"We're going to run a little sting operation."

CHAPTER THIRTY-SEVEN

My walking boots came off on Tuesday morning. My ankles felt weak but stable. I needed to get away from here, but first I had a little more competition to eliminate.

The police department provided me with a set of supportive red walking shoes. I still needed crutches, but they had cleared me for action. The plan was for me to find my way to a nearby ice cream vendor, make a purchase, and then sit and wait. There would be people all around. I just had to act normal.

When the young mom with the three-year-old twin boys sat down on the bench with her back to me, I was immediately suspicious. For ten minutes, she fussed over them and fidgeted with their clothing. She doused them with suntan lotion and nattered at them to quit their whining. Then she got up and left.

Five minutes later, a young Asian couple plumped themselves down and spoke in Cantonese. They didn't seem to notice me at all. A wiry middle-aged man with yellowed teeth, a nervous twitch, and a tanned leathery hide stopped by the garbage can to rummage for pop cans or beer bottles. I saw him eyeing my red shoes and my nerves started to fray just a little more. He stared at my water bottle a long time. I took a final swig and handed it over to him.

When those three evacuated the area, I felt the heat starting to take its toll. I pulled my baseball hat a little and rubbed my nose to make sure the suntan lotion was doing its work. A couple of teen guys with a rugby ball strolled by. One dropped the ball and it rolled under the bench. As I bent over to retrieve it for him, he leaned over me and said, "Two, tomorrow." I handed him the ball, he tossed it back to his friend, and they were gone.

Fifteen minutes later, an attractive young woman in Nike jogging gear rested herself on the bench. Her ponytail hung loosely over her right shoulder. As she leaned to catch her breath, she whispered, "Any action yet?"

"Nothing obvious," I said.

The redhead persisted. I watched her pull at her wrist bands. "Anyone leave you contact information?" I looked at her closer and saw that it was Corporal O'Conner, my guardian from the hospital. "Anybody say anything in passing?"

I thought back. "Mom with twins was here. Just nattered at her boys. Chinese couple didn't say anything I understood. Dumpster diver just wanted my bottle. Rugby guy said something about 'Two, tomorrow,' but I thought he was talking to his friend. He didn't even say thanks when I gave his ball back."

Corporal O'Connor moved closer. "Someone said 'Two, tomorrow' and then just left? Sounds like maybe a contact."

I stared back at her as if things were starting to click. I hadn't been at all suspicious of those boys, which goes to show that I probably wasn't cut out for undercover work.

She told me to wait five minutes and then join everyone back at the meeting room at the condominium. When we met, the team was very excited, thinking our sting just might work.

I had some pretty significant nightmares Wednesday night after all that. Alexis obviously had a wide network of contacts and I didn't know who was with her and who wasn't. For all I knew, this activity with the police could be another elaborate hoax.

At 1:30 Thursday afternoon, the team dispersed again from the meeting room to take up their places. I'd never spot these people in a crowded park area. A young couple pretending to be lovers. Two young guys in shorts and no shirts throwing a Frisbee. A middle-aged woman walking her poodle. Several others dressed in casual wear and mingling around. Even Sergeant Richardson was decked out in khaki shorts and navy blue t-shirt. His cover would be to sit on a bench about fifty feet away, reading the paper.

I waited until five minutes before two, at which time I shuffled my red shoes out to my bench. At five minutes after two, an ice cream vendor in a musical golf cart made his way along the sidewalk, stopping every few feet to make a sale to the children who crowded around. I didn't pay much attention until the cart was about ten feet away. I thought I noticed a black arm giving out the treats and taking money. In a multicultural city like Vancouver, that wasn't at all suspicious.

When the cart was within reach, an ambulance with siren blaring rolled into the park toward a man who seemed to be screaming and convulsing on the ground. The crowd quickly gathered around him. People pressed by me, trying to get a look. I noticed that the undercover policemen posing as Frisbee players were among the first to intervene. The other officers had shifted their attention to the action on the field.

When the cart came alongside me, there was no question that Anthony sat in the driver's seat. His smile shone as big as ever.

"Hop in," he said.

I didn't know what the police were planning, so I jumped in. We began to slowly work our way through the stragglers who were still crossing ahead of us. Several children came running up, but Anthony said he was sorry—we were sold out. He turned off the ice-cream jingle and picked up speed toward the parking lot.

Without even looking around, Anthony escorted me out of the golf cart and into the back seat of a black Lincoln Continental. The windows were all darkened. The Porsche and Mercedes may have gone, but this man still liked to travel in style. I tried not to look around before getting into the back seat of the car, as the one warning I remembered from Sergeant James was to not draw suspicion to those who might be following us.

We were out of the park and nothing happened. The car locks clicked on and there was no way out. That was when the sweat really started pouring down my back.

Anthony looked at me through his rear-view mirror, his smile confident. "Your chaperones got a little distracted."

He waited for my response. When I didn't give him one, he told me to take some clothes out of the bag on the floor and change my outfit. There was also a brunette wig and some shoes.

This hadn't been part of the plan I'd heard the officers talking about. I bunched over by the door to obstruct his view and changed as discreetly as possible. There was a navy halter top and pair of white capris. There was also the blue topaz Egyptian cross. I'd seen all this before. I saw Anthony trying to adjust his rear-view mirror, but I snuggled in close behind his headrest and successfully made my transition. I kept waiting for the sirens, but they never came.

Anthony pulled into an underground parking lot. Two floors down, he stopped by a cherry red Grand Caravan. Alexis stepped out of the driver's door and motioned for me to get out. She eyed me approvingly. When Anthony drove off, I had no idea what was supposed to happen next.

I got into the passenger's seat. Alexis wasted no time backing out of the parking stall and heading for the exit. Her left hand was constantly tucking strands of hair behind her ear.

"Okay. We know you're a serious player," she said. "You've taken out the Monk and you've taken out Ivan. We know you'll go to any length to win. Taking him over that jump was brilliant. I couldn't believe the look on his face. His neck and leg snapped like a pretzel. Our team finished him off quick. They couldn't get to you in time, but we're here now. He was going to take you down while you were sailing, but you got him first. You won the showdown, so you get the whole team."

I was stunned by what I heard. I tried to keep any expression off of my face. I tried not to even look in the mirrors in case there really was no one following us. I didn't want to believe I was all alone.

Alexis kept checking her mirrors. She turned corner after corner until she was finally satisfied. "I'm dropping you off so you can get the deal done. It looks like you've had a little extra attention lately."

My only defence was my words. I tried to sound harsh. "Natalia, you know I like to win. You and Sebastian are a little too careless."

Her head jerk in my direction showed her surprise. "So, Tommy Lee was right. There's no fooling the Kat Woman. He told us you would have the nine lives of a cat and we better not double-cross you. It won't happen again."

I pressed my advantage and became as assertive as I could manage. "Pull over into that McDonalds."

She looked my way briefly but did as I asked. I got out and motioned for her to follow me inside. I took her into the washroom and told her to change clothes with me. She was perplexed, but stood with her back against the door to make sure no one else entered. I handed over the white capris for her blue shorts. She handed me her white blouse for the navy halter top I'd been forced to wear. I gave her the blue topaz Egyptian cross. I threw the wig into the trash. She was already a natural brunette.

We both looked at ourselves in the mirror and made some minor adjustments. She might have an inch on me at five-eight, but our body types were almost identical. Her brown eyes definitely went better with brunette hair and my blue eyes definitely went better with strawberry blond. My skin tone was more olive than her porcelain, but otherwise she looked almost exactly like I'd looked five minutes previously.

Before we could say anything, a couple of teen girls walked in. We exited and went back to the car.

Alexis couldn't help talking. "Did you notice Anthony got his fourth gold ring? That's for Ivan. Those rings should all belong to you. All that brute has to do is take one more of us out and he'll complete the set. You and I need to stick together. That man is more than just the muscle, but I guess you knew that."

I kept quiet, realizing for the first time that Anthony flashing his rings was more a warning signal than anything else. If I failed, I could one day be represented by a thumb ring on the hand of a killer.

Ten minutes later, on the outskirts of the city, Alexis pulled into a strip mall parking lot. "See the Iranian Dhosa restaurant? Last table in the back. Your contact is there."

I continued my play. "You'll make the deal. I'll wait. If we're partners, I have to make sure you know the secret of the art."

I saw a smile come to her lips as she summoned all her feminine charm. Her left hand began to work that hair around her ear and she played with her topaz earrings. She seemed to relish the opportunity.

She clenched the car keys. "You'll wish you were there to see me in action," she said. She gave me a wink and stepped out of the van without another word.

She was met by two men at the door. As she made introductions, making sure all the attention was focused on her, I slipped out of the van and relocated myself into a telephone booth near the main road.

The three of them moved out of view. I crouched and watched.

Fifteen minutes later, two men carried a duffle bag out of the restaurant. It was heaved through the open side panel door of a white Ford Explorer. One of the men checked the Grand Caravan where I had been sitting a few minutes before. He seemed satisfied and drove off with it. Alexis didn't come out in the next fifteen minutes.

I finally called 911 and waited.

CHAPTER THIRTY-EIGHT

By Thursday evening, I was back in my apartment, packing under the watchful eye of two bodyguards. Anthony's Lincoln Continental and Alexis' van had both been found by the police.

Sergeant Richardson assured me that they would have Anthony in custody soon. There was apparently a tracking device in the red shoes they'd given me to wear and the shoes were still in the car.

Alexis had disappeared, but from my story about the duffle bag, the police didn't hold out much hope for her.

Sergeant Richardson announced to his squad that the men had likely been targeting me, and with the change of clothing they'd taken out Alexis instead. It was a good time to put me in a safer place.

The force needed their personnel working on another major case, and right now they would examine alternatives to keep me safe while freeing up the constables who had been watching over me around the clock.

When I mentioned the option with Bruce in Virginia, Sergeant Richardson began to work his phones to see what possibilities might exist. Perhaps, while Bruce and I had been unable to do anything, God was still doing more than we could ask or imagine.

Late Thursday night, I said my airport farewells to Hanan, my constable bodyguards, and Pastor Gary. I didn't know what Bruce or the police had to do to get me away, but I didn't want to say or do anything to spoil things. I eagerly put some space between myself and those who had taken Alexis. For once, I just did what I was told. I was wheeled onto an Air Canada plane for the first of several shuttle flights leading to Williamsburg International Airport in Virginia. I would transition through Chicago.

Barbara Saunders agreed to let me stay in her guest suite. The FBI re-established jurisdiction over me. Lizzy would meet me on Saturday, after she flew in from Minneapolis through Chicago and Richmond. I looked forward to being with Bruce.

The taxi cab dropped me off at Barbara's place in Jamestown Village on Friday afternoon and I was welcomed like a long lost friend. Barbara seemed to be about five-eleven. She gave me a hug, her black hair cascading over her shoulders and down onto my face like a grand waterfall. She wiped the hair out of the way and cupped my face in her hands. Her chocolate eyes seemed to devour me, piercing my soul.

Her civilian clothes kept her from standing out in a crowd, but she was definitely in the Armed Forces—her square shoulders and posture, her demeanour and confidence, her acceptance of what was and what had to be done next. She tipped the cabbie extra for hauling my luggage to the porch, grabbed hold of my hand, and walked me up the three stairs into her suite.

We talked from the moment we met. After several minutes, she finally stopped to inform me that Bruce would be by in two hours. I settled into my room and then attempted one of the first showers on my own without bags over my hands and feet. I sat on a small plastic stool Barbara had rounded up.

Smelling the apple scent of my new shampoo, feeling like I was really clean, and taking the time to splash on a touch of Irresistible put me in a whole new mood for my man. But my mind was still scattered and filled with all kinds of different thoughts.

Yes, I was nervous to see him again. I could tell by the ten or twenty times I'd been applying my lipstick. I didn't even usually wear this shade. I spent way too long in front of the mirror trying to get my hair just right. My dress just didn't seem to fit right, and even though I changed five times it was still the one right for today. I wondered if any of this extra work would even be noticed. I wanted to just hide away and not have to go through this.

I began to realize that you can't be controlling and self-sufficient if you want your man to protect you. He had to know you needed him. That you wanted him. That you believed in him. That you desired him at the core of who you were.

Forgiveness was such a hard road. I'd really been a bitter person. I knew, as a counsellor, that we're all wounded in some way and we all wound each other in ways we don't even realize. But as a person, I was struggling.

I wanted to be one of those girls who glowed from the inside-out. I wanted my man to look into my eyes and never want to look away again. I wanted him to be mesmerized and hypnotized with the wonderment he saw in me. Of course, fantasy was still fiction.

Without a doubt, I knew that Bruce needed me to be soft and tender. Gracious and gentle. To call him out as my champion. My hero. My protector. For too long, I'd been hesitant about being his woman. For too long, I'd let my own woundedness get in the way. He may have had an artificial leg, but I'd been living with an artificial heart. He couldn't do much about his leg, but I knew I could do everything I needed to do with my heart. This was my greatest prayer: *Abba, give me a heart that knows how to love and be loved.*

All my adult life, I had longed to be needed. To be wanted. To be cared for. I'd worked so hard for these things. It just took so much time—so much energy—and I was never sure I'd get what I looked for. For the first time in my life, I thought that maybe I didn't have to be wild after all.

When the knock on the door came, Barbara let me answer it. Bruce had healed up and looked as good as I'd ever seen him. While my eyes surveyed that strong, square jaw, those expressive brown eyes, that short-cropped black hair, and that mile-wide smile, he pulled me into his arms and kissed me without inhibition.

When I came up for air, I felt almost shy. I stroked his cheeks, his lips, his nose, and examined his eyes again. The past few months faded away and it seemed like we had never been apart. Before I could say a word, he scooped me up and bundled me into the living room where he dropped me gently onto the couch. He dragged out a chair and propped my feet on his lap. He began to massage away all the aches and pains of our separation.

He said his first words. "I've been listening. Welcome home."

All I could say was, "Aaaaaaaaaahhhhh."

CHAPTER THIRTY-NINE

D ifferences didn't take long to show up. When Bruce dropped me off, after a tour of the base on our third day together, I grabbed a laptop and banged out a message to Sarah. I needed help. The message was meant to be clear and straightforward. When I read it on the screen, I realized I might not have succeeded.

Sarah: I don't know if we can make this work. We're so different. I'm not sure what's wrong with me anymore. Will I ever do this relationship thing right?

Bruce is a meat and potatoes guy. I love biriyani, samosas, sushi, sakuma wiki, wat, and any other food that's out of the ordinary.

Bruce solves his problems alone, in his own head and in his own time. I need to talk them out immediately until everything is resolved.

Bruce lives his life facing wildness and looks for a little tameness along the way. I live a lot of tameness and go out of my way to find a little wildness.

Bruce loves to watch sports. I'd rather get out and do anything that doesn't involve sitting still.

And of course, there are the usual differences between how we hang the toilet paper, how we squeeze the toothpaste, how we shop, how we handle budgets and financial investments, how much care we take of our vehicles, how much time we like to spend on the phone with friends, and our understanding of what true listening really means.

And what's more, Bruce has way less training about God than I do, yet sometimes I think he has more faith and trust than I do.

We've talked for two days since I got here. His almost-foster sister, Barbara, has been really good about giving us our space, but I'm sure if she had her way she'd take a shot at my guy. He seems so distracted sometimes that I'm not sure he really has his focus in my direction.

Not once has Bruce offered to bring me breakfast in bed or massage my back. I've tried hard to stay calm. I've tried hard not to compare him to other guys I've spent time with. What irks me is that I've bared my soul to this man and let him know what I would love. He even told me he got my message and heard my heart. His emails were really responsive once he got going, but in person I don't feel like we're making any breakthroughs. He did massage my feet the first day. Love, Katie.

I had plenty more I could share with Sarah, but I just needed to get a little steam out of the pressure cooker and let her in on what was happening.

Bruce only had a couple of days off work and we needed to make the most of them. Barbara kept heading into the base to keep the project going. I realized it was awkward for me to be living with Barbara and to be the one driving Bruce around. I think my taking control made him even more self-conscious about his leg and limitations.

When we went out, Bruce would give me instructions on turns too late and I would respond too slowly. We often missed our first choice of routes, which kept us scrambling. These drives didn't do us any good, so I suggested walks closer to home. But my feet hurt from the walks if they got longer than a few blocks.

Bruce kept insisting that I needed to be using my feet and he needed to be using his legs. My right ankle felt increasing pain from working the gas pedal and brake. On Tuesday night, I told Bruce that he would have to drive from then on.

In the morning, we walked almost halfway around the Big Bethel Reservoir. My feet were slowly getting stronger even as the pain persisted. The noise from the takeoffs and landings was already becoming background noise for me. Our plans to try a round at the Eaglewood Golf Course was postponed when we realized how much torture we had already put our feet through.

Barbara was great at helping me work out with my feet through her foot massages at night. Bruce gave me the opportunity to work out by walking me around all day. He insisted that all this was part of his therapy and my rehabilitation. He kept his arm around me and kept me walking. And talking. One thing we did do was sweat together a lot.

The Thursday after my arrival, Bruce drove me through the curvy mountain roads of the Shenandoah National Park. While it was very different than British Columbia, I appreciated the beauty of the mountain ranges, the waterfalls, and the wide diversity of plants and trees.

I was so glad for the cloud cover. As we sat in a rest stop along Skyline Drive, we saw a black bear checking vainly for abandoned garbage. We also saw a fox scurrying along the edge of the clearing and a couple of red-tailed hawks scouting for mice.

Holding hands used to be a normal part of our routine, but not anymore. There was no question that Bruce was intentionally courting; it was just taking a lot for me to get past my shame and guilt. We'd had our talk about Damian yesterday, which had been a long day. We were still working out the aftershocks and this long drive was a good distraction.

Most of our talks happened away from Barbara's place. We had survived the issue regarding his prosthetic limb. He'd taken it off and put it on to show me all he could do with it. We even spent an hour in the community pool. I still wondered if I should have worn the one-piece instead of the bikini. I think I attracted the attention of too many guys apart from Bruce, which seemed to make him feel uncomfortable. Maybe he was the possessive type.

Bruce had very few limitations once he got moving. To prove it, he climbed the stairs on the eighteenth-century lighthouse at Fort Story. Then we walked around and looked at the three hundred species of birds at the Back Bay National Wildlife Refuge. Finally, we visited the aquarium. Up until that time, we'd had nothing serious to fight about.

Dean had told me once about the nineteenth-century Danish philosopher, Soren Kierkegaard. This influential thinker had once pictured most Christians to be like students who preferred to look in the back of their textbooks for the answers to math problems instead of working them through.

Kierkegaard was also a theologian and psychologist. He focused a lot of study on the area of personal choice and commitment. He believed that growth came through perseverance and experience. The difficult would inspire those noble in heart. He explained that in the early grades of faith, our Teacher often made the answers clearer and easier to find. As we grew, the help grew less frequent and the answers harder to find.

I was starting to see that this reality worked not only in our personal lives with God, but in our personal relationships with each other. Unfortunately for Bruce, he was getting the brunt of my learning and experience.

When we came home from our trip to Shenandoah, I decided to email Sarah for some insights on building trust in intimate relationships. I'd taught this stuff to others, so I had the exercises and words in my head, but somehow it didn't happen the same way in person with Bruce.

Early Friday morning, Sarah's reply was waiting for me.

Katie: Looks like you're in love with a man. Have you ever thought that perhaps Bruce is just trying to keep a tiger in its cage by not unlocking the door? You really are a lot more irresistible than you realize. A good relationship always takes longer than a day to build. Try focusing on planning your trip to Kenya. Tell him what to expect. Talk about something neutral other than your relationship. Let it happen naturally. Love, Sarah.

Considering the way my life had been going since meeting Bruce, I wasn't sure I really had more than a day, but Sarah's advice helped me take three deep breaths the next time Bruce and I met. I took an extra half-hour of preparation to get ready for our Friday dinner. There was no way he wasn't going to notice me. The impact was there, but I still wanted more. Like Queen Esther in the Bible, I invited my prey back for yet another feast the following day.

I had to ask Lizzy to postpone her visit for a few more days. We agreed to stay in touch and keep working on our dreams for the wedding.

CHAPTER FORTY

Barbara moved near the top of my best friend list by giving up her three-hour Saturday morning appointment with her favourite beauticians. She even went with me and made suggestions along the way. In my twenty-eight years of adventures, I had never experienced the complete package of a beauty salon before.

I wasn't sure all the Biblical descriptions of heaven could touch what it felt like to be pampered as a queen this way. In those first hours, I could almost feel my hair transforming under the magic touch of these specialists as they highlighted, washed and conditioned, cut, and blow-dried me into euphoria. The scalp massage almost had me levitating out of my chair.

If that hadn't been enough, the French pedicure, manicure, and massage drained me of every ounce of tension and moved me to a place of bliss. Barbara covered most of the conversation for me and left me daydreaming about my evening with Bruce. For a moment during the manicure, I had the thought that this man of mine had better appreciate all I was going through for him. During my facial, I had the thought that I could care less what he appreciated. I was doing this for me.

The last thing I wanted to do when all was done was get up out of that chair. Barbara drove home and I couldn't stop looking at my complete makeover. I felt as giddy as a teenager on her first date. Barbara had taken a picture of the finished product with her Nikon and I could hardly recognize the gorgeous model who peered back at me from the screen.

For a few minutes, I debated asking Barbara to take me shopping as well, but after looking at my bill again I decided I'd spent enough. I had a knockout blue-patterned Hawaiian sundress that I'd been saving for a night just like this. Just the swish of the skirt made me feel like a princess. The open-toed matching sandals were good for dancing, walking, or just dinner.

When I twirled in front of the full-length mirror in Barbara's guest room, I felt my confidence rising. There was no way Bruce wasn't going to be focused on me tonight. I was going to have to manage keeping him interested—just not too interested.

The minute I made my grand entrance in Barbara's living room, Bruce was captivated. His eyes opened wide. He inhaled quickly and then slowly let out his breath as his mouth formed a tight little "wow." He didn't even notice the Sport Illustrated magazine I was holding in my hand as a test. No matter how awkward I might have felt, I'd decided to play this for all I could get out of it.

I twirled and gave him a coy little smile. I even batted my eyelashes.

His smile grew as big as his face would allow. His khaki pants and light blue polo shirt definitely weren't going to be taking the attention when we dined tonight, but at least it matched my outfit.

Bruce's embrace and kiss didn't make me want to leave for dinner. As usual, he broke it off, but redeemed himself when he held me at arm's length and twirled me like a ballerina to get the full effect of my ensemble.

When we got near the restaurant he'd chosen, he made me close my eyes. I was probably overdressed for the atmosphere inside, but Bruce had brought me here for the scenery and the food; that was romantic enough. The appreciative glances I got from the waiters and other customers encouraged Bruce to request a table in the back.

The shrimp was mouth-watering and the company exhilarating. I found it quite a game to flirt across our small table and to drop double entendres to his remarks. Several times he had to stop and look at me again to see if this was really me.

Finally, he started talking on a personal level.

"Katie, you confuse me." He took my right hand in both his hands and stroked my wrist. He locked his deep brown eyes onto mine. "Tonight you look amazing. You're doing everything possible to let me know you want us to work. I just don't understand what's been happening while we've been apart."

I could feel myself wanting to squirm and maybe scoot out of there, but I hadn't come this far to back off now. Still, I needed clarity on Bruce's issues.

"Bruce, I know I hurt you. I asked your forgiveness. Do we have to talk about it again tonight?"

He pled with me through his eyes until I bowed my head and consented.

He went on. "I thought you'd be excited by all the plans about Kenya. There's only a month until your sister's wedding. I thought you'd be doing all you could to get us back together. It's been really hard to hear you've been with this Damian guy. It's hard to understand why you haven't once responded to my emails about Kenya. I hoped we could have our trip planned out by now."

This was the first time I could remember hearing anything specific from him about Kenya and my defences began to kick in. Then I remembered all the messages I had deleted when I'd been overwhelmed. The shame and guilt poured over me again. I started feeling like all my efforts were a waste, but then something wild and powerful grew inside me and I actually sat up straight.

"No," I said aloud.

I could see the surprise in Bruce's face. I had to reassure him and myself. I took back his hand in mine.

"Bruce, you're the most important man in the world to me right now. I wanted this to be the most special evening. I wanted to take your breath away and have you fall down on your knees and beg me to spend the rest of my life with you."

I could see that I had his attention and he kept his mouth shut.

"I am fighting for you and I need you to fight for me. I cannot possibly explain everything that was happening to me in Vancouver, but one thing I want to make clear: I had over a hundred emails when I got back into my account. I was just too overwhelmed. I panicked and deleted most of them. I'm sorry, but I never saw one of those emails about Kenya. Of course I want to go and show you my home. It's where my heart and soul connect."

For some reason, my impromptu speech persuaded him and we spent the rest of the evening dreaming, planning, and scheming about Kenya. Somehow, a walk along the beach helped bridge the romantic side of things and by the time Bruce finished up his goodnight at Barbara's door, I was glad for every penny I'd spent. I didn't get the proposal I'd hoped for, but I'd sure knocked away all the barriers in the way of it happening soon.

CHAPTER FORTY-ONE

izzy and I spent three wonderful days dreaming, remembering, and trying
to organize everything through email, Skype, and phone calls. The hardest
part was sorting out travel plans with our contacts in Africa.

It could be difficult enough trying to do things in person in Kenya, never
mind trying to organize a trip from across the world. We had to constantly figure
out time differences, locate numbers through the internet and operators, and
figure out substitutes when what we wanted wasn't "in stock." It was a great
bonding time and I hated to release her. We were set to fly in two weeks.

Sometimes I had a sixth sense when something was up with Bruce. The signs
were subtle. The look in his eyes. The way he hesitated a little longer than usual.
The hand in the pocket playing with a coin or something. Maybe it was just the
full moon.

While makeovers couldn't last forever, I got a good week out of mine.
Every day we made our Kenya plans and played backgammon, Hearts, and
card games that took our minds off each other. Lizzy's wedding was less than a
month away and she and I had spent considerable time on the phone meshing
our ideas for the trip of a lifetime. I envied Lizzy and Dean for their dream
coming true.

On Saturday, Bruce let me know that he was making dinner at his place. He
told me to wear the knockout Hawaiian sundress again. That was another thing
that got my instincts going. He picked me up himself and ushered me into his
little brick bungalow. While I'd been there a few times before, never had I seen it
decorated so extravagantly. Candles were lit, the table was set with fine china and
linen napkins, and soft jazz was playing in the background.

A new four-by-eight mirror above the flickering fireplace made the place look larger than it really was. We did look good together. I raised my eyebrows at Bruce and gave him a questioning look. He just smiled and twirled me around in a ballroom dance step. I watched us in that mirror, feeling my smile and confidence growing.

We started with Samosas, which Bruce had picked up somewhere. Dinner was chicken cordon bleu, asparagus tips, and small roast potatoes. The food was artfully displayed and made by the hand of Bruce himself. Sparkling grape juice showed sensitivity to my conservative side. Blueberry cheesecake showed his knowledge of my weaknesses. Sometimes food laced with the right spices—and the right love—tasted better when others made it.

When we were done, we finished up the dishes and kicked off our shoes. Bruce cleared the living room and took me through a number of slow dance pieces. When I felt the strain on my feet, he sat me down and gave me a good foot massage. I felt loved again.

However, Bruce told me he wasn't done for the night. We were going for a drive. He grabbed an old backpack on our way out the door and refused to tell me what was in it. We made our way to Chesapeake Bay and Fort Story. Somehow Bruce was granted entrance even though visiting hours should have been over. He kept the backpack slung over one arm and cradled me with the other.

The full moon shone brightly over the black and white lighthouse being used for navigation today, but that wasn't where Bruce led me. We turned toward the other structure. I knew from our first trip here that the old Cape Henry Lighthouse stood as a majestic sentinel at the spot where a cross had first been placed by English colonists in 1607 to thank God for the safe crossing of the Atlantic. It was a lasting tribute to answered prayers. The octagonal stone monument stood, at its peak, some seventy feet above the sea. George Washington himself had appointed the first lightkeeper.

The last time we'd been here, Bruce had climbed to the top to prove himself, but I had stayed below with my sore feet. This time he looked me in the eye, winked, and led me up the stone steps and through the door. An inner staircase wound its way toward the platform at the top. At each window on the way up, he paused to look at me in the moonlight and kissed me gently and passionately.

When we finally reached the top, he took me out on the platform overlooking the bay. Only a few ships were still making their way into the harbour. A single seagull rode the night sky in the light of the new lighthouse. We soaked in the scene, and it did feel magical.

I wasn't sure how long we stayed there, but as we stood and stared Bruce reached into his backpack and took out an iPod with earphones. He put one of the earbuds into my right ear and the other into his. My hands were around his neck as I looked up into his eyes. I could see his smile growing. I was anticipating another dance.

The song played. It was a Lou Reed special and one of my favourites. I closed my eyes and swayed with Bruce to the soft jazz and crooning as the sound came clearly to my heart.

The song was about magic moments that lovers find in each other's eyes and arms. Moments that catch you by surprise with their sweetness and softness. Moments that meld and last in a kiss and a dance.

Somewhere in the middle of the second verse, I sensed Bruce pulling away from me and I stopped moving to see what was happening. Bruce had bent down as if he had dropped something.

As the moon washed over us, as the lighthouse called out for peace and life and safety to all who could see, as the music played on in my ear and the lone seagull floated on the gentle breeze, Bruce took my hand and asked me to spend the rest of my life with him. I'm not sure whether the ring went on before I said yes, but it sure did sparkle in that moonlight.

The whole world could have watched us kiss. I didn't care anymore. I had found my man. The prayers of my heart were answered.

CHAPTER FORTY-TWO

Being engaged two weeks before my sister's wedding was a big enough surprise, but Bruce let me know he wasn't done with surprises. It must have been 4:00 a.m. when I got to bed, and at 9:00 a.m. Barbara shook me awake to congratulate me and tell me it was time to get ready for church.

I wasn't sure my makeup did all it was supposed to, but we made it. I held Bruce's hand through the service and hugged and smiled at hundreds of people, but it all felt like a daze. While we were sitting at lunch, Lizzy and Dean walked in and joined the festivities. I couldn't stop squealing and dancing around with Lizzy, hugging her and Dean, and showing off my ring. They all patiently endured my crazy dance.

It was obvious that the three of them had something up their sleeve. I saw their knowing smiles with each other, but I didn't get in on the secret until the meal was done.

Bruce reached into his pocket and pulled out an envelope. He raised his eyebrows up and down several times and winked. I took the envelope and opened it. Inside were tickets to Kenya. I smiled and gave him a hug, but it was clear Bruce wasn't satisfied with my reaction.

He took the tickets from me and held them in front of my eyes. "Look at the date," he said.

I did. I'd almost lost track of time with the scheduling. Finally, it clicked. "Tomorrow? We're leaving tomorrow?"

My life suddenly felt out of control. This was a week earlier than expected. I needed to shop, and I had less than twenty-four hours to do it.

Bruce and I met Lizzy and Dean back at Barbara's house. Lizzy called me to join her in the back bedroom. When I walked in, I saw the most incredible wedding dress hanging from the curtain rail.

It was better than a Cinderella ball gown. Layer upon layer of lace. A basque waist. Ruffles, billowy tulle, pearl beading. Brocade fabric. A huge train. I loved it. I could already see Lizzy in it.

As I stared in fascination, Lizzy moved to the bed and opened a box. She removed a stunning diamond-covered tiara. She saw the smile threatening to split my face.

"Like it?" she said.

"I love it," I replied. "You'll look like a princess. Daddy would have loved this day."

Lizzy kept smiling as she moved toward me and placed the tiara on my head. I looked in the mirror and loved the look.

"Too bad I'm just the bridesmaid," I said.

Just then, Bruce walked into the room and took both my hands. "Actually, you're the bride. We've decided to have a double wedding in Kenya."

My mouth went dry. My heart threatened to beat its way out of my chest. I had trouble focusing.

Finally, I found my words. "But... but, I haven't got time to get a dress."

Lizzy kangaroo-jumped toward the hanging dress. "Ta-da. This is your dress!"

I couldn't believe it. "What? But how? When? Wow!"

"Remember when you helped me dream about the perfect wedding dress a year ago?" Lizzy asked. "Remember how I got your measurements for the bridesmaid dress design? It was all a cover. We wanted to surprise you."

The panic clutched at my throat. "But what about my other clothes? I'll still need to shop."

Lizzy sashayed her way over to the closet, which she slid open. She pulled out two suitcases. "All packed except for the lingerie. We're leaving that to you. We've got a few stores set up for tomorrow. This time, you don't have to play shy with me."

In a single day, my world had changed. Again.

CHAPTER FORTY-THREE

Lingerie shopping with Lizzy brought out my conservative side more than I thought it would. Shopping with a specific man in mind was a different experience for me than for my sister. In her innocence, she could be brazen, and she had every right to be. I couldn't pretend innocence and the emotions inside me felt like a straitjacket. I was a robot making purchases without entering into the spirit of pleasure the designers had envisioned.

I was still numb when we reached the airport and checked through customs. I knew Bruce was guiding me through the process with his gentle hand in the small of my back, but he was more like a shadow lurking at the corner of my vision. Airports were where you always said goodbye to those you loved. There was no one to say goodbye to anymore.

A great emptiness seemed to swallow my heart and put the squeeze on my stomach. I was moving into my future and Bruce was holding onto my hand with an energy I couldn't give back. He'd been great to get us the seats by the emergency exit. We had room to stretch.

Lizzy and Dean were just across the aisle and seemed so focused on each other. For Lizzy, this was like finishing a great adventure she'd been dreaming about all her life. She'd prepared for it and planned for it.

For me, it was like having no warning before being thrown back into a whirlpool I'd once been pulled out of. Yes, I wanted to be married. And yes, there was no better man for me than Bruce. And yes, Kenya was the perfect place to marry the perfect man. I just hadn't had time to process it all and I couldn't get my feelings on track fast enough to catch up with life as it was happening to me.

I confessed my fears at meeting faces and friends from long ago. How would my emotions flow when I came face to face with those who had been so much a part of my identity almost thirteen years before? I told my attentive fiancé that I may not be the woman he thought I was. Bruce whispered his love and encouragement to me over and over again.

Somehow, dinner came and went. The lights in the cabin were dimmed and I whispered to him that I didn't think I could do life at the pace it was happening. I hadn't had the chance to say goodbye to my home. He assured me that I wouldn't be doing life alone anymore and that I'd never have to say goodbye to my home. Wherever we went together would be our home. He told me I could start another journal to capture my new life.

By the time we reached London's Heathrow Terminal Five, I'd shed another waterfall of tears. Bruce kept making trips to the washroom and bringing me wads of toilet paper. I wasn't sure how long he could keep this up.

Dean led us onto the tram and into the city to do the tourist thing. Everywhere we went, we were told to "mind the gap." I remembered Robert, Lizzy, and me having so much fun with that phrase after our last trip through London. Signs urging us to be aware of the small space between the tram and curb were everywhere. In addition, conductors were always warning us of the same danger. The sign was even plastered on coffee mugs in souvenir shop as if it was some national joke.

Time seemed to melt away as we took the double-decker bus tour to see Big Ben, the parliament buildings, the changing of the guards at Buckingham Palace, and Westminster Abbey.

It was a whirlwind eight hours and, despite my lack of sleep the previous night, it was a needed reprieve from my self-absorption.

Neither Bruce nor Dean had been to London before, so Lizzy and I enjoyed having some inside knowledge and experience on our guys. We barely had time for fish and chips at one of the Kings Crossing pubs before we had to catch the tram back to Heathrow.

In the lounge, as we waited for our boarding call, I made two comments that I regretted as soon as they were out of my mouth. Perhaps it was my foggy brain or my untamed tongue. I turned to Bruce in front of Dean and Lizzy and said first, "How do I know you're the man God wants me to marry?" If that wasn't enough, I turned to Dean and said, "You haven't answered my questions about unanswered prayer or trusting God." Lizzy tried to distract the conversation by suggesting we get some coffee, but I could tell that things were pretty strained as we boarded the next flight.

Soon after takeoff, Bruce asked if I'd mind talking to Dean. The two men switched seats. Dean was gentle in initiating the conversation we needed to have. After checking to make sure I was okay, he started right in.

"Katie, I know you settled this issue on another level when you were thinking about suffering and God's goodness. Remember when we talked about Rabbi Kushner's response to his own son's premature death? He said that he could only see three options when we think about God and suffering. God must not be good, God must not be strong enough to stop bad things, or God must be unwilling to use his power to remedy our pain. Kushner concluded that God just wasn't powerful enough to stop all the evil that humans face in the world. Katie, is that what you think today?"

I had no problem responding. "Dean, I believe God is good, powerful, and caring. I just don't always understand his plans and how they involve me. He doesn't seem to answer my prayers."

"Unanswered prayers are the ultimate test in our understanding of who we believe God to be. Without going into a lot of personal detail, I can tell you that God has often said 'no' to my prayers. The silence in my heart was deafening and mind-numbing." He hesitated for a moment. "I know God said 'no' to Jesus in the garden of Gethsemane when his own Son asked him if there was any way to avoid drinking from the cup of suffering before him. God said 'no' to Paul when his best messenger asked God to remove his thorn in the flesh, the messenger of Satan. God said 'no' to David, the man after his own heart, when he prayed that God would spare his innocent son."

I knew all this and cut in. "I just need to be clear in my own mind how to be sure what God wants from me. You asked me what I would accept as proof for the four questions. I feel like my life has been in chaos ever since then. When I think of these questions, I just get verses and images in my head."

"Like, which ones?" Dean asked.

I didn't even hesitate; these verses had been swirling around in my head for days. "When I ask myself how I know God cares about me, the words *'Cast all your anxiety on him because he cares for you'* comes to my head."

"That's 1 Peter 5:7," said Dean. "The verse right before it tells us to humble ourselves under God's strong hand. When the time is right, he'll lift us up."

I pressed on. "When I ask how I know God is being fair, the words *'Will not the Judge of all the earth do right?'* come to mind."

"That's Genesis 18:25. It's taken from Abraham's bargaining with God over the destruction of Sodom and Gomorrah. Abraham finally had to rest his trust in

God that somehow God wouldn't destroy the righteous with the wicked."

I was amazed that Dean was able to pull these references out of his mind without any resources in front of him.

"When I ask how I even know God's there, I get a verse from Hebrews. *Without faith it is impossible to please God, because anyone who comes to him must believe that he exists and that he rewards those who earnestly seek him.*"

"You're right," said Dean. "That's in Hebrews 11:6. Verse one of that chapter says that faith is being sure of what we hope for and certain of what we do not see. All of the heroes of faith listed in that chapter held onto their belief in God and what he was doing, even when they didn't get to see the outcomes in their own lifetime."

I unloaded the last of my burdensome insights. "And when I ask how I know if God has ever said anything we can know or trust, 2 Timothy 3:16–17 plays in my head. *All Scripture is God-breathed and is useful for teaching, rebuking, correcting and training in righteousness, so that the man of God may be thoroughly equipped for every good work.*"

Dean patiently persevered. "It all comes down to whether we really know God and his word or not. Once we do, the rest is growing up in our relationship with God. Katie, I can't tell you anything you don't already know. You need to have trust and faith every day you wake up and every night when you lie down to sleep. I don't have all the magical insight on prayer, but I hang onto a few verses as I'm praying. Isaiah 65:24 says, *'Before they call I will answer; while they are still speaking I will hear.'* The psalmist says in Psalm 17:1–2, *'Hear, O Lord, my righteous plea; listen to my cry. Give ear to my prayer—it does not rise from deceitful lips.'*

Having a conversation with God is as much about listening as it is speaking. It's paying attention to what he wants to tell you right now, right where you are."

He paused, watching me closely.

"Here's the way I think prayer works as an interaction between us and our Abba," he continued. "God already has all the answers we need before we pray, but he has chosen to work through our prayers, so he develops life circumstances to get us to pray. Usually, that means he brings about a need that makes us seek out his will for our life. As we seek his will, we make the changes that his word instructs us to make. As we adjust our lives to his plan, his blessing is given. By paying attention to Scripture, to the Holy Spirit, to the insight and wisdom of God's people, a believer discerns God's will. In faith, you ask God's will to be done in your life. God responds to bring about his will on earth as it is done in heaven."

My brain felt thick, but I got the gist of what Dean was saying. "So, with all that's been happening in my life, God wants me to marry Bruce in Kenya?"

Dean unbuckled his seatbelt and prepared to leave me. "Katie, why don't you take some quiet time and let God tell you that?"

CHAPTER FORTY-FOUR

Since the 1880s, counsellors and workshop leaders have tested their clients with images that are designed to look like two things at once. I would often use a drawing that revealed both an old hag and a young beauty, depending on how one perceived the merging strokes of ink. Another design might show a mug profile or two faces looking at each other.

Stepping into Kenyatta International Airport in Nairobi early Wednesday morning was like flipping the image from one perception to the other. As soon as I smelled the familiar air and body odours, as soon as I heard the tongue of my childhood, as soon as I saw the swarthy black faces and military garb of soldiers, as soon as I saw the familiar halls and walkways that had absorbed my last sobs so many years ago, as soon as I approached the immigration lineup, everything changed.

It had started before the final leg of the trip, when my ear picked up the familiar Swahili of Kenyans in the Heathrow terminal lounge. It started when my eye picked up the colourful swirl of colour on Kikapus and Kitange cloths. It started when I heard their laughter and felt the rhythm of my pulse accelerate. It continued on the plane, but now, in the lineup of tired, sweaty, noisy, jostling Africans, home felt close.

I hardly even noticed Bruce hesitating as I dragged him through the crowds in an effort to reach the next phase of our processing. Finally, we presented our papers, exchanged our greetings, answered the questions, paid our fees, and received the big smile and welcome to Kenya. Lizzy and Dean were right behind us as we cautiously skipped down the stairs to the waiting luggage belts circling round and round with belongings arriving from all over the world.

The crush of bodies was already three deep around the belt, so I raced to find a cart from a blue-uniformed porter. Shouts of welcome poured through the doorway from those who had come to pick up fresh arrivals. I sensed again the waiting hugs and enthusiastic hellos of my friends and I found myself looking for familiar faces.

Lizzy's whisper in my ear was corrective. "There's no one there. It's only us."

My sister took the cart from me and left me feeling a strange mix of contentment and sadness. I'd come home to a place where my family and friends were no more.

At the moment, I just had to make sure that my wedding dress had made the trip. For a few minutes, I felt like a salmon fighting to move upstream as I worked my way through the crowd of bodies toward Bruce at the carousel. In the end, he was the one who found my prize and held it up with a cheer.

For our first hour in Kenya, we rode a taxi through the traffic to Nairobi. The one we chose appeared to have fewer scrapes and dents than some of the others. And the driver was as enthusiastic as an old friend.

An endless stream of billboards announced the latest cell phone plans and other products of Kenya. I saw both the ostriches and zebras first, then pointed them out to the others. Civilization and wildness had found an uneasy mix in this land.

Everywhere, along the edges of the road, were masses of Kenyans. I rode in the front seat with the driver. Lizzy chattered all the way, acting like a tour guide from her place in the back middle seat. All I had to do was to sit and absorb.

Although there was a mostly-paved two-lane roadway on our side of the divided highway, by the time we got close to the first roundabout, there were at least five or six lanes of trucks, buses, matatus, taxis, motorcycles, and cars jockeying for position.

Most of the vehicles weren't even on the pavement and the pedestrians on the edge seemed to put their lives at risk. Although it was only mid-morning, the sun already bounced its scorching rays off the surrounding metal. The dust swirled into our open windows.

I knew our guesthouse could be reached within ten minutes at night from that roundabout, but today it would take another hour.

Bruce and Dean perched on the edge of their seats in the back and I saw their heads craning to find the spaces ahead. This was a kind of driving Dean hadn't experienced before and one with which Bruce was uncomfortable. It felt good to be one ahead of the guys. I looked back at Lizzy and we winked.

The driver lurched, squeezed, and honked along with everyone else as vehicles towering over us groaned and grinded within inches of either side. The dints and scrapes along many of the cars didn't give any of us much confidence as to what could happen next.

Two young men clung to a ladder on one side of a bus as we tried to pass at less than walking speed. One of them swung out and planted his feet on the top of our car, then jumped back laughing. Dean's eyes were wide. Bruce gave me a raised eyebrow and a smile, but nothing more.

A policeman stood in the middle of the road at the roundabout blowing a whistle and waving wildly at drivers to keep moving. Young men were darting out into traffic to hawk rolled newspaper cones full of peanuts, paintings, magazines, and jewellery. There was no question I was home.

Several things impacted me on this trip. Apart from the number of cars on the road, I was blown away by the fact that almost every second person was texting on a cell phone. Mothers with babies on their back walked along the side of the road texting. Drivers in the middle of a traffic jam were texting. A policeman at the roundabout was waving at traffic with one hand and texting on his cell with the other. I even saw a Maasai warrior pull a ringing cell phone from under his blanket and start texting. When I'd left Kenya, we didn't even have internet or cell phones in Kijabe.

We finally reached the guesthouse and unloaded our luggage.

Bruce took me by the hand and looked me in the eyes. He spoke to my heart. "Katie, welcome home. Right now, and right here, I pledge you my love. In just over two weeks, you'll be by wife. You'll never be alone again."

Lizzy wanted to show Dean everything at once, so before we even stopped for lunch, she had us riding a taxi to the giraffe center where Bruce tried his luck feeding special battery-sized capsules to the long-necked giants using just his mouth. My fiancé got that long, slimy tongue slurping up at his neck and jaw. He released the pellets from his lips as we all laughed and took turns. The pictures turned out really well and we laughed all over again as we reviewed them.

Next, we headed to the ostrich center to feed greens to the birds. Dean got his fingers snapped at for releasing his vegetation too slowly. Lizzy hovered over him as he winced, allowing her to examine the damage. Bruce caught the exact moment of tragedy on camera. The expression on Dean's face as the beak closed on his fingers would make the shot worth saving.

On the way to the Sheldrick Wildlife Center, we stopped for samosas, roasted corn, and Cokes from a small shop *duka* at the side of the road. The orphaned elephants and rhinos at the wildlife center were a hit with the guys and we had fun posing with the wildlife.

By evening we were tired, but Lizzy insisted on beating jetlag by keeping us awake putting our wedding plans together. She finally conceded that if we spent the next days focusing on getting all our wedding details down, the last week could be reserved for sightseeing and going up to Kijabe. The romantic getaway at the coast would have to wait for the honeymoon.

Before much else happened, I needed to get out to Kijabe to see the place of my birth and last goodbyes.

CHAPTER FORTY-FIVE

A person's reticular activating system (RAS) filters out everyday noises like airplanes landing and taking off and keys us in to details we need to know about. With a week to go before my wedding, my RAS was quickly tuning in to everything about Bruce. I noted the keen interest he took in the lack of medical care available in the Kibera slum area, where a million disadvantaged Kenyans huddled in makeshift shacks of cardboard and tin. Lack of good water and sewage disposal made it a perfect trap for diseases of all kinds. His heart went out to the children especially.

On the streets, he noticed the hardships of the lame beggars and the handicapped. He talked with the street boys who cajoled him for shillings. He ducked into the shops with the East Asian merchants and chatted them up about their businesses and families. He was obviously familiar with the African scene in more ways than I had realized and his artificial leg didn't slow him down.

We rented a car and Bruce tried to drive it, but with all the roundabouts, nonstop traffic in undetermined lanes, and cars all driving on the opposite side of the road from what he was used to, it almost proved a fatal effort. When we were nearly run down by a city bus coming at high speed with its horn blaring, Bruce said he had visions of me crumpled in the wreck. We ended up swerving onto the edge of the sidewalk and had several people banging on our doors after what turned out to be a near miss. Bruce was shaken up and I finished the drive back to the guesthouse, even though I had never driven in Kenya. Bruce did seem to recover once we decided to stick with taxis.

Lizzy and I continued to meet up with old contacts. Most of the shop owners we had known now had their own children running the stores, but just a mention of the name we knew would be enough to send a messenger to fetch our old friends. It took longer to shop than we scheduled, but we also saved a lot of money as we were given great discounts as part of the owners' blessings on our celebrations.

We indulged ourselves and our men with all the mouth-watering fresh tropical fruits we'd been missing—loquats, bananas, coconuts, mangoes, papayas, custard apples, dates, figs, and gooseberries. We relished the flower stands with the heavenly scents of frangipani, jasmine, oleander, and gardenias.

By mid-Friday afternoon, we had completed our orders and purchased the supplies we wanted. Our contact, Solomon, from the Rift Academy, came straight to the guesthouse and ferried us to our next stop. The traffic was chaotic and the crowds of people along the edges of the freeway were just as plentiful.

My first look at the Rift Valley from the escarpment road made me gasp. The beauty was everything I had imagined. As we rode along the knife edge, at over nine thousand feet, the skies came ablaze with a sunset to defy anything I'd ever seen in National Geographic. Cotton candy clouds floating in a baby blue sky wrapped themselves in brilliant shades of pinks, yellows, reds, and oranges while a brilliant golden orb dove for the horizon beyond the hills.

The setting was magical. I could even hear Bruce take in a quick breath as he surveyed the wonder. It reminded me of one of the Academy's young staff members who had just seen the sight for the first time. He raced to the edge of the ravine we were standing at, raised his finger in a salute, and shouted, "Man, that guy can paint."

As if to accentuate things even more, a ring of fiery silver outlined the clouds as the sun prepared to disappear. Mount Longonot, the lone dormant volcano rising out of the valley floor, was etched in its own shimmery glow. The night winds were already reaching through our windows to welcome us home. I felt Bruce squeezing my arm, and when we looked at each other the magic seemed to reach into our very souls.

It was dark as coal by the time we descended over two thousand feet of winding road to Kijabe. The bush babies, owls, and other nightlife were already into their chatter. While I had expected some of our old missionary friends to be waiting, I didn't expect to see the number of Kenyan friends who had put themselves at risk by waiting into the darkness for our arrival. The greetings, handshakes, and hugs came easily and Bruce and Dean had little trouble following my lead into the fray.

Twelve years melted away and I was sixteen again—home, free, and at peace with my world. While some of the faces I knew were missing, and some had creased up a little more with age, there was no doubt that heart connections didn't die just because of time or distance.

Although we talked to our friends long after all sense told us to retire, we eventually made our pledges for future connection and dropped into bed. When the unshielded sunlight pierced through the bedroom curtains at six in the morning, like it always did, I pried open my eyelids and looked across at Lizzy. She was already smiling.

It didn't take too many bangs on the guys' door before Bruce stuck his greasy head out and begged for a few more minutes to clean up and prepare for the day.

After a breakfast of sausages, eggs, and toast, Lizzy and I led our men on a tour of the campus—the dorms, classes, gymnasium, alumni court, fields, cafeteria, chapel, library, and all those special places that carried our own memories. We saw the corner stone of the main Kiambogo Building, laid by United States President Teddy Roosevelt in 1909. The dedication stone marking one hundred years of quality education to missionary kids stood out as a new memento since I'd left. The gardens were a favourite of mine. I loved the purple jacarandas, cacti gardens, multi-coloured bougainvillea, daisies, calla lilies, and poinsettias standing as tall as houses.

When we came to the chaplain's office, where Dad had helped so many of the staff and students, I could feel my eyes misting up and legs getting weak. Lizzy eased the moment by telling the story of how a green mamba had almost got my dad as he stepped out of this office.

The students all looked a lot younger than I remembered them looking in my day. Some of the buildings also looked a bit smaller. A lot of new construction had happened. The one consistent thing was the gorgeous view, phenomenal gardens, luxurious sunshine, happy people, and overwhelming freshness brought over us through each touch of the breeze.

With every new place there were stories to tell. Of course, all along the way we met friends who had to be introduced and invited to a pre-wedding celebration we were having in two days.

When we came to our old house, Lizzy and I stood in awe. My small cactus garden had plants over six feet high in places. The tree fort in the backyard olive tree had been modified and expanded; three little boys chattered like monkeys as they scaled the trunk toward it. The chickens, tortoises, and dogs were gone, but most of the layout remained the same. Story after story tumbled out of us as we competed to share the adventures that this place held for us.

As we prepared to walk away, I noticed an elderly man pedaling furiously in our direction. Before he even came into the driveway I already knew who it was.

"Francis!" I screamed.

Lizzy joined me as we raced up to our friend and flung our arms around him. Francis was the yard worker who had faithfully looked after all our needs for the last ten years we had been here. Although he was retired now and still living an hour's ride away, there was no question the community grapevine was working just as well as it always had.

We introduced him to Bruce and Dean and made arrangements to bring all our guests to his house on Thursday. I slipped him some shillings so he wouldn't be burdened by the hospitality costs. After catching up on all the news of the family, we said our farewells.

Midafternoon, we had a meeting with Chaplain Taylor and Pastor Njoroge. The two clergymen, one from the Academy and the other from the local church, would be combining their roles to perform a multicultural wedding ceremony that combined the worlds Lizzy and I had grown up knowing. Bruce and Dean were just going along with whatever we set up. Lizzy had been emailing the chaplain for months, so most of the changes involved adjusting her plans to include Bruce and me. My sister had let me have so much input into her ceremony that it already felt like mostly mine.

After two hours of sitting over chai and mendazis, and ironing out the details of the ceremony, we needed to get some exercise. Pastor Njoroge prayed a long, eloquent blessing over our lives and marriages before releasing us on our way.

After hiking down a ravine and exploring the Mau Mau caves, where warriors had once hidden as they anticipated an attack on the school, we headed down to the *duka* shops and some of the best stew and chapattis available on the planet. With a warm Coke, to wash it down, and a samosa to fill in the gaps, we couldn't have asked for anything better. On the way home, we saw a troop of baboons warily spying out a chicken coop that might provide a future dinner if other hunting proved unsuccessful.

The evening was filled with more friends, pictures, and stories. We sat in the yard overlooking the Rift Valley, watched the deep purple line of the Mau escarpment start to take shape. Whether Bruce and Dean wanted it or not, our friends gave them the inside story on what we were really like as young girls. I knew Sarah would have a lot more of her own stories to add when she and her husband Keith flew in on Monday.

To finish off the day, we took a walk to gaze at the stars. Bruce almost created a fiasco when an African *askari* stepped out of the shadows with his German Shepherd guard dog and shared a greeting in Swahili. As usual, the guard had a dark full-length coat and a knitted mask covering everything but his black face. I had forgotten to warn Bruce about this part of life on the mission station and he made an aggressive move to protect me. I had to yell at him as the dog began snarling and pulling hard at its handler's chain.

It took a few minutes for me to explain things to the guard in Swahili as best I could. By the end, we were laughing and wishing each other a good night. Our walk was probably a little shorter and tenser than I had envisioned it.

It probably didn't help when I told Bruce that the guard dogs had once been Rhodesian ridgebacks, which were used for hunting lions. "They could rip your throat out in a second," I crowed. Our first dog, a Golden Retriever, had died of tic fever, but our second dog had been a Rhodesian double ridgeback. I think he was impressed, but I noticed him doing several shoulder checks as we turned toward the guesthouse.

On Sunday morning, Lizzy and I took Dean and Bruce to sit in with at least a thousand other Kenyans as they worshipped. The colourful Sunday dress and hairstyles of the women was enough to make me glow inside.

Three hours on a crude wooden bench proved to be a bit challenging for all of us when we combined it with the excitement of the past week. It was still great to see that God was actively at work in believers of every tribe, tongue, and nation and to realize that one day these brothers and sisters would join us around the throne of Jesus in one great choir.

In this place, we met many more good friends we had missed. Although we had at least a dozen invitations for lunch, I had made commitments to take Bruce and Dean down to the valley on a few motorcycles I had arranged to borrow. These guys were in my world now and before I gave my final commitment to Bruce, he needed to see the rest of the world I had captured in my journals and photo albums.

CHAPTER FORTY-SIX

I remembered a message from Pastor Gary where he said that until the thirteenth century, a lot of believers prayed and read as a group activity and did it out loud. Very few people had mastered the art of reading and praying silently within their own heart and mind. God was still there. What we think of as normal seems to have changed through the ages.

The thing I'd learned to love about God is the way he shows up in all the places and times one least expects him. Today, God showed up in the surge of wildness galloping beside me as I rode a Honda 250 motorcycle over the plains of Africa. Although Dean and Bruce constantly lagged behind, I wasn't going to miss my chance to ride in the heart of the herd. I deliberately targeted the lead zebra stallion and squeezed past several gazelle and antelope to reach his side. He tossed his head and flashed his teeth but took up the challenge.

Twice he tried to shepherd me into thorn bushes, and once he even hesitated long enough to buck and kick out his powerful hind legs in my direction. The race was on, the wildness pumping, the adrenaline working. In the middle of that ride, I felt God's pleasure flowing through me. Within a few hundred yards, the ground proved too challenging and I broke away as the herd rushed on.

When Bruce and Dean caught up to me, I was standing by my motorcycle smiling wider than a Cheshire cat. When Bruce clutched down and stopped beside me, I could already see his smile through the helmet visor.

"You are one crazy woman," he shouted above the noise of the engines. "And I love you."

With the advance of civilization in this area, we'd had to ride further out to find the wildlife. I turned to take us home. Twilight was short on the equator and most of the sunlight was already gone by the time we turned off the main tarmac road and onto the last five miles of gravel road leading to the Academy campus.

I tried not to move too far in front of the guys as I guided them over the unfamiliar road. There were no streetlights or homes with welcoming lights. In my chase for my own pleasure, I'd forgotten that this was a road where car hijackers loved to do their work.

As I looked over my shoulder to see if the guys were keeping pace, I noticed a shadow moving along the bank beside me. The headlight of my motorcycle gave just enough light to reflect off a wild eye and razor sharp teeth. The killer of the night was within six feet of me and keeping perfect pace.

My heart threatened to beat its way out of my chest and my wrist wanted to crank the throttle and gun the motorcycle as fast as possible. A black leopard had chosen to hunt me as the isolated target away from the pack. At least, that's what my mind told me.

At that moment, my mouth felt as dry as the Sahara. Any prayer I might have had sounded like the last gasp of a dying woman. All I saw was darkness and wildness.

Bruce's Tai Kwon Do training came into play in the middle of my fear and I told myself to breathe and focus. Instead of making a break for it, I slowed myself down. Instead of moving away from the leopard, I made a feint toward it. The unexpected move threw him off and his stride faltered.

I slowed the bike down quickly, made a swerve in the road, then turned the headlight to expose the master of the night. His snarl was mind-numbing and I almost froze in place. Just then, Bruce and Dean rounded the corner and saw the cat starting to move toward me. Bruce revved his engine and made a direct run for the leopard, screaming at the top of his lungs. The cat dodged, turned tail, and escaped into the brush up the hill.

Bruce held me while Dean stood guard. Two thoughts kept me from collapsing. I had enough wildness now to last me through the wedding and my prince and protector had literally saved me. Who knew what could have happened if the leopard had really attacked me? At the moment, all I cared was that I was safe in the arms of the man who loved me.

Lizzy had been spending the afternoon working out menu details with some of our community friends, but she was seriously fretting by the time we pulled into the driveway of the guesthouse. She ran to Dean and embraced him before he could even turn off the engine. We probably should have texted her on our way home.

Dean tried his best to turn off the bike, kick down the stand, and hug Lizzy all at the same time. Instead he almost spilled the bike, plus himself and Lizzy as well. I managed to reach out and steady the bike until his balance was back under control.

Lizzy directed her comments at me. "What are you thinking? You had me scared to death that one of you had been hurt, kidnapped, or half a dozen other things that can happen when you get into your wild moods. Katie, we're getting married this week. Don't you dare mess things up when we're so close."

I reached out for my sister. Instead of responding, she turned away and grabbed Dean by the hand. Before he even had his helmet off, she was dragging him inside.

As she went through the door, she called back over her shoulder. "Katie, we can talk later. I just really need some space right now."

Bruce came up behind me, wrapped his arms around my waist, latched onto my elbows, and snuggled his chin into my shoulder. "Hey, wild woman," he said. "Cat got your tongue?"

I would have whirled around and slapped him, but he had such a strong hold on me I could only give him a head butt to his ear. "Oww!" was the only response I got. Then a deep-hearted chuckle.

After a few vigorous wiggles from me, Bruce stepped away and, still smiling, said, "Now I know why they call you the Kat Woman. You face down leopards, you get into cat fights with your sister, and you turn men wild."

I threw my helmet at him, but he ducked out of the way and danced around the motorbikes chuckling like a mad man. His artificial leg didn't seem to be slowing him down much at all.

In a minute, the madness was done and Bruce helped me put the four motorcycles in the shed for the night. Bruce knew nothing needed to be said about Lizzy, so he just gave me another hug and a quick kiss goodnight. He gave me a knowing nod.

"I think I'll take a shower and read a little," he said. "Those two have a few things to work out before any of us are getting any supper or sleep tonight."

I crooked my little finger at him and motioned him inside. "As soon as we both get cleaned up," I whispered in his ear, "we better use our cooking skills to get a little peace back into this place. I'll meet you in the kitchen."

By the time Lizzy came back to our room an hour later, she was in a sombre mood. I lay on my bed reading the Psalms when she peeked sheepishly around the doorway.

"Guess I blew that one," she said. "Dean told me about what happened with you and the zebra and the leopard. I can't believe how that happens with you. It really freaked him out. Glad you're okay."

I looked up and smiled as best I could. "You're forgiven." I got up and gave her a hug. "Supper's on the stove. We better get eating and sleeping before we leave to get Sarah in the morning. If you think you've been consumed with wedding plans so far, you ain't seen nothin' yet."

CHAPTER FORTY-SEVEN

By five o'clock in the morning, the headlights of our minibus pierced the darkness while the engine groaned up the thirty- and forty-degree switchbacks leading up to the one cross-country highway at the top of the escarpment. With sheer rock on our left and significant ravines on our right, I was happy to have Solomon at the controls.

With lighter traffic, we made good time into Nairobi and avoided the morning glut at the roundabouts on our way to the airport. Within an hour of our arrival, Sarah and Keith appeared at the top of the stairway leading down to the luggage carousels. We waved at them from our side of the immigration barrier. Soon after, Barbara Saunders confidently made her way down to our level.

Barbara wore a sensible ensemble of khaki slacks and a white button-down blouse. Behind her, I could see an American family all dressed in jeans and wearing an assortment of bright t-shirts. They seemed less confident and stood looking at the mob scene below them. I knew instinctively that this was Dean's family.

When Dean's mom and dad, Carl and Vickie, and two sisters, Sandra and Heather, finally stepped cautiously down their last flight of stairs, Dean and Lizzy started yelling and waving. The noise and confusion was too great to get them to look our way, so Dean finally gave an ear-piercing whistle. The younger sister, Heather, heard and looked our way. Soon everyone was waving and smiling.

As I hugged Vickie at the entranceway, I chanced to look one last time up the stairway they'd all come down. Leaning on the wall in the shadows of an artificial bougainvillea plant was a tall black man with reflective sunglasses. He was definitely watching us. He looked a lot like Anthony. I stiffened so quickly that Vickie asked if anything was wrong.

I excused myself and tried to move nonchalantly toward Bruce. When I got his attention and explained the situation, he looked calmly where I indicated. No one was there.

"Honey," he said, "we're in Africa. You'll probably see a lot of black men wearing sunglasses. Relax. Let's let everyone enjoy their time without worrying about something from the past."

We were delayed an extra hour trying to find the suitcase for Dean's mom. Everything else arrived as scheduled. The airline representative assured us they would deliver the suitcase as soon as they located it.

The usual traffic clogs at the four main city roundabouts gave us plenty of extra time to explain the scenery to our new arrivals and assure them that everything was going to be fine. The endless line of pedestrians along the road was normal. The dirt and garbage was also normal.

When Dean's sister Sandra involuntarily gasped at her first sight of the Rift Valley, a shiver of pleasure snaked its way up my spine. When Barbara lost all composure and shrieked with joy at her first sighting of a zebra herd, my smile broadened so wide it started to hurt my face. Lizzy kept everyone captivated with her commentary. I just snuggled into Bruce and drank it all in.

At five o'clock in the afternoon, the hall we had reserved for our pre-wedding ceremony was flooded with community friends. They buried us with gifts of fruits, vegetables, potatoes, chickens, eggs, flowers, and colourful baskets and cloths. In the next three hours, we feasted on a beef stew combined with rice and chapattis.

Dean's family was tired, but managed to stay awake through the choirs and speeches and cutting of the cake. Lizzy and I were celebrated like queens. I knew this had a lot to do with my parent's legacy.

We gave Barbara, Carl, Vickie, Sandra, and Heather one day to settle in, adjust, tour the Academy campus, and then we blitzed ahead. We visited the Mayer's Ranch, where the garden wedding would be held. At one time, this British settler's holding had extended to six thousand acres across the valley floor. When Kenya gained independence, it was cut back to six hundred. The property manager, Crispus, responded to Carl's question on size by saying the current government was thinking of reducing it to one or two hundred if they had their way.

The plush oasis held greenhouses with some of my favourite cacti. It also had some of the few lush grass lawns and flower gardens in the area. The greenery surrounded beautiful falls and a lake where spring water was captured, bottled, and exported around the country. Towering acacia provided a canopy over it all.

The owner, a proper British woman who was introduced to us as Lady Roslyn, had been born and raised in Kenya. She showed us the grounds with pride and invited us in for tea. Dean's mom, outfitted in a borrowed dress from one of the missionary ladies, couldn't quit pointing out the fifteen-foot poinsettias that grew everywhere. The neatly trimmed eight-foot bougainvillea hedges also gained awe.

A local group of Masai entertainers, who usually performed for tourists, sent some of their representatives over in full regalia to finish negotiations on the cost of their dancing. Their bodies were smeared in red ochre and their hair was plaited. They were a proud people who believed they were favoured of God. They reminded me of Egyptian pharaohs.

Three of the young morans conned Barbara and Dean's sisters to engage with them in some impromptu dancing. When Sandra and Heather claimed that they couldn't dance, one of the young men suggested, in passable English, that they should pretend they were jumping out of the way of a puff adder. This made the girls more nervous than ever, but they somehow improved their performance.

The Masai men were of marriageable age and began to express their obvious interest in Dean's sisters. The rungu clubs and cowskin shields, combined with their spears and bows and arrows, marked them as true warriors. The girls' white blouses and pastel slacks didn't set them apart as obvious choices to milk cows, build mud and dung huts, stock charcoal fires, and serve their men. I was glad Dean's family really didn't understand the dialogue and intricacies of body language in those few minutes.

After the arrangements were done, we scooted with the minibus for half an hour along the Valley Road through the canopy of thirty-foot acacia trees toward Lake Naivasha. As we passed Crater Lake and Hell's Gate, I filled Dean in on my stories surrounding these sights.

As I pointed out the old volcano, I told him that the locals said the lake was bottomless. We had actually gone here as a family with friends of ours and tried to swim in the lake. The water burned our skin and left us with serious rashes for weeks. Near the rocky formations of Hell's Gate, I talked about our rock climbing adventures and our almost fatal encounter with a herd of Cape buffalo in one of the small canyons.

Naivasha was a haven for flower farms, wildlife ranches, and old colonial settlers and it was in this garden of Eden that we stopped for a lunch of tilapia and rice.

The roads were now paved, but when I was a girl the dust came up to our hubcaps during the drought. The same plumbago hedges, with their pale blossoms, lined the property line. The bamboo, bananas, and canna lilies were plentiful here. Spiky rows of sisal plants still lined the pathways in several places. Pepper trees and acacia thorns were in abundance.

Several of the vendors hawked freshly picked pineapples, oranges, potatoes, and bananas. They bundled their wares with branches of maroon and white bougainvillaea. The bushes grew everywhere.

As we gawked at a band of frolicking Vervet monkeys, a flock of pelicans took flight and swished right over our heads. We all ducked in a gale of laughter as if we were avoiding seagulls at work. Vickie loved the delphiniums and candelabrum trees that seemed to grow in abundance everywhere we looked.

Once again, Lizzy filled everyone in on the adventures our family had enjoyed in this area of Kenya. Our near brushes with death before charging hippos and Cape buffalos sounded more terrifying than I remembered in my journals, but this time I could laugh. The flood of mud that had washed over our tent and campsite sounded more like something equalling Noah's watery experiences. The sailing feats we accomplished on this lake sounded like something that should have made it into the Guinness Book of Records, but this time I could feel the wind and spray as I closed my eyes and experienced the story. One day, I would do it all again.

After stuffing our faces, we strolled to the lakeshore and watched hippos cavorting in the *marula*—the wide swatch of papyrus reeds along the shore. The water surface itself was still and smooth as green glass. Giraffes nibbled on the lower acacia branches. Water buck and wart hog wandered only a few hundred yards away. Seven zebra, six gazelle, a pair of miniature dik dik, and three wildebeest all formed a strange herd at the water's edge. Of course, overhead was the constant chatter and movement of Vervet and Colobus monkeys as they performed their acrobatic manoeuvres among the treetops.

Dean's dad was a birdwatcher and Naivasha had some three hundred species of bird life he continued to rave about. He checked them off his list as if he'd won a lottery—maribu storks, fish eagles, crested cranes, Egyptian geese, spoonbills, herons, ducks, cormorants, and dozens and dozens of other feathered creatures intent on displaying God's glory.

A group of Japanese tourists repositioned themselves to be closest to a flock of peahens gaining the attention of a very active peacock. One of the group was actively snapping photos with a high-powered digital camera. Dean's mother seemed a little shocked at this attempt to get a picture of nature in action.

Our last stop before nightfall was up to Nakuru to take a look at some great wooden carvings and some special crafts and paintings designed by true local artists. The works were much the same as they'd always been, but I loved to feel the smooth ebony and olive carvings on my face. On the way there, we saw a family of wart hogs scurrying along the road with their tails high in the air.

I saw Bruce watching me and, before I could warn him, he reached for a cheap black image of a hippo and rubbed it against his cheek in mockery of what I was doing. I smiled as a smudge of shoe polish stayed behind. This man of mine was going to learn some things the hard way.

With purchases and trophies secured, and plenty of new friends made, we urged Solomon to cover the two hours home as quickly as possible. All along the roadway were stands selling fresh oranges, pineapples, plums, and other temptations. We stopped once for a quick refreshment.

Although the road had sections with significant potholes, Solomon attempted to oblige our request for quick passage. We hung on for the ride of our lives. Twice, Dean's sisters screamed as they were nearly tossed from their seats. All along the road we could see the remnants of tires that had blown apart, vehicles that had broken down, and repairs that had been neglected.

Another spectacular sunset bid farewell to our guests as we rose up the escarpment to a viewpoint overlooking Mount Longonot. By the time we reached our 9,200-foot escarpment summit, we came to our turnoff. The steep descent of S-turns toward Kijabe began in pitch black. Solomon slowed down as this section had been responsible for the deaths of many impatient drivers.

Halfway down, as we passed the rock quarry hairpin turn, Solomon brought the minibus to a lurching halt. There on the road stood three men gesturing wildly with machetes in their hands. Both Lizzy and I had seen this before. This was a carjacking corner. Our one carjacking experience flooded over my memory as I tried not to yell at Solomon to reverse quickly.

One man approached Solomon and began an intense discussion. I heard my name being mentioned and moved up quickly beside the driver.

Solomon interpreted. "Katie, this man says that someone has come asking about you. He says it is a strange black man from America. The community is suspicious. They have told him that you are gone from here and the man has returned to Nairobi. They will continue to watch, but would like some instructions from you to see if he is a friend you are expecting."

Bruce immediately scrunched up next to me and expressed his concern. I reminded him about seeing Anthony at the airport when we picked everyone up. I thanked the man in Swahili and, after basic conversation, I got Solomon to translate into Kikuyu. I let them know that this man wasn't good and that they should continue to warn me if he was seen in the area.

I asked him if he had noticed any rings on the man's hand. Solomon's translated the exchange and told me that the man had five gold rings. I shuddered, because I knew that the last ring represented Alexis. I wouldn't have to think about red slip-on shoes any longer.

My anxiety now threatened to rise higher than Mount Kenya. All I wanted was to run and get rid of all this adrenaline. Instead, I had to sit back and hope that my past life didn't once again ruin everyone's future.

With three days to go before my dreams became a reality, I was more unsure than ever about how I could put the man I loved at risk. I had one arrow prayer in my quiver: "Not now, Lord."

CHAPTER FORTY-EIGHT

Going to Francis' house with the gang was like taking an adventure back in time. We bought sacks of rice, beans, maize meal, flour, sugar, and tea from the *duka* shops. We also picked up some bread and two crates of soda. Lastly, we stopped by the butcher to get him to wrap ten pounds of stew beef in newspaper. We knew Francis would have his whole family onsite.

For forty-five minutes, our van followed the twists and turns of a dirt track that resembled the surface of a prune. Rain and drought had worn away any stable surface on the roadway. Bruce could hardly believe Francis had ridden his bicycle all this way, every day, for all those years. And yet he had. I was impressed again at the toughness and resiliency of the Kenyan people.

Almost all the homes along this stretch of road were the typical mud-and-wattle huts of poor Kikuyu. A few had stone walls topped with corrugated tin called *mabate*.

When we finally pulled into Francis' yard, our van was mobbed by multiple generations of smiling faces. Our food offerings were quickly whisked away into the *mabate* tin shack, which still served as the kitchen for Francis' wife, Lucy, after fifteen years.

We met brothers and sisters and aunts and uncles and grandmas. Everyone chattered away in Kikuyu, Swahili, and English like we were old friends. Bruce and Dean joined right in on the hugging and even Carl, Vicki, Sandra, and Heather got into the act.

The mud-and-wattle stick construction that served as a bedroom and living room stood in the same condition I had last seen it—only more rundown. The plank-board bedrooms and ladies' workroom still had the same gaps in it I had seen years before. A Holstein cow and calf grazed contently at the edge of the corn field, stopping occasionally to eye the activity. There were still a few scrawny chickens in the pen and two turkeys constantly protesting the invasion of their domain.

Lizzy won the day by presenting lollipops to everyone. Bruce and Dean played soccer with the dozen children who were permitted in the yard. Carl talked with Francis, who began telling stories about Lizzy and me growing up. I joined in the chatter of the women and showed some of the teens and young adults how to use my digital camera.

Several of them had never seen themselves on camera before and when we took group photos, they posed strangely so they could identify themselves in the picture.

Food preparations rarely got started until the company had arrived, so it was at least an hour before we were invited in to feast. Francis proudly showed off our family photos, which he still kept tacked to his wall. I could see myself as a confident sixteen-year-old standing with my arm around Robert and Lizzy. Mom and Dad smiled joyfully. None of us looked like we were ready for the changes that would come in the next few years. My family had changed unbelievably. Francis' family hadn't changed much at all.

The picture sparked another wave of loss for me, but it sent Francis into a round of stories about how great Mom and Dad had been. He reminded us again how all the people in the community felt about them. I sensed again the importance of the years my family had spent here and the good changes that had taken place in the people. Some of those changes had endured despite the impact of our absence.

Lucy did her wifely duty and bathed our hands in warm water so that we were cleansed and ready to use our fingers for eating. The chai and chepatis were next, followed by rice, beef stew, and sakuma wiki. I explained to Bruce that sakuma was like swiss chard or spinach. Finally, we get *irio*—a mix of corn kernels, mashed potatoes, and sakuma ground up together. It was all good.

Since guests were served first, children outside, and women in their own space, we had to encourage Francis to change up the custom a little so we could visit with everyone. He relented and allowed a few children to join us for a few minutes before they were ushered outside again.

He let me know that there would be time for visiting with all the others later. Now was the time to eat.

When all the feasting was done, the visiting was finished, and the pictures were taken, we gave our final farewells. I invited Francis and Lucy to the weddings on Saturday and promised the family that we would send a little something to help them finish up their home and pay for school fees in the coming year. They told me to remember to send enough copies of the pictures for all of them. They would likely put the pictures on their walls and spend years with their friends and family remembering when the *wazungu*—the white ones who ran in circles—came to visit.

On the way home, the prune-like road hadn't changed. We were jostled and battered back and forth for most of the forty-five minutes, but we also had new memories we could talk about with all our friends and family for years to come.

Thursday night was just for games—Pit, Rook, Crokinole, and Hearts, among others. In every room there was laughter, stories, snacking, and bonding. Weddings were a good way to remember that while some things change, other things stay the same generation after generation.

CHAPTER FORTY-NINE

The hiss and sparking of burning olive wood demonstrated one thing: once something was consumed, it couldn't go back to being what it used to be. At four o'clock in the morning, the day before my wedding, I realized that the only choice I had was what kind of fire I chose to consume me.

I knew the flames of fear and anxiety were strong and could easily take everything and everyone I loved. They had done their destructive work many times before. I also knew the flames of passionate love for Bruce could consume me and leave me without any excuse for hanging onto the pains of my past. The Bible said that perfect love casts out fear; that meant the fire of love was stronger than the fire of fear. I had to believe that was true and I prayed one more arrow prayer: "Lord, burn me with love."

Although I did the occasional shoulder check to see if Anthony might be in the vicinity, I found myself growing more and more confident that I was about to start a new phase of my life for which God had been preparing me. Every time I looked at Bruce and saw the way he was interacting with the world I'd grown up in, I felt more and more attached. He genuinely was connecting the dots in my life.

Several times in my last week as a single woman, Bruce asked me to take out the journals I'd written as a sixteen-year-old in my last months here. He got me to sit in the places where things had happened and just read my thoughts aloud. An incredible healing was happening.

Although so much was the same, so much was also different. Many of the faces in this place were different. Some of the buildings were different. The life experience and feelings were different. And I was different. This time, I wasn't afraid to leave. I had someone I wanted to be with.

Sarah had gone over the details of the ceremony and reception with me so much that it felt like I had it all memorized. Whenever Lizzy and I caught each other staring at our guys our smiles grew bigger and bigger. This was going to be the best day of our lives.

The Friday evening wedding rehearsal dinner was like a huge class reunion. Classmates from both Lizzy's and my Academy school days made the trip. Missionary kids were like that. They'd fly across the world for a chance to be together to relive old times. We sat in two huge circles and Bruce had to listen to stories of endless adventure from my friends just like Dean had to sit and listen to stories from Lizzy's friends.

Of course, so much more had happened after we left the Academy that we weren't a part of and an old ache started gnawing at the pit of my stomach. I honestly did feel glad for my friends; I just felt sad for me.

Sometime around ten o'clock, we dismissed all the guys to another room and began to do our girls' things. Several of our friends were experienced in all things feminine and French nails were on the menu. Our hair was braided, styled, and played with over and over. We were the queens of the harem and enjoyed every minute of it.

Three of my friends, and one of Lizzy's, had gotten married before us and they began to fill us in on the fine art of living with a man. I really tried to listen when it came to intimacy, roles, finances, shopping, personality differences, making choices together, praying, and deciding where to live. When the girls found out I hadn't even had the chance for premarital counselling yet, they inundated me with everything they could remember from their sessions.

I felt like the biblical Hadassah on the night before her one chance with the king. Fortunately, she had pulled off everything she was supposed to do and became Queen Esther. I may never reach the height of being Bruce's queen, but I was ready to settle for being his princess.

We finally dismissed everyone at 2:30 in the morning. When I was alone in my room with Lizzy, I felt the old ache return. So much had happened without me. I could see my sister felt the same way.

"We missed a lot," I said.

She took me in her arms. "We lived a lot, Katie. We lived a lot."

Lizzy and I took a walk just as the sun was rising. We wanted to see our last African sunrise as single women. We held hands as the warming rays washed over us and showered us with the glow of life from the tips of our toes to the tops of our heads. We raised our hands and sang together. We joined the birdsong in praising our Maker. We hugged and cried and just rested our heads on each other's shoulders as we took comfort in the relationship that had lasted so many years.

"Thanks for sharing your special day," I said.

"Thanks for making it twice as special," she replied. I could hear her smile in the words.

Breakfast involved an energetic mob of twenty or so bodies milling around the guesthouse kitchen. Dean was the only one of us who had parents or other siblings to coach us through the day, but we had each other, and Carl and Vickie were generous with their words for all of us. I could see that Lizzy was completely impressed with her sisters-in-law and they loved her, too. I envied her and I could see Bruce glancing often in their direction as they huddled and laughed with each other.

Bruce and I took one last walk together overlooking the Rift Valley and Mount Longonot. We took an hour to lie on our backs and watch the clouds drift by. We identified the drifting images above the Kinangop hills and Mau escarpment in the distance. First the fluffy travellers were sailing ships setting off to explore new worlds. Then they were dolphins leaping, and turtles swimming, and then they were seniors having a potato sack race. This man knew how to make me laugh!

The hills were spotted with drying fields of maize and the white flowers of the pyrethrum flowers, sold for insect repellent. Eucalyptus trees still grew in small sections among the wild olive and indigenous trees of the Kikuyu escarpment. A small section of the tarmac road, built by Italian prisoners of war, was visible as it wound its way down to the valley floor.

I drilled Bruce one more time to make sure he knew what he was getting into. He reminded me of God's love and grace and forgiveness and said that both of us were starting fresh and new with each other.

As we watched a hawk soar by, he pulled up his pant leg, removed his artificial limb, and asked me if I could honestly accept him as he was now—not as the man I had first fallen in love with, not as the man who had saved my life, but as he was right now.

To answer him, I bent down and kissed his stump, then replaced his prosthesis.

We pledged our unending love to each other and then headed home.

A couple of the girls, Laura and Rachel, took on the task of final preparations for my hair and makeup. They readied the supplies while I had a shower. When

I finally felt clean all over, I settled in for my last hours of single bliss. While I enjoyed my friends' jesting, I inwardly prayed that God would be gracious and let everything stay peaceful. At least for today.

CHAPTER FIFTY

Since we didn't have a dad to walk us down the aisle, Lizzy and I had Francis take us both. The gardens were in absolute perfect glory at Mayer's Ranch as we took our places behind the rows of white plastic chairs that took care of the two hundred guests we had planned for. Dozens of others were left standing on the periphery, but no one who came was turned away.

The Academy family loved a celebration. If school hadn't been in session, I might have even thought about using the large Centennial Hall for the ceremony, but right now there wasn't a more glorious spot in the world than this one. Lizzy was adorable in her veiled hat and long trained gown. I could see Dean eyeing her hungrily. I wasn't yet ready to look Bruce in the eyes.

Chaplain Taylor and Pastor Njoroge stood on the far side of the archway that had been covered in red and white bougainvillea. Bruce and Dean stood proudly in their black long-tailed tuxes on either side of the clergymen. Six groomsmen and six bridesmaids had already finished their processional to the Academy's stringed ensemble, playing Paco Bell's Canon.

Today, daughters would not be given—only taken. Sarah finished arranging the long trains of our dresses, then fussed with the veils and bouquets of red roses we were carrying. She even adjusted Francis' tie a little. He smiled at all the last-second details. He had never been part of anything like this before and he was eager to make us proud. Two of the Masai women joined us and placed a special bead necklace around our necks.

When the wedding march sounded, and the guests all rose, Lizzy and I gave our stand-in dad a playful tug. We were off. My face felt like it would split. My life was about to change forever. Several of the women from Francis' family ululated with their high-pitched crescendos and danced us all the way to the front. Those familiar with African traditions joined in the celebration and by the time I came face to face with Bruce, I could see that he was enjoying my wild side.

I looked into the eyes of my future husband and the rest of the world disappeared. I knew things were happening, but it all seemed like a dreamy fairy tale schemed up by a little girl who just wanted all her life to be perfect.

Francis handed us off to the right men, we all said the right vows, we received the right rings, we signed the right marriage licenses and registers, and we even kissed the right partners. The message from Chaplain Taylor was about finding our roots and our wings in Christ. From Pastor Njoroge, the message was about the unity and love we find in Jesus. The Masai dancers enthralled the audience through the signing of the registry and beyond. It all ended far too quickly. Especially the kiss.

Only once did I check the crowd to see if there was any way Anthony had found his way in. I chided myself that the community was watching out for me and that I had nothing to worry about. Once I was satisfied, there was little to limit me from expressing the freedom I felt in being loved and wanted.

For the next hour, I was mobbed by guests all wanting to give hugs and hellos and little snippets of their lives. Bruce did his best to support me, but I could sense that he had sacrificed a lot to let me have my dream wedding come true. Almost everyone had come to support Lizzy and me. Dean had his family. But apart from Barbara, I was all Bruce had.

The caterers had done a wonderful job of laying out traditional African and American foods for the guests to enjoy—trays of samosas, fancy sandwiches, tropical fruit plates, vegetable

platters, roast goat, hot dogs, stew, bread and jam, sodas, and many different cakes. There was something for everyone and I had neither the time nor stomach to eat any of it.

When the ochre-smeared Masai dancers wound up to the peak of their action, they had Lizzy, Dean, Bruce, and me jumping up and down with the best of them. I had no doubt that the red dirt was going to be a challenge to any dry cleaner. At least I had put the veil and train away for safekeeping.

Once in a while, I felt like I was going to jump right out of my bridal gown. I had to clutch the top of my dress and adjust my leaping enough to not embarrass myself completely. This may not have been all that dignified in the halls of Vancouver, Seattle, or Chicago, but it felt like it would last a lifetime. I didn't want it to stop or even slow down.

The friends who knew me from school told me repeatedly how surprised they were by the wild transformation of the calm and conservative scholar and athlete they had once known. Lizzy surprised no one. She had always been as bouncy as Tigger.

As the event wound down, a single raincloud skittered across the sky and we all felt the briefest of sprinkles. For the Africans, this was hugely significant because rain was an indication of God's blessing. The setting sun dazzled us again with its creative palette of colours on the clouds and soon the torches were burning brightly.

The guests slowly evaporated away to their homes as time passed. Finally, Bruce took me by the hand and pulled me aside. "We need to say an official goodbye to everyone before they all leave," he said.

"If we say goodbye, it'll all be over," I replied.

He pulled me closer to a torch, where he could see my eyes clearly. "It's just beginning," he whispered. "Sometimes it's okay to say goodbye to one thing so you can say hello to something else. Like me."

I looked into his eyes and it seemed like I really saw him for the first time. This was my husband. The man of my dreams. The man who had committed his life to me. He wasn't going anywhere. And neither was I.

With that reinforcement, we gave our official thank-yous, goodbyes, hugs, and kisses. My classmates promised to see me at the next reunion, somewhere in Michigan in two years. Slowly, I released my friends. Letting go of Francis, probably for the last time, was heartbreaking. I bawled like a baby when I released Sarah and Barbara. I was the saddest, happiest bride there ever was.

Solomon drove up the decorated minibus and Dean farewelled his family, Bruce checked once more to make sure Barbara would be okay without him, and we were off on our honeymoon.

That night, we would stay in a couple of cottages forty-five minutes away at the Kentmere Club. In the morning, we would take taxis into the airport and fly down to Mombasa. That was where the real fun would get rolling.

CHAPTER FIFTY-ONE

Travelling to Mombasa could be done in six or seven hours by car or bus, by overnight train, or in an hour by plane. There was no way the four of us wanted to delay the rest of our time together by taking the slower options. By God's grace, the plane left on time and Bruce and Dean were able to see the country from the air while escaping the intense heat being experienced by those on the ground.

Perhaps it would seem weird to some that I had a joint wedding and honeymoon with my sister, but we just lived out our own experience with our own guys and almost ignored each other. We'd talked off and on about a Mombasa honeymoon for so long that it wasn't a big deal to know my sister and Dean were somewhere in the same hotel complex.

Being welcomed as Mr. and Mrs. Southerland and being given a key and license to run right through temptation's door was a little like I imagined Alice felt in Wonderland. Everything was somehow different than I remembered, yet all of it was vaguely familiar. As a married woman, it was far better than I dreamed and simpler than I had hoped.

The king-size bed sat in the center of the room, which also had a small table and chairs with a loveseat. There were no televisions or computers or other distractions. We were on the top floor, overlooking the ocean and the tops of the coconuts and palms that spread the length of the glistening white sandy beach.

I was eager to get into my bikini and get out into the Indian Ocean with its bathtub-like waters. I was determined Bruce was going to experience the best possible time with me, but I wasn't sure how he felt about going into such a public experience with his artificial leg so obvious for everyone to see.

He surprised me. I had teased him about how my swimsuit was going to knock his eyes out of his head and then ducked into the bathroom to change. When I came out in my beach coverup, he was already standing in his swim shorts ready to go. He looked a little disappointed that he'd have to wait until the beach for a preview, so I had to give in, delaying our swim for a while.

It was in this state, as we lay in bed wrapped in each other's arms, that he told me about my surprise honeymoon gift. I released him and watched as he walked to his carry-on case. He pulled out a single envelope and walked back toward me without shame.

I opened the envelope. Inside was a picture of Lancelot. I smiled but felt a deep sadness as well.

"He's yours," was all Bruce said.

"I don't understand."

Bruce sat down on the bed and took my hand. "I've been in touch with Uncle Bob ever since I found out Lancelot had been shipped to Belgium. The man who bought him says that while Lancelot had done his duties as a stud, he was wild and uncontrollable. They couldn't find anyone who was able to ride him. I knew how much that horse meant to you, so I've arranged to get him back for you."

I screeched for joy and jumped on Bruce to give him the most passionate kiss I could manage.

When we came up for air, I still had one question on my mind. "Where are we going to keep him?"

He smiled mischievously. "The farm hasn't sold and I've arranged with Uncle Bob to lease the old farm for our first year. After that, we can decide where we'll live and what we want to do with our lives."

Of course, this kind of announcement meant that swimming was delayed all over again.

When we joined Lizzy and Dean for supper that evening, it was obvious that I was the last one in on the secret about Lancelot. We celebrated and enjoyed the African dancing and all-you-can-eat barbecue. Somehow life had flipped from tails to heads overnight. Time was flashing by.

We rode camels, went snorkelling along the coral reef, swam in the pools, and ate our fill of seafood and wild exotic meats that are part of the Kenyan tradition. While we spent an hour or two at supper together, as couples the rest of the evening was spent in our own rooms.

The honeymoon passed quickly. We took a trip down to the spice island of Zanzibar and toured the historic evidences of the slave trade that had been part of the coast. We ventured up to Lamu by the ancient dow sailing boats and explored the Muslim island with its narrow passageways that allowed for foot passengers only. We explored nature preserves and saw exotic snake shows.

Our last week of honeymoon involved a safari tour through Amboselli to see the elephants and lions in their natural habitat. We also stopped by Treetops for more wildlife at their watering hole. This was the place where Queen Elizabeth II had been staying at the age of twenty-five when she found out she was the new sovereign of England, Canada, and the entire Commonwealth.

At Masai Mara's Keekerok Lodge, we saw a pride of lions bring down a zebra. We also saw a pair of cheetahs hunt a Grant's gazelle from our perch in a hot air balloon tour that Bruce and Dean surprised us with.

Our last stop was at Nakuru Park, where we saw the rare white rhinos.

On our way back to Nairobi, we made one last stop in Kijabe to say goodbye to old friends before leaving. I'd tasted again the deepest joys and beauties of the country of my birth and it had been worth it all.

When the British Airways 747 lifted off from the tarmac at Jomo Kenyatta Airport, this time I didn't cry myself blind. Sitting by the window, looking down on the ostriches that had welcomed me, I felt Bruce squeeze my hand. I could smile and say hello to the rest of my life.

CHAPTER FIFTY-TWO

Bruce and I said goodbye to Lizzy and Dean in London as we went our separate ways. Two weeks in the Hamptons got us off to a good start on the American side, and then we moved into Bruce's place to wait for the arrival of Lancelot. I learned to love his mirror over the fireplace as my dancing and passion improved.

It was late November when the news about Lancelot's arrival came and I was delirious with excitement. Bruce made arrangements to lease out his unit while we were away. We jumped into his Durango on Tuesday morning for the 1,400-mile trip to the Red River Valley in Minnesota. We were pulling a large U-Haul trailer with everything we owned. Lizzy and Dean and Uncle Bob were going to meet us at the farm on the weekend.

We made quick stops in Richmond and Charlottesville and then picked up the pace. The rains were steady and the winds were chilling when we made our coffee stops. We decided to call it a day at Charleston and get to bed early. I've never been one for driving too long.

Bruce slipped out of the hotel room just before dinner and picked up some ribs. His dramatic entrance afterward caught my attention. He charged in, slammed the door, and backed up against it. When I bounced to my feet in response, he waved me off. He was drenched, but smiling.

I was about to relax when my new husband raised my anxiety again by saying he'd almost got run down by some guy in a red Lexus. He brushed it off by saying that the rain was blinding and his leg had slowed him down as he tried to cross as the light changed. The driver likely just hadn't seen him with the weather conditions. We had a peaceful night.

On Wednesday, we drove through Cincinnati and Indianapolis, where we called it another day. The weather hadn't shown any signs of improving and forecasts indicated there may even be flurries ahead. I was feeling the effects of sitting so much, but I knew we could finish this off with one more push.

It was my turn to pick up supper. I went down the block from our hotel for Chinese takeout. As I stood at the counter making my order, I chanced to look out the window. I noticed a red Lexus pulling out of a parking spot across the street. A shiver went down my spine. Imaginations can really play with a person's mind, so I didn't bother telling Bruce. Besides, this Lexus had been pulling a small trailer. A strange combination.

On Thursday, we drove north to Madison and then west into Minneapolis. We were too close now to stop, so I urged Bruce to press on to the farm. We made it at dusk and found the key, hidden in the flowerpot where Uncle Bob had told us it would be. I knew Lancelot had been brought in earlier in the morning but decided it would be best to meet him the following day. Bruce and I needed to get the house in order if we were going to live here for the next year.

After Bruce brought me breakfast in bed on Friday morning, I couldn't wait any longer. We explored the barn and found the old Yamaha 250 that I had used to race Lancelot so many times before. Uncle Bob had brought it back and left it here for my use. It was all cleaned up, fuelled, and ready to ride.

I felt a surge of adrenaline at the first rev of the engine and Bruce looked at my face in amazement.

"Wild child," he said. "Your eyes are on fire. What are you thinking?" I smiled wickedly and he held up his hands. "No, no, no. You cannot just go and race that horse on your first day here."

I pouted and winked. "Only if he asks," I said.

Bruce shook his head and told me he'd be up in the Durango in an hour. "Just be careful," he said, looking skyward. "It looks like we're in for a rough storm."

"Best time to race," I replied as I fastened my helmet and pulled down the visor.

When I arrived at my usual gate for entering the pasture where Lancelot was king, I didn't see any sign of the black Arabian stallion. I knew he had a lot of territory to refamiliarize himself with, so I entered and waited patiently. I revved up the engine and still there was no horse.

A glance at the dark shadowed bellies of the thunderheads made me think twice, but I'd committed myself. The waterfall wasn't going to wait too much longer. The wind that usually tugged at my hair dropped to nothing as quickly as a Canada goose that had been shot out of the sky. Not a leaf or blade of grass even twitched.

I decided to do a little exploring of my own and rode the trail that Lancelot and I had faced many times before. This time the trail was slick and muddy from the recent rains. I reached all the way to Denman's Gulley with no trace of horse life. The gulley was filled with rushing water. There wasn't even a hoof mark anywhere. I wondered if Uncle Bob had been unable to deliver the stallion as expected.

The moment I decided to head home, I heard the distant whine of a motorcycle engine. My only thought was that somehow Bruce had found a way to get a motorbike and join me. I decided to surprise him and took a back route through the woods.

As I moved out through the brush, the rain began to fall again. Twice I stopped to listen and gauge where the other rider might be and I adjusted my path to come out behind him. It was difficult to judge exactly, as the thunder rumbled in the distance.

When I flew up at full throttle near the entrance gate, I saw the rider coasting down the hill below me. I could tell immediately that it wasn't Bruce. The rider was too big.

When the rider heard me behind him, he immediately kicked into gear and started a quick circle back in my direction. I could see that his back wheel wasn't giving him the grip he needed and that he moved much too quickly in these conditions.

I slowed down, assuming he was coming back to talk to me. He seemed to be carrying a bat of some kind in his hand, so he really only had one hand to control his machine. For some reason, as he got closer he increased his speed and I felt a streak of fear down my spine.

Instinctively, I opened the throttle and let out the clutch. I almost slipped and lost control of the motorbike, but then managed to hold on as the front wheel landed again. The bike fought me like a bucking bronco.

The rider actually swung his bat at me as my bike lurched forward and just out of his reach. In that second, I saw the eyes and the wicked smile through the visor; I knew that Anthony was looking for his sixth and final ring.

He pulled a quick 180 with only one hand. That act of strength and control alone nearly froze me in place. He was on me before I could set. As I ducked to the left, his swing glanced off my right shoulder and shattered my rear light.

Fire erupted from my shoulder and down my arm, but I didn't let go of the throttle.

My path to the gate had been cut off by my assailant's recent manoeuvre and I had little choice but to head back to the path I had just travelled. Although I had at least a hundred feet and momentum on my side, his was a more powerful bike and he had determination on his side. He began to swing his bat like a Spanish matador closing in for the kill.

I knew my one hope was to reach Denman's Gulley and make the jump. Within a few hundred yards, I saw the lone oak in the field ahead. I charted my path as I neared the crest of the last hill before my descent. I could tell there was no way my escape was going to happen.

Anthony had plenty of power and swung wide to my right. The ground was soggier out there, but muckier where I rode. Both bikes strained as we pushed them full out. Despite my throbbing shoulder, I minimized my fishtailing in the cottonpatch muck.

I briefly looked behind me to see how long I had, when out of the corner of my eye I caught a glimpse of a black stallion in full gallop heading in my direction. Lancelot was coming from Anthony's right and Anthony was so focused on me that he didn't see the horse.

The first streaks of lightning flashed almost in sync with the thunder. As I passed the oak, the lightning sent a jagged fork that hit the proud sentinel with full intensity. The sound was ear-splitting as the giant tree cracked under the strike. The smell of charred wood spewed out like volcanic lava.

I almost ditched the bike from the shock, but I held on. Anthony was momentarily distracted and gave me a little extra space. His planned intercept point had been frustrated. With

my course change, he was forced to make another arc. He sped up to end this chase once and for all.

When I glanced again, Lancelot was within lengths of Anthony's bike. If my attacker had noticed him, he didn't give any evidence of concern.

The unsteady ground didn't seem to be slowing Lancelot down at all. The rain was streaming off his satin hide and, although I couldn't see his eyes yet, I knew they were wild.

For now, I had to focus on finding my sweet spot for the jump. I was within five or six hundred feet. While Anthony likely didn't know my plan, it appeared he wasn't going to wait any longer. He angled his bike toward me and raised his bat.

It was then that Lancelot made his move. Surging with an extra effort, he cut to the inside, between the two of us. Anthony was taken totally by surprise.

Lancelot continued to surge ahead until he was even with me and we were eye to eye. I could feel his life energy. We merged. Wild with wild. Strength with strength. It only lasted a moment, but the bond we shared spoke for us in this act.

I wasn't sure how the final act would go, but I made no effort to slow my bike. I either made this jump or I had raced my last. Anthony wasn't even in my thoughts anymore. I wanted to make this for Bruce and for all the love and life I had left to give.

The sweet spot was only five feet wide and had to be hit at just the right angle. There was another flash and another rumble as I launched into space. I looked back and saw Lancelot had firmly blocked the good path for Anthony.

The last thing I saw was Anthony's bike reaching the edge of Denman's Gulley a full twenty feet from my sweet spot.

I focused on aiming my bike as high and as far as possible.

I barely managed to catch the far lip of the gulley. The bike slid sideways on the muddy embankment and there was no way I could control it. I was thrown off and landed in a painful heap with my head hitting the ground hard. I'd never been so thankful for a helmet.

I wanted to lie there and groan, but then I remembered Anthony and raised my head. Without thinking clearly, I loosened my chin strap and tossed my helmet to the side. There was no sign of another motorcycle this side of the gulley. In fact, there was no sound of any bike, just the river racing by and the victorious whinnies of a stallion who I knew was up and pawing at the sky.

The rain poured down on me, but that was the least of my concerns. I still didn't know what had happened to Anthony. Could he be wading across to finish me off with his bat?

I crawled toward my twisted motorbike. Five feet away from it, I heard crashing through the brush behind me. The terror was soul-numbing, but the scream was lost in my throat. I fixated on the spot and couldn't believe my eyes when Lancelot struggled up and over to be with me.

He trotted the few paces to where I knelt and nuzzled my cheek. I patted him and struggled to my feet. My foot was hurting bad and I knew it was going to be very hard to walk all the way back to Bruce. I placed my hands on both sides of Lancelot's face and looked him in the eyes. All I said was, "I need you."

My wild stallion hardly flinched as I led him to a stump, grabbed his mane, and hoisted myself onto his back. No one had ever ridden him before, but there was something between us. I urged him toward the edge of the bank and moved along until there was a clear spot. I could see part of one wheel from a motorbike barely sticking above the surface of the raging water. Anthony was nowhere to be seen.

I turned Lancelot toward home.

Bruce was waiting in wonder as we rode up. I fell into his arms and sobbed with relief. He carried me inside and gently dealt with my wounds. Both inside and out.

When I could finally get my story out, Bruce called the local sheriff's office. A patrol came by and Bruce went with them. Two deputies stayed with me while I shivered in terror. They allowed me to warm up by taking a bath and then spent the time taking my statement about exactly what I saw.

Two hours later, I heard a siren. An hour later, Bruce returned and the deputies left. Anthony's body had been found downstream. A red Lexus with a trailer for a motorcycle had been located two miles down the road.

Strong flashbacks overwhelmed me. Bruce almost being run down in the rain in Charleston. The Lexus in Indianapolis. We had been hunted like animals. All that was over.

I was so relieved that I tried to squeeze Bruce with my best one-armed bear hug. I hobbled and pulled him to the door. We stood in the doorway, watching the rain come down. A hundred yards away, Lancelot looked in our direction. When another streak of lightning forked, the mighty stallion rose up on his haunches and pawed at the sky with a fierce cry. He was truly king of his domain.

"Are you sure it was Anthony?" I asked Bruce. "How many gold rings were on his left hand?"

Bruce looked at me blankly. "There were no gold rings at all."

I felt a twinge of fear but knew somehow that my last pursuer had been vanquished.

"Thank you, God," I prayed out loud. "Thanks for answering all my prayers through Lancelot and Bruce."

My husband held me, kissed me, and welcomed me home.

CPSIA information can be obtained at www.ICGtesting.com
Printed in the USA
LVOW050838140313

323936LV00005B/16/P